THE SCHOOL OF
ENGLISH MURDER

Ruth Dudley Edwards was born in Dublin but
now lives in London. After a period of teaching
and academic research, she worked in telecom-
munications and then the Civil Service. Since
1979 she has been a freelance writer. Her other
Robert Amiss mysteries are *The Saint Valen-
tine's Day Murders*, *Corridors of Death* and
Clubbed to Death. She has written a number of
biographies, including the official biography of
Victor Gollancz, and is currently writing the
official history of the *Economist*.

D0958869

THE SCHOOL OF ENGLISH MURDER

by

Ruth Dudley Edwards

GOLLANCZ CRIME

Gollancz Crime is an imprint of Victor Gollancz Ltd
14 Henrietta Street, London WC2E 8QJ

First published in Great Britain 1990
by Victor Gollancz Ltd

First Gollancz Crime edition 1992
Second impression September 1992

A catalogue record for this book
is available from the British Library

ISBN 0-575-05176-0

Printed and bound in Great Britain
by Cox & Wyman Ltd, Reading

To Elizabeth Bawdon, Susan Chadwick, Nina Clarke, Vincent Guy, Ivan Hill, Maureen Lenehan, David and John Mattock, Tina Moskal, Richard Pooley and all those other friends who have taught English as a Foreign Language properly but who nevertheless inspired, helped or encouraged me to produce the present travesty.

THE SCHOOL OF
ENGLISH MURDER

PROLOGUE

'Do you want to know another of the bitter ironies of life?'

'Probably not,' said Rachel. The weariness of her tone was not lost on Amiss. 'But carry on if you must. It might be one I hadn't heard of yet.'

'It's that people who take principled decisions that cost them money are always those who can't afford to. Catch any of those sods with fat savings accounts and a twenty-year build-up of pension entitlements walking out on a safe job.'

Rachel eyed him levelly. He could see her lips contracting into thin lines. When they opened and he heard her teeth snap he warded off trouble hastily.

'OK, OK. You're about to point out that I walked out in a fit of rage, that principle had nothing to do with it and that I could have returned if I hadn't been too proud. And, knowing you, I expect you've got a list up your sleeve of well-heeled people who gave up all for honour.' He stubbed out his cigarette savagely.

'Good guesses,' said Rachel. 'You, on the other hand, will now point out that not everyone should be expected to be accurate and objective in times of crisis. You'll add that at a time like this a chap needs a woman who'll bolster up his ego rather than one who subjects his every remark to rigorous logical scrutiny. You may even go on to elaborate on why, being only a gentile, you can't be expected —'

'Will you shut up?' yelled Amiss. 'You're talking like a bloody civil servant.'

'I *am* a bloody civil servant. I thought the whole problem was that you wished you still were.'

'Not me,' declared Amiss, leaping to his feet and striding up and down the room purposefully. 'I can't wait to embark on an exciting new career. You'll see. I'll become a nasty, greedy insider dealer and drive a nasty, flashy Porsche.'

'Fine,' said Rachel. 'In the meantime, don't forget to sign on the dole. I suppose if you can't find a job you can become a Foreign Office spouse. It'll do wonders for my career if you're free to travel with me, protect me from liaisons with dubious foreigners and engage in intelligent small-talk at cocktail parties. Most of my competitors have liberated wives who object to doing that kind of thing. You'll be a great asset.'

'Is that a proposal of immediate marriage?' asked Amiss hopefully.

'Call it a statement of long-term intent.'

They looked at each other and Amiss grinned first.

'You're an impossible cow,' he said, 'but I love you. I can't wait till you're stationed back in London. Now before you bugger off back to Paris, take me out, buy me a wonderful dinner and let's get down to considering seriously how I go about finding a decent job in Thatcher's Britain.'

1

Amiss arrived at the Unemployment Benefit office five minutes before his nine o'clock appointment and was delighted to be interviewed punctually by a motherly Jamaican of such cheerfulness and optimism as to mitigate the effect of the bad news she conveyed. She helped him fill in his claim form and then surveyed the result.

"Sorry, love. Nothin' doin'. I can tell you now you won't get no dole for about six months. From what you've said you're sure to be classified "Voluntarily unemployed without a good reason."'

'Six months? I thought it was six weeks.'

'That was in the old days. Didn't you know there's been reforms? This is one o' them.' She grinned so disarmingly that Amiss was forced to grin back.

''Course you'll be able to appeal.'

'No point. I've no case.'

'Why'd you jus' walk out?' she asked with unprofessional curiosity.

'Bad temper mainly, I suppose. I got fed up with stupid bureaucracy. And I'm too proud to go back. Besides, I need a change.'

'I didn't think high-ups did that sort of thing.'

'I didn't think of myself as a high-up.'

'Well, compared to me you were.'

She took pity on Amiss's embarrassment.

'Cheer up, love. With your looks and your brains you'll be fixed up in no time.'

'But in the meantime I haven't any money.'

'Go on. What were you doin' with it?'

'Don't know really. Taxis? Eating out? Going abroad? I was never the saving type.'

'Well I suppose if you're really stuck, Social Security'll help. But you'll be lucky to get the rent and enough for one night a week out at McDonalds. The good days is over.'

'Well, anything helps when you've got nothing,' said Amiss lugubriously.

'Off you go then. It's two buses to get to the Security. Pity you're called Amiss. The L-Z office is much nearer. Now if you'd been called Robert Mugabe you'd have it made.' And giving him a crisp set of directions, she sent him off with a smile and a wave.

With a lift in his step Amiss set off in search of the first bus. He had been waiting for fifteen minutes when the rain began to fall. The woman in front of him struggled to pull up the rain hood on the baby buggy with one hand, while her elder child tugged at the other and screamed to be allowed to go to the playground. By the time the bus turned up, mother, children and Amiss were all suffering from fractured nerves. With difficulty he helped the family on to the conductorless bus and fled upstairs out of earshot.

A second lengthy wait in persistent rain finally put him in the appropriate mood for his first look at the Social Security office. It was an uncompromising piece of concrete neo-brutalism, whose barracks-like appearance was subtly enhanced by its perplexing adornments. The one piece of graffiti — BANK OF DRESDEN — was new to Amiss and only marginally more comprehensible than the three rows of posters each showing a clenched fist, a great deal of barbed wire and a lot of Arabic writing. Underneath these was a small poster picturing the late Shah of Iran, which accused the 'Criminal English Freemasonry' of having put their agent Khomeini in power and then concealed his death for years. The said freemasonry was additionally charged with being at the head of world terrorism. To raise further the spirits of its putative clientele — or perhaps to make the indigenous population feel at home — officialdom had put up a sequence of its own notices outside and immediately inside the glass door. The first explained that the building served another purpose: it was additionally a centre for artificial eyes, limbs and appliances. The second stated that no dogs were admitted, the third that no cycles or dogs were admitted and the fourth gave details of the correct procedure in the event of escaping gas. The fifth was the *pièce de résistance*:

MEMBERS OF THE PUBLIC PLEASE NOTE
No person in possession of alcoholic liquor
nor severely affected by drink or drugs will
be admitted to these premises. The police
will be asked to remove those who fail to
comply with this notice.

The only positive note was struck by the friendly doorkeeper who confirmed that Amiss was in the right place at the right time and sent him to a door at the end of the corridor. He was less than surprised when he found himself in a room of dreary awfulness. It contained perhaps thirty bucket seats, all of them occupied, with a line of people standing waiting for the next vacancy. The dirty yellow walls contrasted startlingly with the floor-covering — a pock-marked reddish lino that erupted in places into what looked unnervingly like large black boils. There were expanses of scratched brown notice-board empty apart from a scattering of small leaflets about death grants. At the far end of the room Amiss could see three officials conducting interviews from behind their protective glass.

He stood at the end of the line and began to read. Every five minutes or so everyone would move up one place to make room for the newcomers. By midday Amiss felt as if he'd been there for half a lifetime. The wailing of the baby behind him was driving him madder even than the smell and incoherent mumblings of the two drunks immediately in front. He shifted uncomfortably on the plastic seat, leafed through his newspaper for the fifth time that morning and failed to find anything he hadn't already digested. The previous time he had applied himself so thoroughly as to become *au fait* not only with the article on the current state of English ladies' hockey, but even with the details of the Commons debate on EEC agricultural policy. He looked furtively at his neighbours to see if there was any chance of effecting a swap of newsprint. Number three down the line was still crouched over his racing paper; number five remained glued to a pictorial magazine engagingly titled *Big Women*; the woman

13

immediately in front was immersed in a religious tract and the two Asians to his right scanned papers in their native languages. It was unlikely that any of them would be thrilled by an offer of the London *Independent*.

Not for the first time Amiss excoriated himself for being so pathetically reliant on reading matter. He searched through his pockets in pursuit of diversion, pulled out his bank manager's letter and read it with a scowl.

PRIVATE AND CONFIDENTIAL

Dear Mr Amos,

Overdrawn £850

It is with disappointment that I learn from our Mr Kersse that far from making proposals to eradicate your overdraft you are now requesting an increased facility.

Since I understand that you have severed your connection with your employers and have no source of income I cannot permit you to increase the monies due to the bank.

In view of this situation we have had to recall your monthly direct debit to Wiggins. This incurs a bank charge of £15.

Please let me have your proposals for repayment as a matter of urgency.

Assuring you of our best attention at all times.

Yours sincerely,

N M MACERLEAN

'Scots git,' muttered Amiss sourly, trying once again to comprehend a system of operation which thought it sensible to levy a charge of fifteen pounds for bouncing a debit of ten pounds. Still, the silver lining was that not the most suspicious dispenser of Her Majesty's welfare benefits could claim that he didn't need money.

It was fifteen minutes later that he realised the line had slowed up so much that he would probably be stuck for at least another half hour. There were six people ahead of him and only two interviewers. And Detective Superintendent Jim Milton, who was due to meet him for lunch at one at a venue half an hour away, was a very busy man.

After a couple of moments of dither Amiss abandoned his seat. The line moved up one behind him. As he opened the door he turned back for a moment to survey the scene. The two men being interviewed finished together, rose and shuffled towards the back of the room. One vacant seat was taken by the woman first in line; the second by a man behind whom the next four people formed a semicircle. With a low moan of disbelief Amiss realised that he had failed to spot that they were a family. He debated trying to regain his place at the top of the pecking-order, thought about stories of punch-ups and murders in the Social Security office, and muttering a curse, left for Milton and the winebar.

'Poor old Robert.' As so often in the course of their friendship — forged during the police investigation into the murder of Amiss's Civil Service boss — Milton found himself simultaneously laughing at and sympathising with Amiss's latest mishap. 'Will you go back this afternoon?'

'God, no. I couldn't face it twice in one day. I'll go back tomorrow morning bearing a hipflask and a complete set of Trollope.'

'You won't get enough to do more than survive, you know. Let me lend you a few hundred until you get a job.'

'Thanks, Jim. I do appreciate the offer, and I promise I'll take it up if I'm starving, but I'm curious to see if I can get through this by myself. You can buy lunch, though.'

'Well, make the most of it. I won't be able to entertain you again for a couple of months. I'm being sent to Staff College.'

'Does that mean your promotion is on?'

'It certainly does. You'll be able to call me Chief Superintendent before long.'

'You'd better buy us champagne then.'

'Cheeky sod,' said Milton, summoning the waitress. 'Lucky for you I've been working since two this morning and am on my way home to bed. Otherwise it would be sparkling mineral water.'

'Yeh. Same for me in the days when I worked. I can see advantages to being unemployed. You can get pissed at lunchtime.'

'On what you're likely to get from Social Security,' said Milton cheerfully, 'all you'll be able to afford is meths.'

Amiss was still hot and cold with a mixture of rage and shame when he got home from the Social Security office the following day. It had been one thing to learn that if anything Milton had been over-optimistic: meths would be way beyond his budget if he had to subsist on what the state was offering. That he had taken in his stride. What had caused the trouble was the attitude of the tiny narg behind the reinforced glass.

'Well, of course it's not for me to say, but you have been very irresponsible, haven't you?' had been bad enough. 'If I were you I'd make a serious effort to get a job soon,' had been marginally worse. Then, when the state of Amiss's overdraft had been discussed, had come, in the same unctuous tone: 'You're sure you didn't put something aside in a building society for a rainy day? We can find out, you know. It's better to be honest.'

'That's what did it,' he wailed to Rachel over the phone.

'Did what?'

'I shouted that no one should ever deal with a man under five feet two and stormed out.'

'Ouch!'

'And now I'm awash with liberal guilt at mocking the unfortunate.'

'And haven't any Social Security money.'

'Precisely.'

'Can't I send you a cheque?'

'Please, no. All this is my own fault and I've got to get myself out of it. I can live on credit until I pick up a temporary job.'

'I can't wait to hear the next instalment. A row with your landlord? Or the credit card companies?'

'Actually it'll probably be the bank. I wrote a letter yesterday afternoon which I rather regret.'

'Irascible?'

'Splenetic is more like it.'

'Robert, darling, I don't think misfortune agrees with you. Let's hope your luck turns soon.'

'Don't you worry. I'm about to tear into the appointments

sections and find my new career. You'll see. I'll be draping you in ermine and pearls yet.'

'Until then I'll settle for a share of a bed in London. Preferably not under the arches at Waterloo.'

2

'Dear Sirs,' wrote Amiss, painstakingly and slowly on his manual typewriter. 'In response to your advertisment in the *Independent*, I should like to apply for the post of Purchasing Manager.

'I have recently completed a year in a senior purchasing capacity in the British Conservation Company, on secondment from the Department of Conservation.'

He paused, read through what he had written, spotted the missing 'e' in 'advertisement', applied erasing fluid to the last four letters, attempted to replace them with five, surveyed the result critically, swore, tore out the page, crushed it into a ball and hurled it in the direction of its fellows.

He got up, made another mug of strong coffee, lit his last cigarette and surveyed his small living-room with distaste. Every surface carried its own variety of mess. The typewriter was barely visible in between piles of blank paper, large white envelopes, stamps and torn out pieces of newspapers; one sofa sported piles of his curriculum vitae while the other bore the newspapers and magazines he still had to scour for job advertisements; on the bookcase were four dirty mugs and two full ashtrays; and the floor was largely covered by discarded newspapers, abandoned drafts and letters of rejection.

He went into the kitchen and searched vainly for a plastic garbage bag. As he returned reluctantly to the typewriter, he reflected on why he seemed incapable of doing such a mundane job without creating chaos. For this, as for so much else, he blamed the Civil Service, which had coddled him for such a long time with filing clerks. He stifled a wave of nostalgia.

He reread the advertisement to which he was currently trying to apply. It required him to live in Birmingham, to travel widely within the United Kingdom and to reorganise a warehousing system for a cosmetics company. Apart from carrying with it a company car which he did not want and private medical insurance of which he did not approve, it closely resembled the Civil Service job which he had so angrily refused.

Systematically Amiss sorted through all the other advertisements he had selected. He threw away the eighty per cent that demanded qualifications or experience which he completely lacked. He had already been turned down for dozens of similar jobs in management, marketing, personnel and business consultancy. Good academic qualifications and a stated willingness to learn were no substitute for pieces of dubious paper from business schools.

Critically he reread closely the other twenty per cent. He knew uneasily that although these seemed open to someone of his background and experience, he laboured under a serious disadvantage. In Civil Service terms his record was excellent: recruited into the élite fast stream, he had bypassed most of his contemporaries to secure one of the most coveted jobs — private secretary to the head of his department. But of course to most businessmen all that was meaningless: the only part likely to make sense was his valueless period of secondment to a wally department in a wally organisation and even that was extremely difficult to write up attractively.

He reflected bitterly on the irony that most civil servants who went out on secondment were offered highly attractive bribes to stay. The talents they revealed on the job: their articulacy, industriousness, clear-mindedness and above all, a mastery of prose beyond the wildest dreams of most businessmen, made them prize captures. But it was not until the outside world saw them in action that these talents were recognised. It was dispiriting how outsiders clung resolutely to the image of all civil servants as dreary hidebound grey men in suits. He could hardly be surprised that so far he had been offered only two interviews, both for commission-based sales jobs he knew he would be incapable of doing successfully.

He and Milton had mulled over his joining the police and had concluded the idea was a non-starter. 'You'd be better working with knaves than fools, Robert. You'd go crazy being ordered about by slow-witted bigots. And with all our efforts we've still got a fair number of those.'

'What makes Ellis able to cope?' Amiss had asked, for Milton's protégé, Detective Constable Pooley, graduate and ex-member of the Home Office, continued to flourish. 'He's like me. Ultimately he's got a vocation that enables him to put up with almost any amount of shit. And besides that he's buttressed by an insatiable passion for crime-solving.'

Amiss felt the old familiar longing for a vocation and an even sharper one for a cigarette. He looked at his watch and realised it was in any case time to go out to his lunchtime job. As he reached for his raincoat he heard the telephone. It was Pooley proposing dinner. 'On me, Robert.'

'That's not necessary,' said Amiss rather stiffly, feeling slightly indignant that his misfortunes were being bandied about the Met. 'I'm a barman now and making enough to finance the occasional feast at a greasy spoon.'

'No, please, I insist. In fact I'd like it to be at my place. I've got an idea I want to talk over with you.'

'Ellis, you wouldn't be trying to get me involved in any boy-wonder detective stuff by any chance? I'm off corpses for Lent.'

'Lent's long over. What about tonight?'

'Well, it is my night off.'

'Done. Come at eight.' And Pooley rang off.

Amiss stood thinking for a moment. Then, repressing his misgivings, he shrugged, picked up his raincoat and set off for the Fox and Goose.

3

'Good God, Ellis. This isn't an interest. It's an obsession.'

'You disappoint me, Robert. What next? Are you going to ask me if I've read them all?'

'Sorry,' said Amiss, surveying in awe the huge book-lined Victorian drawing-room that made up three-quarters of Pooley's flat. 'How many books, roughly?'

'Ten thousand, at a guess.'

'And the proportion that are crime-related?'

'Maybe seventy per cent.'

'Give me the guided tour.'

'When I've got you a drink,' said Pooley, and led Amiss into the kitchen.

'It all started with Sherlock Holmes when I was eight,' he said, mixing their gin and tonics. 'I became an awful bore trying to make deductions based on people's appearance. Even now I practise on the tube, though I doubt if even Holmes would have found it that easy in a multi-racial society — stretches one's knowledge pretty thin. It's more than I can do to tell the Dutch from the Germans or the Indians from the Pakistanis. Anyway, then I progressed through Edgar Allan Poe to general detective fiction.'

He led Amiss over to the far right-hand corner of the room.

'That's what makes up these two walls.'

'They all look pretty elderly,' remarked Amiss, as his eye was caught within seconds by Margery Allingham, Freeman Wills Crofts, Anthony Berkeley and Dorothy Sayers.

'No. They go chronologically, not alphabetically. So at the end you'll see a few that came out only last month.'

Amiss walked over and scrutinised his host's latest acquisitions. 'Playing it safe, aren't you, Ellis? Ruth Rendell? Reginald Hill?'

'I have to be highly selective now,' said Pooley sadly. 'I confine myself to the authors I'm sure will still be read in thirty years time. Otherwise I'd have to live in a warehouse.'

He waved across the room. 'The other shelves have great trials, lives of the great advocates, encyclopaedias of crime, dictionaries of poisons, general forensic stuff, popular psychology and so on. And to prove I'm not a monomaniac, there's also a fair bit of history, literature and country stuff.'

'Country stuff?'

'Yes. Topography, reminiscences of country life, picture books. That sort of thing.'

'I didn't have you down as a rural type.'

'Well I shed my Devonian accent at school.'

'Where were you at school?' asked Amiss idly. He looked towards the sofa and scanned the tables at either end.

'You're looking to see if I have ashtrays, aren't you? Hang on, here's a saucer you can use.'

'Are you sure you don't mind? Most people do.'

'Well, I'm not most people,' said Pooley, with a slight hint of sanctimoniousness. 'Anyway, what's the use of inviting you here and having you a nicotineless nervous wreck all evening.' He waved Amiss to the sofa and sat down in the rocking chair himself.

Amiss lit his cigarette. 'I was asking where you were at school.'

'If I tell you, you must promise to keep it a secret — even from the Superintendent.'

Amiss looked narrowly at his host. 'Not Eton or Harrow?'

'''Fraid so. Eton actually. But I'd never live it down in the canteen, so for Christ's sake . . .'

Amiss began to laugh. 'Oh, Ellis, don't tell me you're seriously upper class. It's not going to be Lord Pooley of the Yard, is it? I know the old jokes are the best, but really . . .'

Pooley looked hurt. 'I'm not even an honourable. And thank God I've got two older brothers between me and a title. Fortunately my old man is a peer of the utmost obscurity — a decent old stick but the original backwoodsman. He hasn't attended the House of Lords for more than ten years so no one's ever heard of him.'

'And what does he make of your chosen career?'

'He's coming to terms, like the rest of the family. They were always at me to be a barrister, which I'd have been hopeless at. There were mixed feelings about my going into the Civil Service. Mother was relieved it was respectable; Father talked about bloody pen pushers.'

'What made you decide to leave?'

'No good at it. I didn't give a toss about policy and I hated drafting all those boring briefing papers. Besides, I was too imaginative and not clever enough. What I enjoy doing is sticking my nose into other people's business and finding out why they're doing what they're doing. So now I can do that more or less legitimately.'

'But how can you survive in the middle of all those thickos? Not to speak of all the yessiring and nosiring and sorryfornot-goingbytherulebooksiring?'

'I went to public school. Remember? I don't suffer from the egalitarianism and intellectual snobbery of you grammar school lot. And besides it takes the upper classes to understand that pecking order is not related to talent.'

'How did you know I went to grammar school? Oh, sorry. You noticed the slight stoop that came from carrying a heavy satchel.'

'Actually your C.V. is on file at the Yard. Now come into the kitchen, help me make dinner and bring me up to date.'

'You know what I think?' asked Pooley half an hour later over the pâté. 'I think you've made a really dumb decision. Whether you know it or not, you're a natural civil servant. You should go back. You know perfectly well they'd welcome you with open arms.'

'I'm sick of people telling me that.'

'Sorry, Robert. I know I don't really know you well enough to presume like this, but I'm going to anyway. What the devil are you doing working as a postman and barman?'

'Trying to raise enough to live and to visit Rachel occasionally. She hasn't been able to get away from Paris for weeks.'

'Now you're being obtuse. You know what I mean. By your own admission you haven't come across any real jobs you want. Why in God's name don't you go back where they'll appreciate your intelligence and integrity?' Pooley cleared their plates and served up the pasta. He left it to Amiss to break the silence.

'I have a reason now.'

Pooley looked at him encouragingly.

'I didn't really at first. It was simple obstinacy. I've been close to giving in. There've been a few overtures from old bosses in the Department.'

He paused to attempt to stuff his fork-and-spoonful of spaghetti into his mouth. Half fell back on his plate, splattering his sweater with bolognaise sauce.

'Damn. That's a Jim Milton trick.'

'Yes. I've noticed the Super is a bit clumsy,' remarked Pooley as he mopped Amiss down.

'Don't you even *think* of him by his first name?'

'Can't afford to. He's my lifeline. Without him I'd never have had a break. I've no intention of jeopardising anything by any undue familiarity. The canteen culture's red hot on favouritism. So the more the Super talks to me informally, the more I treat him like a Field Marshal. Anyway back to you.'

'I've had a lot of time to think over the past few weeks, especially on my early morning postal round. And a lot of my thinking was about the Service. Then last week I read Peter Hennessy's book on Whitehall.'

He took another forkful of salad and appeared to fall into a reverie.

'And?'

'Oh, sorry, Ellis. I spend so much time alone at the moment that I forgot I wasn't talking to myself.

'There was a lot in there about the kind of person who becomes a civil servant, essentially the safety first type who wants security. And the point was made that even those who come in thinking they don't fit into a stereotype almost inevitably do by the time they reach the top. He quoted an observer's description of the process as "the velvet drainpipe". You stuff your young élite up it and out they come at the top uninfected by any outside influences.'

'So?' asked Pooley encouragingly.

'So I don't want that to happen to me and I'm the kind of malleable person to whom it might. I've been horrified at how badly I coped with the real world in the first few weeks of unemployment, culminating in that scene I made in the Social

Security office. My God! There I was surrounded by poor bastards at the bottom of the heap who have to put up with whatever's dished out to them, and I throw a tantrum because I feel patronised.'

'Do you mean you'll never go back?'

'No. In fact I'm beginning to think I'll ask to have this year counted as leave of absence and review things at the end of it.'

'And you'll do what with it?'

'The most attractive thing would be to stay in Paris with Rachel during her last few months there. But I won't. I'll probably spend my time in a variety of jobs learning how the other three-quarters live.'

'You don't feel you did that last year on secondment to BCC?'

'No. That had little to do with real life, and anyway I was in a negative frame of mind throughout.'

Pooley looked at him eagerly.

'So you're about ready to move on to something new?'

'I suppose so.'

'I've got just the job for you,' said Pooley.

4

'Let me give you the background first.'

Pooley picked up the coffee tray and led the way back to the living-room.

'Coffee?'

'Please.'

'Help yourself to milk and sugar. Brandy?'

'You're trying to soften me up, Ellis. Yes, please. I prefer this approach to the rubber truncheon. And besides tomorrow's Sunday. God bless whoever abolished the Sunday post.'

Pooley poured brandy into two glasses and thoughtfully put the bottle beside his guest. Amiss grinned at him, made an expansive gesture with his cigarette and said, 'Carry on. And make it interesting. I want a story of love and hate, greed and retribution, death by moonlight and the downfall of a beautiful woman.'

'I'll lend you a Dornford Yates to take home with you. *My* story begins with an accident in a language laboratory in a Knightsbridge English school.'

'I might have known. At least it wasn't in the lavatory.'

'Robert, do you think you could keep the interruptions to a minimum. Otherwise we'll be here all night.'

'Sorry, sorry. Fire ahead.'

'About two months ago, there was a 999 call from the Knightsbridge School of English. One of the teachers, Walter Armstrong — known as Wally and please don't make the obvious joke — had been electrocuted. He was dead on arrival in hospital.

'Central Area CID were called in and concluded it was probably an accident. It looked as though Armstrong — in the process of trying to fix a fault in the equipment — had reversed a couple of leads. He was alone in the school at the time of the accident, and so never had a chance.'

'Why was he alone?'

'It was eight in the morning and no one had arrived.'

'Did he fancy himself as an electrician?'

'Slightly. Although the principal couldn't understand why he was bothering. He thought he'd told him a proper electrician was coming at nine.'

'Odd.'

'Yes. But then one of his colleagues said it wasn't out of character for him to try to fix it first; apparently he enjoyed showing off his technical knowledge.

'In any case, there seemed no motive. He was an amicably divorced man with grown-up children, and he seemed to do no more harm than occasionally get on his colleagues' nerves. He was a bit of a fusser.'

'Inquest?'

'Accident.'

'So where do you come in?'

'I used to work in Central Area CID before being transferred to the Major Investigation Reserve at the Yard. And I had a drink last week with a DC from there who was unhappy about the verdict.'

'Because?'

'Because he thought no one in his right mind would be tampering with the thing between the mains and the step-down transformer. And if the principal was right, it was extraordinary of Armstrong to come in early just to outsmart the electrician.'

'Didn't those points come up at the inquest?'

'No. Because my friend's superiors thought he was making something out of nothing. And he's too junior to press a point like that successfully.'

'Is that it?'

'Not quite. Last week the principal was attacked on the way home and escaped serious injury or death only by chance. He was wheeling his bike in the dark up the alleyway behind his house when someone came up from behind and began to hit him unmercifully about the head. He had two strokes of luck. The first that he was wearing his Russian fur hat fastened under his chin and that dulled the blows. The second was that a neighbour with a bag of garbage happened to emerge from a

27

back garden at the crucial moment, causing the attacker to run away.'

'A small point. But what the devil was he doing wearing a fur hat in May?'

'The wind really gets to you around Hyde Park Corner and Nurse is susceptible to ear infections.'

'Nurse?'

'Yes. Ned Nurse.'

'Ned Nurse?'

'Ned Nurse. Shall I go on or do you want to make a joke?'

'Go on.'

'There was no sign of the assailant and no apparent motive for the attack.'

'Hmm.'

'Quite.'

'And another thing. It's sheer chance that my pal got to know about this incident. Nurse got away very lightly and the local coppers in North-West Area would've had no reason to pass the information on to Central CID. It was Nurse himself who mentioned it when he called in at Central to deal with a bit of paperwork.'

'Suspicious,' observed Amiss, who was losing interest rapidly.

Pooley got up and began to lope up and down the long Persian rug in the middle of his room. From his supine position Amiss noted the pent-up energy in his long thin body. 'Take up a postal round, Ellis, and you'll begin to appreciate immobility.' Pooley paid no attention. He was rapt in contemplation and periodically he ran his hands through his reddish-fair hair.

Amiss's mind drifted off on to thoughts of Rachel. He was pulled back to reality when Pooley sat beside him and gazed at him earnestly. 'You've guessed what I want you to do, haven't you?'

'Oh, sorry, Ellis. I'm afraid I was thinking of something else.' Amiss tried to concentrate. Illumination suddenly dawned.

'Jesus, you're not going to try to get me to take a job in this poxy school, are you?'

Pooley nodded anxiously. 'It's the only way, Robert. I'm convinced there's something peculiar going on there and the only thing to do is to plant a spy in the camp.'

The effrontery of the suggestion almost took Amiss's breath away. 'Why me?' he asked faintly.

'There's no one else,' Pooley pointed out. 'The Wally Armstrong case is closed as far as the police are concerned and the Nurse attack is just another statistic in North-West Area. Nothing else can be done officially, even supposing anyone wanted to.'

'Who would I be doing this for?'

'Well, I suppose me,' said Pooley in some embarrassment. 'I'm the one who wants to pursue it. I did have a word with the Super about it on the quiet when he looked in last week and he told me he hadn't heard what I said. He also said it might be an interesting distraction for you but that he wouldn't like you killed.'

'Kind of him. Why should I do it for you anyway?'

'Because I'm pursuing it for the sake of the common good,' said Pooley with spirit. 'Trying to find out if someone's been murdered and someone else is in danger is hardly vulgar curiosity. Besides, you're an old hand at this kind of thing now. And you'd be better off in a language school than in a shop or in whatever masochistic line of work you've been intending to try next.'

Amiss realised that the sheer preposterousness of the idea carried some attraction.

'I'm thinking, I'm thinking,' he said, pouring out some more brandy.

Pooley had the sense to stay quiet. Then light broke through Amiss's slightly fuddled brain.

'What are we talking about anyway? How the hell could I get a job there even if there was one. I've neither experience nor qualifications.'

Pooley looked at him with some asperity. 'What sort of an idiot do you take me for, Robert? Of course there's a job. It's been advertised in the local job centre this week and there's also a notice outside the school saying there's a vacancy. Apparently there's a very high turnover there, and from what my friend had picked up, at least a couple of the teachers are novices. Someone presentable with a degree would stand an excellent chance.'

'What would be my cover story?'

'Straightforward, though I'd say you left the Civil Service because you were unhappy with its political direction. Old Nurse is a bit of a romantic lefty and he absolutely abominates Ma

Thatcher. I'm sure you can work out the rest of your pitch without any help from me.'

Amiss smoked meditatively for a couple of minutes. 'But I hated being mixed up with those two murder cases,' he said.

'You hated seeing people you liked die, but this time you'd be trying to find out after the event if someone you didn't know at all had been murdered. That's quite different. And what's more, you know bloody well you enjoyed all that snooping and conspiring with the Super. It was really very like your job as a private secretary.'

Reluctantly Amiss recognised the truth in Pooley's remarks. He sighed gustily. 'That was another thing in the Whitehall book.'

'What?'

'That the sort of people who join and flourish in the Civil Service like private power. Otherwise they'd be politicians. They get their kicks out of knowing that the public don't realise they're actually running things. Makes us sound like a bunch of cradle-rockers. Or come to think of it, maybe we're talking about the prerogative of the harlot.'

'Which is why you were quite happy for the Super to take the credit?'

'That's the theory.'

'I see. And to think I thought it was altruism. Well, that's a weight off my conscience. I needn't worry about anything happening to you, since your motives are purely selfish.'

'If I am stupid enough to go after this job and if they are stupid enough to take me and if anything happens to me, my bank manager — or rather Rachel, since I am temporarily without a bank manager — will have instructions to pin up in every CID canteen in the Met the information that Ellis Pooley is a loaded, pinko aristocrat.'

Amiss spent his Sunday morning dithering. He had no one to talk to about his dilemma. Rachel was accompanying the Ambassador on a visit to Lille, Milton was off on his course and Ann Milton was spending a term at an American university on a business fellowship.

He speculated about talking it over with someone else. His parents? His father would tell him not to be daft and his mother would have hysterics. Come to think of it, he hadn't even summoned up the nerve yet to tell them he had left the Civil Service. Poor devils, he thought, they set such store by common sense. How did they ever produce me?

Mentally he ran down the list of his friends and failed to come up with anyone with sufficient discretion and good judgement. He decided to do something useful. Motivated by the memory of Pooley's orderly flat, he spent a quarter of an hour cleaning up the worst of the mess before taking off to the Fox and Goose to resume his duties.

It was a predominantly Irish pub, which meant that fast service was required even though the majority of the clientele were in no great rush to head off for their Sunday lunch. Only the prevalent good humour compensated for the sheer physical demands of the job. So far Amiss had had no dispute with customers except over his refusal to allow them all to buy drinks for him and by now he had perfected a line of banter that disarmed all but the most truculent troublemaker. His evident enjoyment of superficially anti-English leg-pulling had won him great support among the regulars, so he could always count on one of them stepping in to tell off a compatriot who was making a nuisance of himself.

When the last customer had left mournfully for home, Amiss helped to clean up, was fed a hearty plate of beef, cabbage and potatoes by Mrs O'Hara, and had cash pressed into his hand by her husband with a request to help out the same evening. Only the previous night he had been moaning to Pooley about the impossibility of avoiding entanglement in the black economy: all casual bar work he knew of was cash in hand. His choice was simple: refuse the job or take the cash. The alternative course — to shop the O'Haras to Inland Revenue — failed to appeal.

When he left the premises at four, he decided on a walk. He felt resigned rather than surprised when he realised he was heading towards Knightsbridge.

It didn't take him long to find the address Pooley had given him. The Knightsbridge School of English was in a quiet side street about five minutes from Hyde Park. Amiss was surprised at the pleasantness of the location and the excellent state of repair of the beautifully-proportioned Georgian building: it seemed seriously out of keeping with the image he had formed of an ageing leftie, bike-riding principal.

He stood reading the two notices on the neat, glass-covered board outside. One invited students to take English courses on a shift-system: 9.00–12.00, 2.00–5.00 or 7.00–10.00. Each course ran for ten weeks and to his surprise seemed to work out at only about two pounds an hour. The second notice stated simply that there was a vacancy for a teacher of English as a Foreign Language.

As he was about to turn away, the front door of the building opened. A balding man with a wispy beard emerged, struggling to manoeuvre his bicycle through the door without injuring the paintwork, the machine or himself. Shit, thought Amiss, if he sees me now he might recognise me if I turn up tomorrow and it'll seem odd. Without any further pause and stifling the temptation to say 'Ned Nurse I presume?', he stepped forward and called 'Excuse me.'

The man jumped and barked his shins on the front mudguard with such force that Amiss winced sympathetically. He waited until the agony seemed to have abated slightly and said, 'I'm awfully sorry to have startled you. Are you all right?'

His victim summoned up as friendly an expression as pain would allow and said, 'Oh, I'm fine, fine. Not your fault at all. On the contrary, dear boy, all mine. Completely mine. Can I help you?'

'I was just wondering if the English teacher's job was still vacant.'

'Well, my dear boy, unless my partner has filled it without telling me — and I'm sure he wouldn't do that — I believe it is. In any case, now that you're here, would you like to come in and talk it over? It might save you a wasted journey if you find you don't like us.' And taking Amiss's 'Oh please, I don't want to put you out' for consent, he began to pull the bicycle backwards through the front door. Amiss followed apprehensively.

'Come in, come in, dear boy,' he bleated. 'Come into the lounge and let's have a chat. Now . . . mmm?' and his brow furrowed. 'Oh, dear. What can I find to offer you?' He looked distractedly at Amiss, who kept up a steady mutter of I'm fine, honestly, thank yous which failed to alleviate his host's distress. 'Here, here. Do sit down here. I think you'll find it the most comfortable of the chairs. Or maybe this is.'

Amiss sat down firmly on the nearest and introduced himself.

'Oh, Robert Amiss, very good, very good. I always find it helpful to repeat my students' names when I meet them first. You can remember them better then. Now what can I find to offer you?' And he cast his gaze round helplessly.

'And you are . . . ?'

'Oh my dear fellow, my abject apologies. I am Ned Nurse. I'm the principal here.' He rushed towards Amiss, who leaped to his feet. They shook hands with great ceremony and Nurse headed off towards a corner of the room. 'Would you like some coffee? Oh, dear no. I remember now, the machine has broken down.'

'Honestly, I'm fine.'

'Oh, I'm sure you could do with something.'

Amiss tried to remember if Pooley had said anything about Nurse having suffered concussion. Surely to God he couldn't be like this normally? It was like trying to have a job interview with a cross between Lord Emsworth and the White Rabbit. Nurse was now wrenching helplessly at a cupboard door that refused to open.

'I think it's locked, Mr Nurse.'

'Oh, not "Mr Nurse", please. Call me Ned and I'll call you Roger. You'll find us very informal here, that is to say if you join us. What did you say? Oh yes, the cupboard. Oh you're so right.

It is locked. And I have the key.' He pulled out a heavily laden key-ring, and to Amiss's bewilderment instantly found the right key and opened the cupboard with a flourish. 'There's only whisky here, I'm afraid. Now wait a minute. I'm sure there's more somewhere else.'Now where would that be, I wonder? Where would that be?'

'Whisky'll be fine,' said Amiss, who by this stage would have accepted hemlock if it would have speeded things up.

Nurse poured an enormous measure into a tumbler and handed it over. 'You must forgive me if I don't join you. Poison to me. Poison.'

'Whisky or alcohol in general?'

'Alcohol, dear boy. I can't handle it at all. Behave most peculiarly. But we don't want to talk about me. Let's talk about you. Let's talk about you.'

An hour later Amiss felt quite wrung out. He had been through what felt like his entire life history with Nurse very much in the style in which he imagined he must conduct his classes. He seemed to want information almost in essay form. 'Tell me, my dear boy. What used you to do on your vacations?' or 'Does an Oxbridge education make one a better man, eh? Tell me what you think. Tell me what you think.' If the object of the exercise was to establish if he could speak English fluently, then it was well conducted. Amiss's gratuitous thrusts at the expense of the Prime Minister had elicited squeaks of approval, but he was at a loss to see what it had to do with testing his ability to teach.

He was emboldened to ask a question about the job, thus sending Nurse into a state of agitated guilt. 'Oh, my dear boy, my dear boy, I've been most remiss. Of course that was what we were really here to talk about in the first place. Come with me and I'll show you round.'

He rushed out of the room, throwing a cascade of only intermittently audible information over his shoulder as he went. He was obviously uninterested in architecture or decoration and hence the tour was undertaken at whirlwind speed. Amiss's initial reaction to the interior of the house was bafflement. It consisted of six rooms, four of which were furnished as class-rooms. Only what Nurse had called the lounge could comfortably accommodate more than eight. The décor throughout was luxurious if slightly flash, conjoining oddly with the low student fees. 'Do you teach most of your students in the lounge, then?' he asked Nurse hesitantly as they said goodbye in the hallway.

'Oh, my goodness no, dear boy. This is only for what dear Rich calls the beautiful people. The others are taught in the prefabs in the garden.'

'The beautiful people?'

'Rich'll explain all that to you in the morning. You will come and see us both then, won't you? Come at eleven, at coffee break.'

By the time they parted, it was almost seven and it was only by spending an hour's wages on a taxi that Amiss was able to get to work at opening time.

'Oh, I'll go, I'll go,' he said wearily over the phone to Pooley at midnight. 'Christ, I'm beginning to talk like him.'

'He sounds as if he's almost under with Alzheimer's.'

'Possible. Or maybe he's just vague. I must admit I took to the old boy, wearing though he is. He's intelligent, well-read and seems terribly sweet-natured.'

'Yes, so did my friend. Said he looked very odd though.'

'Well, it's his clothes rather than him really. He's clean enough, but his clothes have washed-in stains and look as if they're hand-me-downs. And the odd socks and open-toed sandals don't help.'

'I wonder what Rich is like. From what you've said it sounds as if poor old Nurse is in love with him.'

'Well, he does sound a bit of a glamour-boy. Ex-ski instructor and all that. I'll have to put on my best frock tomorrow.'

'Good luck. I'm almost sure I hope you're offered the job.'

'I feel the same. I'm getting curious now, though I know it's against my better judgement. God rot you anyway, Ellis. Sleep well.'

6

'These two jobs definitely don't go together,' said Amiss to himself as he responded to the alarm at six the next morning. Carrying out his postal round in a heavy drizzle confirmed in him a growing sense of hope that Rich might offer him the job. He was beyond caring about the danger of working with hypothetically murderous colleagues. More than anything else he wanted to be able to stay in bed until a reasonable time and work protected from the elements. He might even make enough money to be able to leave Seamus O'Hara as well. He was great company, a delightful man and a generous employer, but his habit of hosting spontaneous parties at closing time was wrecking Amiss's health. He felt his youth was going in the service of what O'Hara, despite recent innovations in the drug world, persisted in calling 'the crack'.

Back home by nine, he had some coffee and toast and soothed his nerves with the magisterial sweep of the *Independent*. Then he set about choosing a suitable wardrobe for a putative language teacher. He decided to dress up to the décor of the school rather than dress down to the level of its principal.

Amiss had never been a natty dresser. Although as a civil servant he had been required to look respectable, there had been absolutely no pressure to look smart. Indeed, there was an unspoken assumption among senior officials that gentlemen were uninterested in clothes. Yet although his preferred garb was that of jeans and sweater, somewhere buried deep within him was a dandy waiting to get out. Amiss possessed a few pieces of rarely-worn finery that bore testimony to these occasional outbursts of foppishness. One was the silk shirt that took half an hour to iron; the other was the blazer.

It had been running into his old Oxford friend Jeremy Buckland that sent Amiss in pursuit of such an unlikely garment.

Buckland had always been a sartorial byword for understated yet exquisite style. Rather as Audrey Hepburn had once made the justification for couture, Buckland made his most uncouth contemporaries long to head for Savile Row. In the five minutes that was all the time they had had together, Amiss had found that his life-long prejudice against blazers had evaporated. Worse. He had to have one. It had taken him a whole Saturday to run the perfect specimen to earth in Jermyn Street, where it cost him half a week's salary. Buying a shirt, tie, trousers and shoes that lived up to its perfection took care of the other half. The accessories had been worn often, the blazer never. On looking at himself in his own home Amiss had been unable to think of any occasion when he could wear it without embarrassment. On Buckland a blazer had looked casually smart: on Amiss it looked self-conscious.

'Just the job for Rich,' he said to himself, unhooking it from the rail and checking its buttons for signs of corrosion. 'Anyway, it's the nearest I can get to looking like a beautiful person.'

By ten thirty, when he conducted a thorough scrutiny, he felt satisfied. For good measure he added a touch of the manly cologne an admirer had given him the previous Christmas. The sunlight broke through the gloom and removed his most immediate worry. There would now be no need to cover his splendour with the raincoat that had seen better days.

The door was opened by a pretty woman with a decidedly tenuous grasp of the English language. Three appeals to see Mr Nurse yielded responses of beaming incomprehension; a request for Ned did no better. 'Rich?' asked Amiss finally.

'Ah, Reech. Yes, OK,' she said obligingly and bringing Amiss into the hall, she pointed towards the doorway at the end. He looked curiously into the lounge as he passed and saw only three inhabitants, two of whom were lamenting in a Mediterranean fashion over the coffee machine.

His knock on the door of what he dimly remembered to be a minuscule office yielded no result, and it was five minutes before Ned hove into view looking breathless.

'Terribly sorry, terribly sorry, Roger. Caught up in class.'

'Er . . . actually, it's Robert.'

'Of course it is. How silly of me.' And Ned repeated 'Robert', 'Robert' to himself three or four times before taking him into the office and seating him in front of the more imposing of the two desks. He sat behind the other one and looked anxiously at Amiss.

'Rich'll be along in a moment, and I'm sure he'll like you. He was just a little, just a very little bit cross this morning when I told him about you.'

'How do you mean cross?'

'Oh, not with you of course, dear boy. With me for being at the school during the weekend. Dear Rich worries about me. He thinks I work far too hard and he's always telling me off for coming in on days off to sort out paperwork and so on.'

Amiss was none too surprised. He imagined that Rich's worries were less to do with his partner's health than that of the organisation. The condition of Ned's desk suggested that his approach was to plunge his hands into a pile of paper, grab as much as he could pick up, close his eyes and scatter the pieces around like leaves in autumn.

'But as I tell him, I'm really awfully healthy, especially since we had a lovely holiday in Crete last month.' He stopped and frowned. 'Now what did that remind me of? Oh, yes. I was going to sort out the foreign currency.'

He opened the bottom drawer of his desk and pulled out first a handful of coins and then a wad of notes. He gazed at the money in utter perplexity. 'Oh, dear, oh dear. I hadn't remembered there was so much of it. Now where can I find the space to sort it all out? Not now. Not now. I haven't got time. I've got to teach.' He dropped the money back in the drawer and closed it.

'Ah, here he comes.' A firm step sounded outside and Amiss braced himself. He was so taken aback by the figure that entered that he feared for a moment that his jaw might have dropped. True, it had a deep tan and striking blue eyes, but there ended all resemblance to any creature of his imagination. Rich was ugly, in his early fifties and under average height even in his stacked heels; his hair, though still blond (dyed, wondered Amiss), was in short supply; his nose was too large and his chin too small. Disconcertingly, he was wearing a blazer which to Amiss's untrained eye looked the twin of his own.

'Rich Rogers,' he said, unleashing a gummy smile that revealed a set of expensive but palpably false teeth.

'Robert Amiss.'

They clasped hands with studied virile firmness.

'I see you're wearing the school uniform,' laughed Rich, gesticulating at Amiss's blazer.

'What? Really?' responded Amiss in confusion.

'Just my joke,' chortled Rich. 'Can't imagine putting dear old Ned here into one of these. He'd have spilled coffee all over it within five minutes.' And all three of them laughed heartily.

Amiss looked at Ned out of the corner of his eye and caught him looking lovingly at his partner.

'Thing is,' said Rich, 'I haven't really got time to interview you properly. But since Ned says you'll do, let's give you a week's trial. Five quid an hour, and if you suit we'll talk about a full-time job on Friday.'

'What would the hours be?'

'You'd do all three shifts. Just to test your stamina.'

'Nine hours a day of teaching?' Amiss hoped it was another of Rich's little jokes.

''Fraid so, old chap. I'm hideously busy this week and we're very shorthanded. Normally it's not as bad as that, of course.'

Amiss tried to choose the words that would save him from humiliation, while not losing him the job. He was thankful he had invented very little teaching when talking to Ned.

'You know I haven't much experience,' said Amiss. 'Only the private tuition I told Ned about. I'd need a little training before I could take on a proper class.'

'Nonsense, old man,' cried Rich. 'Nothing ventured, nothing gained.'

Amiss had heard of cowboy English schools, but this seemed pretty ridiculous. Still, with a couple of days of frenzied study in the library he might be able to master enough teaching theory to see him through the first horrors.

'When would you want me to start?'

'No time like the present, old chap.'

'What! You mean now?'

'Got it in one, old bean.'

'But I can't.'

39

'Why not?'

'I've got to have time to think, to make arrangements.'

'Look, Bob. We need someone now. If you don't take it, I'll have to give it to the girl who's coming to see me at twelve.'

There was a brief silence while Amiss tried and failed to summon up the nerve to call Rich's bluff. 'Oh, all right,' he said faintly. 'I'll do my best.'

'That's the spirit, that's the spirit,' said Ned, getting his oar in. 'There's Rich for you. He can charm anyone into anything.'

'That's enough, Ned. Now take Bob to the lion's den.' Rich burst into great chortles of laughter. 'They'll be wondering where I've got to. 'Fraid I've got an urgent job to do here, Bob, or I'd introduce you myself.'

Amiss summoned up his courage. 'Do you mind, Rich? I prefer being called Robert.'

'That's too bad.' Rich sounded really sympathetic. 'I'm afraid we've got a rule here that everyone has to have a monosyllabic name. It's easier for the punters and it gives the school an engaging aura of informality.' He stood up and bared his gums at Amiss. 'Now look here, Bob, just because you've been a civil servant doesn't mean you've got to be an old stick. Live, laugh and enjoy, that's my philosophy. Now off you go and sock it to the tarts and the waiters.'

As the chuckles began, Ned got up and beckoned to Amiss to follow him. 'A real character, isn't he?' he said lovingly, as he led the way to the back of the house and across the long garden. 'Now don't you worry. You've only got to get through the last half hour of this class. I'd stay with you, but I'm teaching next door. Anyway, Rich wouldn't approve. He's a great believer in people sinking or swimming.'

They entered the first of the prefabs. It was furnished with benches and tables, the better to squash what looked like forty people into a space suitable for twenty. Amiss's dazed glance took in skin tones from Nordic to African; eye shapes from round to almond; costumes from mini-skirts to saris.

'Here we are, class.'

'Here we are, class,' they repeated.

'Say hello to Bob.'

'Say hello to Bob.'

'That's the first thing to teach them,' whispered Ned. 'They're new, so all they'll have learned so far is to repeat everything. I'd start at page one of the manual, if I were you.'

And with a sweet and genuine smile of encouragement, he faded out of the classroom.

7

Amiss had never taught in his life and had not the faintest idea how one went about it. As he gazed in dread at the expectant faces in front of him, his mind ranged wildly over teachers he had had at school. The good ones were those who could keep discipline — clearly not a problem here — and interest the students. Interest the students? He had no idea even how to communicate with them. His classic anxiety dream had become a reality, except that this time it was a job — not an exam paper — for which he was completely unprepared.

As instructed, he looked at the manual. Page one seemed to be pretty hung up on 'Hello', to which it awarded an exclamation mark every time it appeared.

'Hello,' he tried out experimentally.

'Hello.'

So far, so good.

'Hello.'

'Hello.'

So he had got them word perfect. Now what? 'Goodbye?' No. Unfortunately it was too early for that.

He looked farther down the page. Ah, of course. 'You Tarzan, me Jane' stuff. It was comforting to think that Jane had managed to bring Tarzan from gorilla grunts to fluent English in only a few weeks, whereas all these people were presumably starting from a base of perfectly respectable and sophisticated languages of their own. But then Tarzan had had the benefit of individual tuition.

As this nonsense was floating through Amiss's brain, he was pointing at himself and saying, 'I'm Bob.' Voices chanting 'I'm Bob' brought him back to reality. This was absurd. How could forty of them know no English at all?

'Wait a minute. Does anyone here speak any English?' Most of them seemed to gather from his intonation that they were not expected to repeat this. 'If anyone speaks *any* English, please put your hand up like this,' and he raised his.

After a moment a boy who could have been Korean or Japanese put his hand up. He was followed by four Asians, an African, five more Orientals, three Arabs and perhaps ten Europeans. As with the class in general, the majority were male.

Amiss spoke very slowly. 'Please put your hands down. Now I am going to say something. If you understand me, please put your hands up again.'

His mind went blank. He opened the manual in the middle and saw a comprehension passage about a businessman. No good. He flicked through and saw something about a restaurant. 'Please bring me soup,' he said slowly.

He looked at his audience. 'Did anyone understand that?' He raised his hand. About eight others followed suit. Presumably the waiters. Now what about the tarts?

'Good-evening. Would you like to come for a walk?' was as close as he felt able to get. That was lost on everyone except four of the waiters. He lacked the inspiration to try tests for *au pairs*, art students, housewives or Shi'ite terrorists.

At least he now had helpers. He caught the eye of the least frightened-looking of the English speakers, a Greek or possibly an Italian, pointed at him and said, 'Please come and help me.'

The man looked at him and said nothing.

Amiss repeated his request slowly, accentuating the 'Please'.

His victim got up reluctantly and shuffled up to the front. 'Thank you,' said Amiss, bowing. He said to him quietly. 'Please. When I say "I am Bob", say "Hello, Bob."'

They rehearsed it in low voices and then tried it out in front of the audience twice. Trying to look confident, Amiss looked at the students and said, 'I am Bob.'

Two schools of thought emerged. The traditionalists wished to repeat 'I am Bob', but they were drowned out by a radical majority who said 'Hello, Bob.' Amiss repeated the sequence until they had all got the hang of it and then said to the Greek, or possibly Italian, 'Who are you?'

'I am Pedro.'

'Hello, Pedro,' cried Amiss exultantly, and the class chanted it along with him. He looked at his watch, saw it was midday, pointed at the door and said, 'Goodbye, Pedro'. Pedro, by now delighting in his role as an auxiliary teacher, stopped by his desk to pick up his belongings, strode to the door, turned and said, 'Goodbye, Bob.' 'Goodbye, Pedro,' called Amiss and almost the whole of the class chimed in correctly with him.

As he was to observe much later, this was to be the zenith of his career as a teacher of English as a Foreign Language.

By nine, the end of his third shift, Amiss felt more tired than ever before in his life. Pausing only to say 'See you tomorrow' to Ned, he fled home to bed, from where he tried fruitlessly to phone Pooley. He then swallowed a large whisky, unplugged his phone and fell asleep immediately. When his alarm went at eight he had the satisfaction of waking up Pooley. 'Odd,' he said, when Pooley's grunts had diminished, 'I had you pegged as an early riser.'

'Not when I get to bed at three.'

'What kept you up? Debauchery?'

'Villainy.'

'Well, that's your job, isn't it? And right now I'd swap it for mine.'

'Fill me in.'

'I can't really now, except to say that I'm on a week's trial which involves me working so hard that I won't have any time to do any sleuthing. If I'm offered a job on Friday, we can make plans at the weekend. I don't even know how many colleagues I've got. Today I was either stuck in the bloody prefabs or was down the pub making apologetic phone calls to my various employers. The Fox and Goose man is distraught. He says he doesn't know where he'll find another Brit who can sing Northern folk-songs.'

'I didn't know you could.'

'Well, I know two. Now, Rich . . .' He gave Pooley a pen-picture.

'He sounds very peculiar.'

'He is. Reminded me of a satyr.'

'Are they a pair of old queens?'

'I really don't know. Superficially it seems so, but Rich doesn't easily fit any mould.'

'Well, good luck. You've done amazingly well to have got so far. Maybe you'll learn to enjoy it.'

'Ellis, you conned me into this. At least have the grace to admit it's a fucking awful job.'

'I do. I do. And I do sincerely hope you at least find an agreeable colleague in the next day or two.'

'As soon as I do that, you'll probably arrest him for murder,' said Amiss. 'What are you going to feed me with on Saturday night? It'd better be good. And make it British. I won't be feeling like anything foreign.'

'Does anyone test these people before their money is taken?'

''Course not. What's the point? Half of them'll drop out anyway and the ones that stay'll learn something — probably. Who cares? It's a growth market.' Amiss reminded himself sharply that he was supposed to be winning friends in this establishment, not alienating members of staff by asking awkward questions. He turned on what he fondly hoped to be his most winning smile and said, 'Enough boring shop. Tell me about you, Jenn. When I've got you another drink.'

It didn't take long for Jenn to confirm herself as the common little bitch Amiss had already spotted her for. It was a relief to him when he realised she was also stupid. After five days of grinding work he would have been incapable of trying to pump someone who might be clever enough to spot what he was at. After he had listened for the best part of half an hour to boastful accounts of how great she'd been as a travel agent, courier, croupier and God knows what else, he interrupted. 'Hey, Jenn. This is great. I'm really enjoying myself. Why don't you let me buy you a meal. Let's celebrate my becoming your colleague.'

'No funny business now,' she said delicately.

'Wouldn't dare, Jenn,' he said, with his best attempt at a rueful snigger. 'I'd say you're well able to look after yourself. Hey, come on. What about it?'

'Oh, all right. Why not? We're only young once.'

Amiss tried to imagine what Jenn saw in herself that made her unsurprised that he would be craving the privilege — on *his* wages — of taking her out. Probably her admittedly impressive tits.

On the stated grounds of convenience and the actual grounds of economy, Amiss tried to steer them towards a curry house, but Jenn outsmarted him. The 'little place' she liked that stayed open late was able to find them a table at midnight, and he saw with a sinking heart that dinner for two was going to cost him two days' pay. At this rate he'd never be able to afford to visit Rachel.

In for a penny. He ordered lavishly. Jenn looked at him admiringly. 'What's a big spender like you doing in a dump like the school?'

Amiss looked shocked. 'Trying out a new career. I think I might like it.'

'Well, it's a funny place to start. Why didn't you try one of the proper places?'

'Why didn't you?'

'Oh, they wouldn't have me. Most of them expect you to be educated.'

'You seem pretty educated to me.'

She tittered. 'In life, maybe. Not in langwidge. But that doesn't matter at the Knightsbridge. Those wogs are getting it so cheap they can't afford to go anywhere else.'

Their overpriced starters arrived. Jenn tucked into her white-bait with gusto. Amiss, who always had a problem with their little eyes, alternated his gaze between his own soup and his guest's face.

'I'd have thought a lively girl like you would find it a bit dull.'

'Well, nothing's dull with Rich around.'

'Really? I haven't had a chance to get to know him yet. Good friend of yours, is he?'

'You insinuating something?' She seemed simultaneously pleased and insulted.

'Nope. I meant friend.'

'Yep. That's all it is. Not that I'd necessarily mind a bit of you know . . .' and she dug him in the ribs. Amiss realised that all that free drink was at last having its effect.

'Like older men, do you?'

'Sometimes. If they're like Rich. 'Scuse me.' She darted off towards the Ladies.

Amiss had five minutes to himself, long enough to ponder deeply over the revelation that Rich could be attractive to a twenty-five-year-old woman. He felt the faint irritation of a nice-looking young man that a pretty young woman could fancy a hideous dwarf nearly thirty years his senior.

She teetered back slightly unsteadily. Her fresh make-up had been applied with more optimism than accuracy. The waiter arrived at the table simultaneously, and the next few minutes were taken up with a particularly irritating carry on about how she wished she'd ordered his *gigot* rather than her seafood platter. When that was resolved she remembered what she had been clearly burning to say when she returned to the table.

'Mind you, I like young ones too — if they're fun.'

'Been many of those around the school?'

'You're joking. I've been here a year and you're the first bit of talent there's been.'

'Sounds as if you're a choosy one.'

'Bighead. No, you should've seen them. God! Well, you know Ned. And then there were a couple of women — Cath's still here. She's a stuck-up bitch.'

'No other men?'

'Oh yeh. There was a young spotty one and an old geezer who got done for indecent exposure in Hyde Park. And Gavs is still here — much good he is.'

'How do you mean?'

'Well, he's you know,' and she treated Amiss to a poor imitation of a camp gesture. She paused for thought. 'Oh, yeah. 'Course there was Wally. Was he well-named!' She fell into a fit of merriment.

'Who was Wally?'

'He was the sort of deputy principal. Here for years. Before Rich came. He went and electrocuted himself in the language lab.'

'Good God. When? How?'

'Oh, only about a month or two back. And it happened 'cos he was an old idiot. Always showing off. "Let me demonstrate this, Jenn." "No, no, Jenn. Not that way. This way." Used to get his rocks off showing how clever he was about everything. Sort of fella if you said you was going to Green Park by the Piccadilly line, he'd want to sit you down to tell you why you should go by the Victoria line instead. Pain in the butt.'

'So what did he do in the language lab?'

'Search me. Mucked around with some wires. Anyway what do you want to know about him for? He's dead.'

'Well, it was the language lab I was concerned about. I don't want to end up electrocuted.'

'Oh, you never have to use it with the wogs. It's only for the beautiful people.'

'You must feel at home with them.' Amiss was finding it increasingly exhausting to be sufficiently flirtatious to keep her happy while not storing up future trouble. 'Is it because of them you haven't done another glamorous job like the ones you were telling me about in the pub?'

'Well, it's fairly glamorous with the beautiful people. You get round a bit. That's why I took the job when Rich suggested it. I don't have to do much with your lot.'

Amiss was encouraged to hear her slur her words slightly. He helped her to some more wine. 'Get on well with them then?'

'Some of 'em. But some of 'em's right bastards and bitches.'

Amiss was finding all this maddeningly imprecise. 'What is it you do with them?'

'That'd be telling.' She looked at him coquettishly.

There was nothing for it. She was clearly a lady who drove a hard bargain.

'Pudding?' he asked, through clenched teeth. 'Coffee? Brandy? And then I'll take you home.'

8

The normally serious-minded Pooley was shaking with laughter. 'And then?'

'The taxi-driver intervened. Said he wasn't having that sort of carry-on in the back of his cab. That gave me a breather to light a cigarette and interpose it between us. Whether he knew she was sexually assaulting me or thought I was attacking her I've no idea. I was too embarrassed to ask after we'd decanted her.'

'You mean you didn't go in with her? You cad.'

'I don't think I'd enjoy being raped.'

Pooley looked solemn again. 'It's a bit worrying, though, Robert.'

'What in particular?'

'Isn't she going to feel rejected? And doesn't that bode ill?'

'I suppose in my shoes you'd have sacrificed your body for the cause. I always knew the police were corrupt.'

'No, no, seriously, have you thought how you'll handle it? After all, if she's that thick with Rogers she could get you fired.'

'All in hand, all in hand, dear boy. What's for dinner?'

'Roast beef.'

'Lead me to it. And don't fret. I've already sorted things out. I rang her up this afternoon.'

'And?'

'She was a bit reserved. Of course I'd no way of knowing what she remembered, but I decided to assume everything. "Jenn," I said, "help, I've a confession to make." Spun her a line about how I was terrified my fiancée would find out — she being madly jealous. I had been unable to resist Jenn's charms and had behaved like a swine in not telling her I was an engaged man. Only mitigating factor that I had resisted temptation, almost overwhelming though it was. Very hard to be well-behaved with someone so madly attractive around. I'd have to keep well away, etc. etc. etc.'

'Excellent. Lovely face-saving job. Mind you, she won't leave you alone until she has her way with you.'

'I hope I'll have finished with the school before that happens. I don't want to get AIDS.'

'Gets around, does she?'

'If my deductions are correct, part of her job with the beautiful people is as a highish-class tart.'

Pooley's eyes gleamed. 'Now we're getting somewhere. Come on into the kitchen and let's get stuck into dinner. And you won't mind, will you, if I take notes?'

'Definitely a fifteen-cigarette problem,' remarked Amiss, stretched sensuously while rocking gently in Pooley's favourite chair. He watched with interest as his host flicked through his copious notes, highlighting parts with the help of two different coloured markers and putting large question marks in the margin.

'What did you say?' Pooley looked up.

'I said it was a fifteen-cigarette problem.'

'Oh, stop being an idiot, Robert.'

'Well, I'm bored. Come on. Let's see you put the tips of your fingers together and run through all the evidence.'

Pooley smiled. 'In the manner of whom?'

'Umm. Holmes? No. You're not a drug-addict. Poirot? No. Too Belgian. Lord Peter Wimsey? Too languid. I can't play this game, Ellis. I hardly ever read crime novels.' He paused for a moment, clearly in deep thought. 'Ah! I have it!'

'Who is it?'

'Miss Marple.'

Pooley threw a cushion which caught Amiss unawares and spilled his drink over his sweater. 'Serves you right,' said Pooley. 'The trouble with you is not just that your humour is infantile — but you bring your associates down with you to nursery level.'

'Well, it's one form of egalitarianism. All right, I'll be sensible for a while.'

'Good.' Pooley got up and embarked on his customary walk up and down his Persian rug. 'Right. I'm putting together what I've had from my mate in Central as well as what you've picked up during the last week from Ned and Jenn. Interrupt if anything germane comes to mind that I haven't mentioned. Now let's start with what we definitely know.

'The Knightsbridge School of English has been in existence for twelve years. Ned Nurse set it up by himself when he inherited the house from an aunt. Up to then he'd been employed at a series of schools round Tottenham Court Road. They were all much alike, usually a few rooms above a shop. Clientele attracted by fly-sheets in the street. The students were generally over-crowded and badly taught but in no position to argue. They were usually desperate to acquire very cheaply the basic English necessary to survive.'

'Tarts and waiters, in fact.'

'Exactly.'

'Poor sods.'

'And that's how Ned felt about them too.'

'Yes. I didn't tell you that he described to me a horrid experience he'd had a year or two before his aunt died. He'd gone to work one morning to find the place closed down. No information, just a locked door. He told the students to come back the next day and tried to find out what had happened. Turned out the school's owners had done a midnight flit with the term's fees. Ned had to break the news to a hundred or so students and he said it broke his heart. Lots of them were in tears.'

'Right. So when he decided to set up his own school it wasn't to make money: he wanted to perform a public service.'

'More or less. And also earn a reasonable income for doing the only thing he could do. Clearly he'd been exploited too. My guess is that what Jenn described as "proper" schools wouldn't have looked at the poor old devil. He's intelligent, and I think he's possibly not a bad teacher, but he's too batty and messy-looking to put in front of discerning punters.'

'This is where it gets hazy,' said Pooley. 'We know how and why he started up on his own, but we don't know what happened then.'

'My strong guess, and I've nothing to go on beyond the odd throwaway remark, is that for several years he made just enough to cover his overheads, pay one other full-time teacher and some part-timers, and scrape a living himself. "Of course before dear Rich we didn't have so many, dear boy, not so many." I interpreted this as meaning that Rich has been responsible for student overcrowding in the prefabs. Not that Ned would have intended to give that impression. As you'll have gathered, he's so passionately loyal that he wouldn't allow himself to see the truth if it reflected in any way on dear Rich.'

'He didn't just mean that Rich had brought in the beautiful people?'

'Don't think so. My impression is that pre-Rich the house was used for just slightly better-off students who could pay a bit more for the privilege of studying in groups of eight rather than twenty.'

Pooley stopped pacing, sat down and poured himself a modest brandy. 'Now from what we can gather, Rich arrived about three years ago, but we don't know from where, and was quickly taken into partnership — to the disgruntlement of Wally Armstrong, who had been working with Ned for some years.'

'I don't know anything about that. It's way before Jenn's time.'

'Central got this from one of Wally's kids. It was very vague. The junior Armstrongs didn't seem much interested in their dad.'

'So Wally presumably had it in for Rich rather than vice versa.'

'Well, yes. Although you reported Jenn as saying Wally was always trying to muscle in on the scene in the house.'

'Rich would hardly have knocked him off for being a bore at their cocktail parties.'

'Well, hardly. But it might have involved more than that. He sounds like the kind of man who could be an awful nuisance.'

'Whatever Rich is,' said Amiss, 'I really don't see him as the kind of raving psychopath that murders someone rather than sacking him. But then I've a vested interest in believing that.'

Pooley was up and pacing again. 'Christ, Ellis, don't you ever relax?'

'Later, later. Now Rich starts to attract a totally new kind of business and a kind of apartheid grows up between house and garden.'

'You're not kidding. I'm surprised us wog-teachers aren't required to use the garden entrance along with the students. I think Rich really *would* murder one of them if they turned up in the house except at the time appointed.'

'Which is?'

'The publicity material is very specific about enrolments. Just the first Saturday morning of the month. Each course starts the following Monday and lasts for four weeks.'

'Now according to Central's information, the beautiful people —'

'Let's call them the BP's, Ellis.'

'OK.'

'— the BP's are students from abroad who come to the school for highly intensive courses in conversational English. According to Jenn, most of them are here as much to have a high old time as to improve their English. At the moment they're taught exclusively by Rich, Cath and Gavs, while Jenn stands in to show them videos, television programmes and that sort of thing. Her main work is as a kind of social secretary cum escort. And of course she's a reserve teacher for the prefabs.'

'That's right. She went on about her important work in arranging what she termed "extra activities" and as I said earlier, the wink, nod and nudge she then produced led me to suppose she organises more than opera tickets.'

'Although as you also said, she might well be a bit of a fantasist.'

'I'd say exaggeration rather than fantasy.'

'Right.' Pooley picked up his notebook. 'Now here are the questions I think we need to have answered. How did Rich get in on the act? How did he and Wally really get on? Did Rich have a serious motive for murder? What is the legal nature of the partnership between Ned and Rich? Are they lovers? Does Rich stand to gain if Ned dies? (We know he had an alibi for the night Ned was attacked, but of course he could always have hired someone.) What are these extra activities? —'

'Stop, stop, for God's sake,' yelled Amiss. 'How in hell am I supposed to keep up with all that?'

'Oh sorry, Robert, I got carried away. I'll write them all out for you before you go.'

'And you'd like the answers after work on Monday.'

'Well, you will have lots more time, won't you?' Pooley looked at him innocently. 'After all you said that as a full-timer you only had to do twelve shifts a week.'

'Quite true. The only snag is that I've very little access to information. I've no excuse to be in the main building except to see Rich or Ned. And I doubt if I'll often be able to coax Ned out to lunch. He prefers to mess up his desk at lunchtime while he slurps yoghurt and eats organically-grown bean sprouts. And I wouldn't fancy my chances of getting any more information out of Jenn — at least not until I can get her drunk again — which I refuse to do before I've invested in a chastity belt.'

Pooley looked crestfallen.

'Don't worry, Ellis, I've got a few ideas up my sleeve.'

'E.g.?'

'I'd rather not talk about them yet, if you don't mind.'

Pooley hid his disappointment. 'Oh, yes, of course.'

'Now, from your end —'

Pooley put up his hand. 'Let me guess. You want me to try to locate some people who worked at the school round about the time Rich Rogers came on the scene and have them discreetly pumped.'

'Got it in one, Ellis.'

Amiss looked at his watch, saw that it was after one and got up to go.

'Why don't you come to me next Saturday? Though I have to warn you it's a small flat and if you want to pace you'll have to do it outside.'

'Great. And obviously if anything much comes up, we'll try to get together during the week.'

'One last thing,' said Amiss, as he put on his coat. 'I'm having dinner with Jim Milton tomorrow. What do I say? It's really very difficult being friends with both of you at a time like this.'

'What would you normally tell him?'

'Everything.'

'Then that's what you have to do,' said Pooley. 'Leave it to him to do the worrying about how to handle this three-cornered relationship. He's the Super, and he's used to making decisions. We have to trust him not to come the heavy.'

9

Bloody young fools, thought Milton. He accelerated into the fast lane, where he remained until he noticed his speedometer was registering almost 85 m.p.h. Guiltily, he joined the law-abiding motorists in the middle lane.

But come to think of it, were they bloody young fools? After all, he had given his tacit approval to getting Amiss involved in the first place. Why had he poured so much cold water on his ideas the previous night, simply because he had been talking about mysterious foreigners rather than about tangible evidence? This was a friend of his who had been a doughty ally in the past, strong on useful information and sound deduction and rarely if ever given to flights of fancy. That was more Pooley's style. Then he remembered that it was Pooley's flights of fancy that had led only a couple of months before to the arrest of the BCC murderer.

Was he old at thirty-nine? Or sliding imperceptibly into the caution of the senior man? He tried to find some distraction on the radio, but the news programmes had nothing that held his attention. He saw the signs for a service station coming up, looked at his watch and pulled into the slow lane.

Amiss jumped out of his shower and dripped over the telephone.

'Hello, Robert. It's Jim.'

'I thought you'd be on your way to Bramshill.'

'I am. I stopped on the way to apologise.'

'For what?'

'For being a middle-aged stick-in-the-mud. I don't know if you two are on the right track, but what you're doing sounds worth a try, and if you ever need to call on me, don't hesitate.'

'Jim?'

'Yes.'

'I never thought I'd be reduced to saying "You're a pal," but I'm feeling inarticulate.'

'That'll be the day,' said Milton cheerily and he rang off.

Amiss's reluctance early on Sunday morning to expose his ideas to Pooley's eager gaze had had little to do with the slight unspoken rivalry between them. It had had much more to do with a sudden embarrassed realisation that they were threadbare in the extreme. Idea One: Charm Rich into giving him a job with the BP's. Idea Two: Hang around Jenn's office pretending to be a bit struck on her. Terrific. Especially since he had no idea how to proceed with One, and was afraid of the consequences of proceeding with Two.

He mulled over the Rich problem on his walk to school. In a whole week he had seen the man only twice. Once to be sent chucklingly to the salt mines and once to be told with a mighty guffaw that he had 'earned his spurs' and was now 'one of the little family'. At that rate it could take weeks to build up any kind of relationship and he did not have weeks. If murdering Ned was on someone's agenda, there was no time to lose.

Amiss knew himself to be a better than average judge of character, and he felt fairly confident he had the measure of Rich. What was imperative was to get the proportions of flattery and cheek right. And, of course, on the assumption that Rich was running some kind of shady outfit, an absence of curiosity and scruple could only be bonuses. Of course, he also needed something to sell him.

He caught him just before nine. 'Excuse me, Rich. Could we have a brief chat sometime today?'

'What about, my dear man? Thought we'd fixed things up to your satisfaction.'

'Yes, sure, but I need some advice.'

'Not on matters of the heart, I trust,' and the 'har . . har . . har' resounded around the building.

Amiss emitted a broad chuckle and stuck to his guns. 'More of the head really.'

That seemed to delight Rich. When he stopped laughing he

pulled his Filofax from under his arm, scrutinised his diary and went through a series of self-important mutterings. 'Seven o'clock,' he said finally.

Bastard, thought Amiss. He must know I finish at five. 'Great. Thanks, Rich. See you then.'

He strode purposefully towards the door to the garden, almost sure he knew how to go about tackling the present continuous tense.

Rich was on the doorstep with an expensive middle-aged blonde and Amiss held back politely as they concluded their business. Rich kissed her hand with tremendous *élan* and a 'Goodbye, dear lady. Arrivederci. I cannot wait', and she sashayed away, turning back periodically to wave.

'You're some operator,' said Amiss admiringly. 'Do you do that to all the girls?'

'Most,' said Rich, eyeing his employee with some surprise. 'Do you always dress like that when you want advice?'

'What?' Amiss seemed puzzled. Then he looked down at his dinner jacket and laughed. 'Oh, this. Taking the mater to the opera. She's a stickler for keeping up standards.'

'Well, come in. Have a drink. You obviously haven't got long.' Rich exerted himself with commendable haste to get Amiss a gin and tonic from a little fridge behind the sofa.

'You're not a man who likes shilly-shallying, Rich, so I'll come straight to the point. Is there going to be a future for me in the class end of the business? Or did you envisage me staying outside with the proletariat?'

Rich was so thunder-struck that he failed to produce any sound at all.

'Fair's fair, Rich. I can take a joke as well as the next man and I played along last week. But you're a student of character and you must know very well that what I'm interested in is the high life and the perks.'

'You were only given the job on Friday,' said Rich in disbelief.

'Come on, Rich. You're pulling my leg. You didn't seriously think I wanted to go into the same line of work as Ned, dear old boy though he undoubtedly is. You and I are two of a kind, for heaven's sake. See an opportunity and go for it. Come on, what do you say?'

'How do you know so much about this side of the operation?'

'The mater again. She met some people skiing who swore by this place and said it was absolutely enormous fun. That's why I applied.' Amiss shook his head. 'Now, Rich, you know women. You can't expect me to tell her what I'm really doing. She'd have a seizure.'

Rich looked bemused. 'Didn't Ned tell me you used to be a civil servant? You don't sound very like one to me.'

'Foreign Office, actually. Loved the parties and all that. Afraid I got dumped for not taking all the backroom stuff seriously enough. So here I am ready and waiting to be your right-hand man. Game for anything, as they say,' and both of them broke into a 'har . . har . . har' in chorus. Amiss fancied that Rich's was a trifle forced.

'Good Lord, is that the time? I must rush. She's an awful tartar if she's kept waiting. Let me know tomorrow, yah?' And Amiss rushed from the room and the house calling loudly for a taxi.

Although Amiss still refused to let Rachel buy him a ticket to Paris, he had put up only a token fight to stop her funding their calls. The phone was ringing as he got through the door, and he took great pleasure in bragging about his *démarche*.

'I never knew you had it in you,' said Rachel.

'Neither did I. Haven't gone in for amateur theatricals since primary school.'

'How did you work up the characterisation?'

'Played it as a cross between Prince Andrew and one of the new breed of Tory MPs.'

'Pretty sudden swing from vilifying Mrs Thatcher to poor old Ned.'

'I hope it's equally effective. Hard to tell. Anyway, if the worst comes to the worst, I've enjoyed it.'

'What's that gobbling sound?'

'I'm eating fish and chips.'

'Well, if the BPs live up to their reputation, it'll presumably be quails' eggs and champagne from now on.'

'I should bloody well think so. Now, have I told you lately that I love you?'

And they fell to discussing matters of more pressing interest.

10

It worked. When Amiss came in the following morning, Rich was waiting for him. 'Enjoy the opera?'

'Awful. Walked out at half-time. Remind me never to go to modern English stuff again. Give me the Eyeties every time.'

'When do you finish today, Bob?'

'After the night-shift supposedly.'

'Well, I'll ask Jenn to take that class for you. Why don't you join us tonight? Some of us are going out on the town. Dinner, dancing. It'll be black tie. Meeting up at the champagne bar round the corner at eight. Hope you'll have more fun than you did with your mater.' They guffawed heartily.

'And the rest of the week?'

'We'll talk about that tomorrow. Let's see how you get on tonight.'

'What's your collar size?'

'Fifteen.'

'Excellent. Yes, I can let you have a dress shirt. Come round at six. In fact you'd better come again in the next few days and choose at leisure from my wardrobe. I've got a lot of stuff I rarely wear that should be perfect for squiring contessas. There was a stage when my mother used to take me shopping every time she came to town.' There was a pause and Amiss heard Pooley say, 'Yes, sir. Immediately, sir.'

He replaced the receiver.

At seven, just as Rich had retied his bow for the fifth time, the telephone rang and he had another of those arguments. 'No,' he said firmly, 'I don't know why you can't accept what I'm telling you.'

'But the offer that I am making to you is excellent.'

'I know that, Sven, but it remains out of the question. My partner will not tolerate it.'

'I think that you are losing a great opportunity. There is much money and tiny risk.'

'I know that, but he is quite adamant. I'm sorry, but there is nothing I can do. Goodbye.'

It was midnight and Rich was in expansive form. Sophie, Galina, Ingrid, Davina, Fabrice and Marcello seemed to be having a whale of a time. Amiss was working furiously to charm the whole pestilential brood while avoiding up-staging his boss. He seemed to be succeeding. He had managed to make a virtue out of his inability to dance: there were squeals and giggles as the women tried in turn to teach him and his exaggerated helplessness underlined the prowess on the floor of Rich and Fabrice, both of whom could have made a living at it.

If nothing else, he was beginning to understand the attraction of Rich. He might seem on the surface to be a fatuous old fool, but to a lot of people, from decent old Ned Nurse through to the jaded cosmopolitan Galina, he supplied an infectious *joie de vivre*. Amiss was beginning to feel that Rich deserved every penny he could wring out of these desiccated people.

It was Rich who called a halt at three. 'Come on, darlings. Beauty sleep.' And he overrode Davina's objections with a hug and a private joke that had her whooping with laughter on her way to collect her furs.

'When ees it you wish us in the school?' asked Galina coquettishly.

'Since the whole group is here, lunchtime will do. Tell you what, darlings. Let's meet at twelve thirty where we started out tonight. We won't want much more than oysters for lunch, will we? Oh, Bob, do your usual day like a love. But then let's you and I have a little drinkie round about — when are you finished? — five or nine?'

'Five.'

'Well come along to the Wednesday cocktail party at five and then we'll go on somewhere afterwards, just the two of us. For a chinwag.'

'A chinwag would be triff.' Their eyes met and they

commenced their job of organising their group ready for the
approaching taxis.

'So he gave me the low-down on the finances. Or what he said
was the low-down.'

Amiss climbed out of the cavalry twill trousers. 'No good.
You're appreciably longer in the leg than me.'

'They can be turned up. Here, try this.' And Pooley tossed him
a magnificent brown tweed suit.

'For heaven's sake, Ellis, we can't start having your clothes
altered to fit me.'

'Why not. Might as well do this thing properly. Try it on. You
might have to take a princess on a country weekend.'

'Too true I might,' said Amiss, clambering into a suit that
Jeremy Buckland would have envied and finding to his delight
that apart from the leg length, it fitted him perfectly. 'Rich tells
me that weekend escorts are in strong demand.'

'Hat!' And Pooley threw across a deerstalker.

'It's too small. My head's bigger than yours.'

'Quite,' said Pooley. 'Now why don't we leave all this for a
while, have a drink and you can finish filling me in.'

'It's primarily an escort agency with English lessons thrown in.
He was quite open about it. It's for people who want some fun in
London but need to be able to justify the time and the expense by
claiming to be learning English. So spouses lie to spouses;
children lie to parents; employees lie to bosses; bosses lie to
employees; training directors lie to exchange-control authorities. Rich charges in the region of two thousand quid a week and
does a roaring trade. Most of the clientele hears about it by word
of mouth.'

'But don't they get found out?'

'There's really nothing to give them away. It is a proper
English school. They do learn English one way or the other.
After all, the escorts are all English speakers and the students
come from a variety of countries and hence have English as the
lingua franca. And if they want to have it off with one of the
escorts, well, I guess that's been known to happen with a teacher
at a normal language school.'

'Well, surely the extra activities cause comment?'

'Again, on the face of it they're no different in kind from the norm. So instead of having occasional theatre trips and gatherings in the pub, they go to Le Gavroche and Annabel's. The central difference is that these students are at the school to enjoy themselves, and Rich is a genius at making that happen. I imagine he also lays on rather more esoteric entertainments for those with unusual tastes.'

'You're being uncharacteristically delicate, Robert.'

'In deference to you, Ellis.'

'And why keep on the prefab business?'

'It's the bread and butter. They may be only paying a couple of quid an hour, but it mounts up. He reckons the school makes a profit of a couple of thousand a week on those poor buggers. Anyway, it's somewhere to put Ned. He wouldn't exactly shine as a BP escort.'

'So what's the escort talent like?'

'Ah, well that's why I came at the right time. Rich has been feeling overwhelmed at the demands on him. He says he's OK on the distaff side. Apparently Cath is brilliant and Jenn OK. He keeps her away from the choosey ones, but she goes down particularly well with Arabs. However he's suffering from a shortage of men, exacerbated by the preponderance of women among the students. Gavs is gay, which limits his appeal a trifle, and anyway his domestic partner is getting possessive and wants him to move to a job with less anti-social hours. Rich said he was resigned to struggling on alone until he could recruit and train someone suitable. He hadn't spotted my potential. However, I am now officially declared a natural who can go on parade immediately.'

'So you're in.'

'As of tomorrow. He's bringing in a couple of part-timers to take on prefab duty. I'm afraid Ned'll be disappointed. He had aspirations to make a dedicated teacher of me.'

'Never mind Ned. Congratulations. Now did you pick up anything about Wally?'

'Only very vaguely. Rich mentioned with a sigh that he was plagued by people who thought themselves suitable for dealing with the BPs. Said it was very hard to tell someone he lacked charm.'

'Do I detect you're warming to Rich?'

'Well, I disliked him so much at the start I could scarcely cool. Let's just say I'm developing a grudging admiration for him. I imagine he's an amoral little shit, but he does work hard and when he drops the asshole façade, it's possible to have sensible dealings with him.'

'Is he a murderer?'

'God knows,' said Amiss. 'Now let's get back to raiding your wardrobe. I've got to get some sleep. Apparently I'm doing a full day's conversation, punctuated by lunch at the Tate to introduce them to its marvellous wine list and then in the evening we're off to a West End musical followed by a late supper.'

'Salary?'

'It's doubled, which helps. There's also a substantial clothes allowance, and of course all expenses are paid. And after six months I can come in on a profit sharing scheme.'

'Robert, you haven't forgotten why you're at the school?'

'No Ellis. I'm there to find out if Wally Armstrong was murdered and to help keep Ned alive. Really, how absent-minded do you think I am?'

'Just checking. Here, try this Burberry.'

However, it was too late to save Ned, who had been knocked off his bike at Hyde Park Corner at seven thirty that evening. The driver whose lorry had killed him swore Ned had ridden into the roundabout right under his wheels. Two independent witnesses corroborated his story. Amiss heard the news with a heavy heart and an indefinable sense of guilt. But the only one to weep for Ned was Rich, who had to identify him at the morgue, where he sobbed so hysterically that they sent for a doctor to sedate him.

11

Pooley spent the morning at a resources allocation meeting of unbelievable tedium. What made it worse was that as senior inspector, Romford was in the chair, standing in for ·Milton. Pooley suffered, perforce in silence and impassively, as Romford held things up with pedantic interventions and irritating objections, looked outraged when anyone uttered the mildest expletive and when in repose exuded that moral complacency that made him so universally unpopular.

'Now, in conclusion, I have an announcement to make. I'm being transferred to Stolen Vehicles. Next week will be my last here.' Grunts and mutters of the ohsirwe'llmissyou variety ensued; Romford reciprocated ponderously, declared the meeting closed and led the way out of the room. Pooley and WDC Simon, left to clear up, danced a jig: it was a moment too deep for words.

His mood was shattered by Amiss's lunchtime phone call; his distress was increased by the constraints on both of them. Amiss was as edgy about being overheard as Pooley, who had had the misfortune to have Romford arrive at his desk the moment he picked up the phone.

'Thanks very much, Bob.'

Recognising the agreed code, Amiss hung up.

Pooley jumped up. 'Yessir.' He lost no opportunity to curry favour with Romford. He had let his contempt show once or twice in the early days and had a great deal of ground to make up — though not for much longer, he crowed internally.

'Who's Bob?' asked Romford.

'Er . . . my garage. Sorry, sir. I asked them to let me know when my car was ready.'

Even Romford couldn't find in this the substance for a homily on time-wasting. 'Here's a copy of my memo to the typing pool.

You'll see I've improved on what you drafted.' Pooley skimmed the proffered document.

'I think you'll agree this shows we won't stand for any nonsense.'

'Oh, indeed it does, sir. Walk all over you if they got a chance, they would,' observed Pooley absently.

Romford nodded and walked away. He reflected with satisfaction on the way that young man was developing. You didn't hear him going on with all that stuff about detective stories any more. Discipline was the thing. Nothing like keeping their noses to the grindstone to knock all that nonsense out of them.

Luckily the table had been booked in the school's name, so it took only a couple of minutes for the obliging receptionist to identify Amiss and bring him to the telephone. 'Robert. Ellis. Can you talk?'

'Sort of. Can you?'

'Yep. Where did it happen?'

Amiss leaned against the desk and kept his eyes on his lunch companions. 'Hyde Park Corner.'

'Time?'

'Sevenish last night.'

'How's Rich taking it?'

'Badly. Not in yet.' Galina caught his eye and waved. 'Sorry. Must go. Anything I should do?'

'Nothing special. Except watch your back.'

'I will. Bye.' He smiled at the receptionist and sped back to his table. 'Sorry, darlings. Honestly . . . mothers!'

Galina smacked his wrist. 'Ees naughty saying bad things about mothers; I am a mother.'

'How am I supposed to think of *you* as a mother?' And smoothly, Amiss drifted into the vein of empty gallantry that was fast becoming second nature.

There were only four lines in the evening newspaper but they made things much easier for Pooley and his friend in Central. Having tipped him off, Pooley spent the afternoon chafing at his desk. He was immersed in routine work on an open-and-shut case: a domestic murder of such dreary brutality as to offer no stimulus of any kind.

Mid-afternoon he decided to console himself by having a chat with Pardeep, the current object of his romantic fantasies. One of the tiny handful of Asian policewomen, she worked on Inspector Pike's team and it was fortunate that Pike was a tolerant man, for Pooley's visits were frequent and without professional justification. Nor was Pooley her only visitor, for even the most deep-dyed racist elements in MIR admitted that she was the best-looking WPC in the Met. Pooley, who prided himself on the purity of his love, believed himself to care more about her mind.

'Tea?'

'Could do.'

They spent a companionable quarter of an hour swapping gossip, and then returned to work. Pooley went into his favourite daydream before catching sight of Romford and guiltily buckling down to his in-tray.

By eight, when they met for a pizza, Doug Layton had a lot to tell. He had met with scepticism first when he had pointed out the news item to his sergeant, but he had been allowed to make a routine call to North-West to get details. The information that Ned Nurse was alleged to have behaved suicidally had incurred mixed reactions. The sergeant, who was determined to believe his death an accident, dismissed this. Nurse was a dozy old devil, he observed, and it would be just like him to ride under a lorry. Their inspector, on the other hand, was prepared to entertain as a very long shot the possibility that Nurse really had committed suicide. Layton was trying to work out how he could have been murdered.

'Well, of course he could have been drugged,' said Pooley.

'That's what I said to the inspector. He thought it a bit far-fetched.'

'Yes. But it's also far-fetched that an experienced cyclist should act like that at the most dangerous roundabout in London.'

'I said that too. And also suggested he might have been drunk. Anyway the PM'll give us some of the answers. It took a lot of arguing, but eventually they agreed they'd ask for a full one, not just the routine.'

'Any word on relatives, friends, all that sort of thing?'

'Only Rich Rogers. There didn't seem to be anyone else to tell. And apparently Rogers said there were no relatives. He's supposed to be in an awful state.'

'No chance it's put on?'

'Not according to North-West.'

Pooley picked thoughtfully at his food. 'I wanted to see you tonight anyway, Doug.' And he gave him the gist of Amiss's involvement to date.

'I have to hand it to you, Ellis,' laughed Layton. 'It's not many DC's have their own private dicks. Hope nothing nasty happens to him.'

Pooley winced. 'Don't. I had a nightmare about that the other night.'

'Well, he's *your* mate. Now, what exactly does he want?'

'Some data on how and why Rich Rogers got involved. More about Wally Armstrong's history. Any scandal about any of them. There must be some people around who were associated with the school at the time we're interested in.'

'See what I can do.'

There had been moments that day when Amiss heartily wished himself back in the prefabs. It had started badly; no sooner was he through the door than Jenn cornered him. 'You goin' to make it up to me that I've had to take your wogs? Jammy bastard, aren't you? Only here a week and you've got Rich in your pocket.'

Amiss's well-bred sounds of deprecation were clearly getting him nowhere, so he changed tack abruptly. 'Hey, girl. Less of that. You and me, we're going to have a great time on these extra activities. Unless you prefer going out with Gavs, that is.' He contorted his face into a wink that was clearly seen by the tall fair-haired man who at that moment emerged from the lounge.

'Oh here's Gavs now. Bob was just talkin' about you,' said Jenn, smirking broadly and leaving them to it.

'I won't ask what you were saying about me. It's probably one of Jenn's wearisome little jokes. I'm Gavin Franklyn, known in this establishment as Gavs. I presume you're Bob.'

'Known outside this establishment as Robert Amiss.' They shook hands.

'Rich has never given me a satisfactory reason as to why we all have to shorten our names: even the dimmest of the punters is quite capable of managing two syllables. Now, business I'm afraid. Jenn's told you about Ned?'

Amiss froze. 'No. What?'

'What a heartless little bitch that girl is. Nothing exists outside her own nasty empty head. Ned was killed in a cycling accident last night.'

'On his way home?'

'So Rich said. Hyde Park Corner.'

'I'm very sorry.'

'Me too. He was a sweet if silly man. But of course the chief casualty is Rich. He rang me this morning and sounded very upset. Hopes to be in after lunch, but we're not to count on it. He's told me which of the punters you're being given. Cath and I will look after the rest. It's a relief to have you here, I may say; our groups have been much too large recently.'

'I don't know what to do with them. Rich promised to brief me this morning. All I've been told is to take them to lunch at the Tate Gallery.'

'Oh, Lord.' Gavs thought for a moment. 'Tell you what. I videoed a programme last night that you can play them. You'll find it gives plenty of opportunity for discussion. It's about money and the fashion industry.' He smiled faintly.

'Thanks a million.'

'Now, come and have a cup of coffee.'

'Love to, but is there time? I thought we started at nine.'

'We do, but they don't. It takes them a good half hour to trickle in and settle down. Come on in. Have you met Cath?'

'Yes. Last night, at the cocktail party.'

'Ah, you've been blooded. Oh, no, of course, I forgot. You were blooded the night before, weren't you? So you've passed the really important tests. Don't worry about the teaching. They don't. Just keep them diverted. And when all else fails, you can take them shopping. Black or white?'

'Black, please. Ah, there's Cath.'

Cath had impressed Amiss at their brief meeting. A pale-skinned blonde, she had the coolness and standoffishness associated with Alfred Hitchcock heroines. Yet although she held out no promise of warmth, she had class and intelligence and would be a partner to make most men strut with pride. It had struck Amiss that she and Jenn complemented each other perfectly.

'Too bad about poor old Ned,' she remarked. 'We didn't see him much but he was a nice old thing.'

'He was an odd old thing at the party,' said Jenn as she came in with more water for the machine.

'He always seemed odd at parties, Jenn. They weren't his scene. He only ever came to see Rich.'

'I dunno. I just thought he seemed sort of high, like as if he was a bit pissed.'

'I don't think he drank,' said Gavs.

'No, he didn't,' said Cath, 'and he definitely wasn't drinking alcohol last night. Never came near the bar.'

'Yeah, I know,' said Jenn. 'He went on about the fruit juice I'd bought. That mango and kiwi one, you know. Said he'd never had anything like it. But I thought maybe he'd had a couple before he came in.'

'Anything's possible, I suppose.' Cath shrugged and walked away. She picked up a magazine and became lost in it.

'Come on, Bob.' Gavs grimaced sympathetically. 'I'll show you your quarters and set up your video machine. Do you know how to use a language lab, by the way? No? Well, I'll show you another time.'

'I heard it was a bit dangerous,' said Amiss, as he followed upstairs.

'Oh, only if you play with what you don't understand. Poor Wally. Goodness.' He turned round on the landing to face Amiss. 'I've only just realised. That's two of us dead within a couple of months. I hope this isn't one of those things that goes in threes.'

'Me too,' said Amiss fervently.

12

Suppressing his distress about Ned as best he could, Amiss got through the morning with less difficulty than he had feared. Much as in principle he disliked his group of spoiled BPs, he was grateful to them for being so undemanding and easy to handle. The television programme lasted until coffee time and — being about people with more money than sense — absorbed them. In the hour and a half of discussion afterwards, he found that as long as he buttered them up and gave them ample opportunity to boast about their wealth, they seemed perfectly happy.

The group Rich had allocated him were to be with him until the end of the following week. They had been chosen for Amiss as the punters least interested in learning English and most interested in having a good time. Rich had explained tactfully that those who had some ambitions to learn were assigned to Gavs and Cath, who could actually teach. Galina, the Italian, and Fabrice, the Frenchman, he knew best: they liked money, nightclubs, dancing, sex and each other. They also had separate interests: Galina liked men; Fabrice liked women. He had met the other three briefly at the cocktail party. Gunther was a fat German playboy whose interests were money, gambling and racing; Simone, the Swiss, was interested in money, keeping germs at bay and finding another husband; and Ahmed, the Saudi Arabian, seemed interested in money, shopping and anything that smacked of depravity.

Lunch had its compensations. As he admitted later to Pooley, he would have been lying if he denied getting any enjoyment out of eating excellent food and drinking superb wines. The deal was that the students picked up the tab for the teacher and split the bill between them. Therefore, as Rich explained to Amiss, the smart teacher handed the wine list to the BP most likely to have a distinguished palate. Amiss had opted for Fabrice on the simple grounds that he was French and therefore had no excuse not to understand wine. It was a wise decision. Fabrice got so excited about the wine list that he persuaded his colleagues to consider this meal a special occasion. The resulting bill made Amiss feel quite faint.

Lunch lasted until half past three, when the conversations about horoscopes began to falter. Amiss's suggestion that rather than go back to the school they would take a look at the gallery went down very well. Ahmed dissented, explaining that representational art was contrary to Islam, and that while they were in the gallery he would go back to his flat and read the Koran. Amiss almost enquired how he had squared with his conscience the alcohol he had just drunk and the pork he had just eaten, but he remembered Rich's advice of the night before. 'You'll pretend to be friends with them, old man: they'll pretend to be friends with you. But they know, and you must always remember, that you're their servant. Play the game the right way and they'll throw you titbits like this.' He showed Amiss his watch. 'Patek Philippe, old man. About three thousand quid's worth. Grateful punter a couple of months ago. Play it the wrong way, and they'll have you fired.' He looked sadly at Amiss. 'Oh, yes, dear boy. If punters complain, out you go, I'm afraid. Their word's law and all that.'

Rich had also been eloquent on the subject of etiquette. 'Now, dear boy. You might think that since they're only here for the beer we should drop the façade of their being students and keep our responsibilities social.'

'It had occurred to me.'

'Two main reasons why not, Bob. First, there's the little matter of visas. Now there's no problem with your EEC BPs. They can come and go to London as they please. And most of the others have no problem in getting visitor's visas, but some of them have — particularly Arabs — and that's where we come in. They book a course; we send them a certificate of registration; they send it to the Home Office; and Bob's your uncle. And while we can be a little . . . flexible, I'm very careful to run a place that could stand inspection from immigration at any time.

'Then — and this is important for all of them — there's the

matter of self-respect. We know they're here to party, gamble, screw and generally have a rave-up away from their nearest and dearest. They need to believe they're here to learn English. It also makes their lies much easier to tell. So we all keep up the fiction that they're with us from nine to five working hard. The only difference between us is that they believe it.'

Amiss and his charges wandered about the gallery for an hour. He showed them a lot of Turner and Stubbs, gave them a few simple facts about each of them, and sent them back to their bases to lie down before the challenges of the evening. He wondered how many of them would shortly be phoning home to lie about having spent a busy day studying English art.

He debated going home for a rest himself, but decided instead to drop in at the school to commiserate with Rich. By the time he arrived, all the students had gone. He found Rich in the study, crying at Ned's desk.

As Amiss retreated in embarrassment, Rich looked up and collected himself. 'Come back, Bob, please. I was hoping you'd come. I have a favour to ask.'

'Of course, Rich. Anything.'

'Shouldn't make offers like that,' said Rich, making a pathetic stab at a laugh. He put his head in his hands for a moment. 'Fact is, old man, I've got to go to Ned's house to collect his cat and I can't face it alone. You wouldn't come with me, would you? I'd be eternally grateful.'

'Well, if it's me you want, Rich. But I'd have thought —'

'Gavs can't. I wouldn't have Jenn. Cath doesn't want to, but she offered to take your group out so you could do it.' Rich got up and grabbed Amiss's sleeve. 'You will, Bob, won't you? Please. I've no one else. There was only Ned. I just lived for the business, you see. Never had time to make friends. Or the inclination, if I was honest.'

'I'll certainly come with you, Rich. When do you want to go?'

'Half an hour OK? And will you sort things out with Cath? She's upstairs.'

'Sure. See you then.'

Amiss went into the lounge and threw himself in the nearest armchair. He told himself firmly that this was a stroke of luck.

Yet he could not shake off a certain reluctance to go with Rich to Ned's house. It was distressing enough to witness grief at the best of times. To do so in one's role as spy made it much worse.

For a few moments he toyed with just walking away forever from the school. Then common sense triumphed and he set off in search of Cath.

Amiss had low standards when it came to housekeeping, but even he was appalled by the condition of Ned's north London house. It was the kind of artisan's cottage that in the right hands would be a little gem. Indeed, it was clear from the appearance of the street that gentrification was rampant. Ned's house, however, was untouched to the point of looking as if no one had painted or even cleaned it in twenty years. There were damp patches on the walls, and torn lino on the floors. The tiny living-room sported a one-bar electric fire, two badly scratched greenish-brown leather armchairs — one leaking horsehair — and an enormous oak sideboard of great ugliness. Around the walls stood bookshelves of various sizes, all full, and piles of books had spread all over the floor and on to the top of the sideboard, where they threatened to engulf the large photograph of Rich that dominated the room.

He followed Rich into the kitchen, which boasted several hundred more books, along with a two-ring electric cooker, the kind of fridge commonly found in caravans, a dustbin, several tins of catfood and not much else. The nearest thing to a modern convenience was the catflap in the back door.

'Do you want to look upstairs?' asked Rich grimly.

'More of the same?'

'Worse, if anything. The roof leaks in several places.'

Rich wrenched open the door and called, 'Plutarch, Plutarch. Damn stupid name for a cat, if you ask me. But then it's a damn stupid cat, and vicious as well.'

'Does it know you?'

'Not really, but she'll come when she wants grub and if you don't mind, we'll wait until then. Sit down inside and switch on the fire if you're cold. I'll find some glasses and bring us some brandy.'

'Brandy?'

'Hip-flask. Ned wouldn't have had any.'

As far as Amiss could see, the books were all related to Greece. Clearly Ned had been fluent in both ancient and modern Greek and his interests stretched from philosophy to modern travel. 'Explain,' he said to Rich as he brought in the drinks. 'What's the background? And why did he live like this?'

'He was a messer — one of life's failures. That's the background. Loved Greek and went to Oxford, but then got a pass degree. According to him it was because he couldn't be bothered working on Latin. Don't ask me, I'm not educated.'

'And then?'

'Nothing really. About twenty-five years ago his aunt gave him enough money to buy this and he never did anything to it. He just didn't notice. Teaching made him enough to buy books and go to Greece sometimes.'

There was a rattling noise in the kitchen. 'Here we are,' said Rich. 'Now hold on here until I call you. Plutarch, Plutarch,' he crooned as he went gently into the kitchen. 'Yummyyummy-yummy. Look what Uncle Rich has got for you. What a lucky Plutarch.'

Amiss, who was well-disposed towards animals, wondered not for the first time why they were so often addressed as mental defectives. Then he speculated about how one should address a mental defective. Finally he remembered how he had occasionally addressed someone with whom he was in love. He tried to think about something else.

'Bob, now please.'

Rich had placed a pile of books against the catflap and was standing in front of a resplendent cat-carrying basket. 'That's very smart,' observed Amiss in surprise.

'Typical. He'd have spent more on the cat than on himself if he'd been able to think of enough things to buy for her. He was the same with me. You should see some of the things he got me — Spode, Meissen. And him dressed nearly in rags. Made me want to weep.'

Plutarch was gross, longhaired and ginger and scoffed her food as if there were no tomorrow. Rich and Amiss stood

75

watching in silence. Finally the beast cleared her plate, stretched and looked round enquiringly.

'Shut the door, Bob. Whatever you do, don't let her out.'

Rich advanced on Plutarch, muttering endearments. These cut no ice with the cat, who launched herself in the general direction of the catflap. The books fell over, leaving the flap accessible and with great presence of mind Rich threw himself to the floor against the cat's only exit. 'Sorry, Bob,' he gasped. 'Can you try to get her in the basket? And watch out. She's a terror.'

From the various scars and bits missing from her ears, Amiss had deduced that Plutarch was no namby pamby. He gazed at her and received a look of startling malevolence. He could not remember chapter and verse, but he knew he had come across such situations on a number of occasions in light fiction. Normally they ended with some human being in great pain. He paused for thought as the cat showed increasing signs of belligerence: its low growls increased in volume. A story about Jeeves and a swan suddenly came back to him. 'One moment, Rich. What this situation needs is a blanket. Any ideas?'

'You won't find any in here.'

Amiss thought of squirming out of the door and investigating upstairs. By hurling herself against the door and scratching it vigorously, the cat indicated a similar intention. Amiss considered the problem. It seemed to come down to a choice between bolting now and incurring dishonour, risking being clawed to death or sacrificing some item of his wardrobe. He took out a coin, 'Heads the blazer goes; tails the shirt.' When heads came up he said, 'The hell with that.' He took it off, unbuttoned and removed Pooley's fine cotton shirt and with a swift movement threw it over the cat. Before the cat had time to regroup or he had time to panic, he had it in the basket and had slammed the lid shut.

'Bravo, bravo, Bob. I don't know how I'd have managed without you.'

'Oh, it was nothing. The only difficulty now is that I haven't got a shirt. Is there likely to be anything upstairs?'

Rich shuddered. 'No, dear boy. Don't even think of it. Put on

your blazer and we'll get a taxi to my place and sort things out.
Perhaps you might let me cook you some supper?'

'Delighted.' And Amiss donned his blazer and went inside to
crouch in front of the electric fire.

13

'I know what you're thinking, dear boy.'

Amiss raised an enquiring eyebrow.

'That this flat is worth about ten of poor Ned's.'

Just as Amiss was about to deny indignantly that his mind ran along such materialistic lines he recalled that it was supposed to. He was finding it increasingly hard to remember that he was supposed to be an unprincipled, money-grabbing shit.

'Oh, yah. Well, it did cross my mind as a matter of fact. Seemed a bit strange. Him being the owner and all. You obviously had a good slice of the action, eh?'

'It wouldn't have mattered how much money Ned had. He'd always have lived the same way. And I'm the same. Even when I'd nothing I lived nicely.'

Amiss had no difficulty in believing that. Although Rich's Kensington flat spelled serious money, it also spelled taste. Here was a man who would have scoured jumble sales for unconsidered but beautiful trifles.

'How long did you know him?'

Rich finished chopping the ingredients for the piperade. 'I'll tell you in a moment. First, are you sure you're comfortable? That shirt's not too tight?'

'No, it's fine.'

'It's too bad about yours. It was so lovely. Where did you get it? Not in this country, I'll wager.'

'Oh, the mater bought it on the Continent, I think.' Amiss was beginning to feel quite fond of his putative mother. 'She's always bringing me back stuff.'

'She sounds very nice. I'd like to meet her some time.'

Amiss hoped Rich was just being polite. He viewed with dismay the prospect of having to borrow Pooley's mother along with his clothes.

'You were saying about meeting Ned . . .'

'It was in Athens five years ago — at the Acropolis, would you believe? I was a courier at the time and I had about a dozen American women to look after; he was on his own. He was wearing shorts, I remember. Grey shorts and an ordinary white shirt with a big orange stain on the sleeve. Oh, yes, and grey socks and open-toed sandals. He looked so ridiculous that I made some joke about him being a possible husband for one of them and everyone went into fits of giggles.' Rich put down the knife, pulled out a handkerchief, dabbed his eyes and blew his nose. When he had recovered he washed his hands thoroughly and returned to the vegetables.

'He heard us and turned round and beamed. You know that disarming smile he had. It made me feel so ashamed that I started a conversation. He was really interesting and helpful and had such infectious enthusiasm that even the most philistine of the ladies took in some of what he was saying about Athens. I was delighted with him. You can't imagine how bored I was that summer. I'd really had my bellyful of trudging round hot places smarming up to people and getting only a pittance for it. Especially after a winter of doing the same on the ski slopes.' He took four eggs from the refrigerator and began to beat them dreamily.

'So we arranged to take a constitutional the following morning at the time when my punters were upstairs slapping stuff on their faces and trying on for each other whatever they'd bought the day before.'

He went through the tears, handkerchief and hand-washing routine again. 'And then we fell in love.'

Amiss was slightly taken aback by a revelation of such intimacy so early in the evening. He took another sip of wine and tried to look like part of the furniture.

'Oh, I don't mean sexually,' said Rich, beginning to cook the vegetables. 'Well yes, I do a bit, I suppose. Mostly on Ned's side. But he had always been celibate, and I wasn't much bothered so there wasn't much to it. Really, though I used to oblige both sexes when I was younger, I could always take it or leave it.' A particularly vigorous stir splashed some liquid on to his apron and, tutting to himself, he removed it and washed out the stain under the cold tap.

'Would you like some more?' The shock of the cold water seemed to have brought Amiss's existence back to Rich's attention. 'Shall we finish the Chablis or would you prefer to move on to red now?'

'I'll stick with the Chablis for the moment, thanks.' Amiss reflected that the cost of the wine he had consumed that day would probably keep a family of four for a week. 'It's utterly delicious.'

'One of my great extravagances, dear boy. Acquired a palate early on; in fact I worked as a wine waiter for a time. But it was only in the last few years I could afford to indulge it — thanks to Ned.'

Rich returned to his vegetables. 'Where was I?'

'Er, in love.'

'Oh, yes.' He turned and looked squarely at Amiss. 'You're sure I'm not boring you?'

'Not in the least.'

'Helps to get it off my chest.' He returned to his stirring.

'I suppose we were both lonely people who were getting afraid of growing old on our own. I loved Ned because he was kind and cared about more important things than money. Funny that, with me being a bit too keen on it. He loved me because I was lively and confident and fun to be with. Yet it was timid old Ned who first suggested we might set up together.' Rich tasted a spoonful of the vegetable mixture and placed the spoon in the dishwasher. 'He invited me to come to London and take a job at his school. "Make a teacher of you in no time, no time, dear Rich. You're a natural. And you don't have to worry about finding anywhere to live. I've got lots of room and you'd be more than welcome to share with me."'

Amiss could not help laughing. 'It must have been like The Odd Couple on an heroic scale.'

'You may well laugh. When I saw his house I nearly cried. I terribly didn't want to hurt him, but what could I do? I didn't get a wink of sleep that night; I was convinced I'd catch fleas.' He poured the eggs into the mixture in the pan and stirred more vigorously. 'Just about ready, Bob. If you'd light the candle and turn out the main light. And pour out the Bordeaux, if you'd be so good. You'll find it over there breathing.'

'So what happened next?' asked Amiss, as he took his first forkful of piperade. 'My goodness. This is wonderful.'

'Glad you like it, old boy. Next? Well, I suppose what happened next was that I took over. I looked at the school — which was pretty dilapidated, I might add — and I had a bit of a think. Then I told Ned there was only one way we were going to have a future together. We could be friends and business partners but on my terms.'

'Which were?'

'I'd kip down temporarily in the most habitable room in the school. We'd get a bank loan to do it up and go up-market. Of course he had to stay as principal — MA Oxon. Always looks good. He agreed to everything. Bit wistful about living apart, but didn't complain. Poor old Ned. He never complained. As long as I was happy he was happy.'

'He didn't have any reservations about the BPs, then?'

'Bless you, he barely noticed them. I didn't encourage much contact between them, though of course I couldn't keep him away all the time.'

'So he never wanted to teach them?'

'Not really. I told him they were too sophisticated for him and he accepted that unquestioningly. The prefabs kept him out of mischief. "Well, of course you know best, dear Rich." That's what he always used to say.'

'And you prospered?'

'Didn't we just!' Rich fell silent and Amiss, reluctant to force the pace, applied himself single-mindedly to his food. When Rich spoke again it was to ask mundane questions about how Amiss liked the job. In his replies Amiss talked generalities, being well aware that Rich was paying almost no attention. When coffee was offered, Amiss sensed that he might be outstaying his welcome. 'Thanks very much, Rich, but if it's all right with you, I'll be off.'

Rich's relief was almost tangible. 'Well, if you must, old bean. I will say I could do with a bit of shut-eye. But I'm most terribly grateful. You were a hero. Oh, and thanks as well for listening so sympathetically.'

'Not at all. Delighted.' Amiss drained his last precious mouthful of Château-Margaux. 'I'll be seeing you tomorrow, won't I?'

'Oh, yes. The show must go on and all that.'

'I hope Plutarch settles in.' Amiss looked through the open door into Rich's bedroom and caught the now familiar unwinking angry glare. The cat had finished shredding Pooley's shirt and was now mauling Rich's duvet. Amiss made a face at her and withdrew.

'You know what I'm hoping for, Ellis.'

'Tell me.'

'That Ned and Wally both had straightforward accidents. I don't want to find out that Rich is a murderer.'

'You're very sentimental really, aren't you?'

'Incorrigibly. I like to believe in true love, and I decline to believe that anyone who didn't love Ned would take on that unspeakable cat.'

'I'm afraid that for the moment everyone has to be presumed guilty until proved innocent. So carry on snooping.'

Amiss sighed and took another gulp of black coffee. 'Oh, all right. When do we speak next?'

'Well, with luck I'll have the PM result unofficially by this afternoon. I'll ring you at work, shall I?'

'Please. Ask whoever answers to call me out of class.'

'And who shall I pretend to be?'

'My tailor, of course. Who else?'

14

The nightmare commenced at eleven, just at the moment when Amiss and Gavs were supposed to avert a human log jam round the coffee machine by shepherding their groups back to the classrooms. Amiss, idly chatting to Gunther, was on his way to the stairs when Jenn called.

'Someone here to see you from the police.'

Amiss's mind filled with sensations of fear and guilt. 'Me? Surely there's some mistake.'

'No mistake,' said the WPC as she entered the room. 'You're Mr Amiss, aren't you?'

'Yes.'

Amiss realised unhappily that neither colleagues nor punters showed any signs of leaving him in privacy for his interview.

'And you live at Lothair Mansions near Victoria?'

'That's right.'

'Well, I'm afraid you've been burgled.'

Amiss felt an overwhelming sense of relief. His loved ones were alive; he hadn't been unmasked. 'Oh, really. Is that all? Well thanks very much for coming along to tell me about it.'

Several of the bystanders looked bewildered, feeling that roars of pain and outrage would be a more suitable reaction. Even the WPC seemed slightly nettled. 'I'm afraid it's rather serious, Mr Amiss. Whoever it was threw paint all over your clothes. I'm afraid they're ruined.'

Poor old Pooley, thought Amiss. Plutarch had certainly set a trend. He wondered vaguely how the problem of ownership could be sorted out with the insurance companies. 'Well, thanks again. No doubt you'll want me to come down to the station tomorrow morning.'

'No, Mr Amiss. I want you on your knees . . . NOW!' She pulled off her cap, and began rapidly to remove her tunic. Oh, no, prayed Amiss. Don't let this be happening to me. Not a Stripagram.

He stood motionless as her clothes continued to come off and the students clapped and cheered. By now they had been joined by the other two groups: every eye in the room was riveted on Amiss and his tormentor.

'Come on, Bob, don't be a spoilsport.' By now she was down to her underwear and was pointing to an envelope tucked into her garter. 'On your knees, Bobby boy. Fetch it with your teeth, there's a good Bobby.'

By now Amiss knew there was no escape. He had to do this or jack in his job. Fuck it, he thought. Give the punters what they want. He sank to his knees as gracefully as he could, leaned forward, and to tumultuous applause plucked the envelope from her garter with his teeth.

'Good boy. Stay. Now gimme.' He pushed his head towards her to proffer his trophy. 'OK, Bobby. That was very good. Come on, everyone. Give him a clap.'

This time the clapping was interspersed with cheers. Amiss could distinguish the raucous 'Hoorays' from Ahmed. 'Now up you get and I'll read you your poem.' This was a more difficult manoeuvre, but through grim determination Amiss managed it with only the slightest tremor. He stood beside her grinning gamely.

'Wait everybody. Where's the champagne?'

On cue, Jenn produced three magnums of champagne from beneath the table. She, Gavs and Cath opened them to more clapping; the students grabbed glasses from the big cupboard and the staff ran around filling them up.

'OK. Is everybody ready?'

'Yes.'

'Let's hear it more loudly. Are you ready?'

'Yes,' they shouted.

'Then I'll begin.' She pulled Amiss's arm around her waist; he made a valiant effort to look as if he were having a wonderful time. It was not that there was anything wrong with the girl; indeed she was very pretty. It was just that his idea of fun was not feeling up near-naked women in public while clad in a light-weight woollen suit of Ellis Pooley's.

'Hi there, Bob,
You ain't no slob.
You're pretty cute,
For a new recruit.
Come on teacher,
Don't be a preacher.
Get off your ass
And lift that glass.'

Glasses were thrust into their hands and the girl raised hers and
cried, 'Happy Birthday!'

'Happy Birthday!' shouted the onlookers. Unclear about what
he was expected to do next, Amiss kissed her with as much
enthusiasm as he could muster. Led by Gavs, the audience broke
into a ragged version of 'Happy Birthday to You', Amiss bowed
his thanks and the show was over. People began to chat amongst
themselves.

Amiss politely helped the girl on with her tunic and faded away
as Ahmed came oiling up to her. He imagined she could look
after herself. He joined Cath at the window. 'You did well,' she
said, 'it must have been hell.'

'It was.'

'I'm grateful no one's tried anything like that on me. I've no
idea what they do for women, but I'm sure I wouldn't like it.'

'I'm sure you wouldn't. I believe they have Tarzanagrams.'

'But it could have been much worse. We had one here once in
leather and a whip who required the birthday boy to take off his
trousers so she could pin his poem to his underpants.'

'Oh, God. What's the acme of these things. A Screwagram?'

'I shouldn't wonder.'

'Anyway, look, Cath. This isn't my birthday. That was weeks
ago.'

She looked puzzled. 'I don't understand.'

'Me neither. I'll find out,' and he called Fabrice over to join
them.

'Is this a present from the group?'

'Yes. The idea it come from Ahmed. He very very much wish
to see one of these girls.'

'But what made him think it was my birthday?'

'No, no. That is joke. At lunch yesterday you have said you are Gemini. Now we are in Gemini. Ahmed says that is enough cause. It is as the Queen and her birthday. This is your official birthday.'

'I see. Well, it's very kind of you all; I very much appreciate it.' Amiss gritted his teeth and set off to thank his group individually.

He was given another present at lunchtime. This too had been Ahmed's brainwave, and had been bought by him the day before, after he had left them in the gallery. It was a cigarette-pack holder made of blue leather with 'Bob' stamped on it in gold; in a slot at the back was a matching lighter. As Rachel pointed out later, he was lucky to have escaped the matching handbag.

'Phone call for Bob!' Jenn's shout carried through the building. It was four forty-five.

'Shall we stop now? Take the last fifteen minutes off as a holiday in honour of my birthday.'

Much laughter.

'I'll see you all on Monday. Have a nice weekend.'

'You also.'

'And thanks again for the presents.'

More laughter.

Amiss ran down to the office phone. 'Ellis?'

'His blood alcohol level was a hundred and twenty, a level at which you're supposed to be five times more likely to have an accident.'

'Shit!'

'So if you're right about his never drinking, someone must have spiked his fruit juice at the party.'

'Fuck!'

'Of course, we don't know officially that he didn't drink. That will have to emerge from routine inquiries next week. So it's not a murder case yet.'

'Bugger!'

'Obviously we can't talk now.'

'Well, there's tomorrow evening.'

'I'm awfully sorry, Robert, but I'm going to have to cry off. There's a massive peace demo so it's all hands on deck. I've been press-ganged into work for the whole weekend. I've no idea if I'll have any time off except for sleep.'

86

'Oh, curses.' Amiss kicked the table in frustration.

'Thanks very much, Bob.'

Amiss slammed down the phone.

'Poor Bob.' Galina was standing by the door. 'You are stood down for tomorrow evening? No?'

'Stood up, yes.'

'Why then you must come out with us. With Fabrice and me. And some of the others — maybe Simone, Ahmed. We will have a good time, no? Dancing, and maybe Gunther take us to play baccarat . . .'

'Dreadfully sorry, Galina. I would have loved to, but I simply can't.'

She looked displeased. 'Say me why not. You have an empty evening.'

'I won't be free. Three of us were meeting. Only one can't come.'

He had noticed before Galina's propensity to get the bit between her teeth. 'Well then you will bring the other one. Is it man or woman?'

The effrontery of the rich still had the power to surprise Amiss; he felt like throttling the importunate bitch. 'It's a woman. But we're meeting in Paris. Now, if you'll forgive me, I have a plane to catch. Bye-bye. Have a dance for me.'

He disappeared at high speed and Galina returned pouting to the lounge, where Rich found her a couple of minutes later. 'What is the matter, Galina my lovely? You look distressed. How can I cheer you up?'

'Bob goes to Paris. It is for that reason he will not come with us tomorrow night.'

'Well, I'm sure you'll have a marvellous time even without him. I wish I could join you, but I have to visit my mother — in Birmingham.'

Galina was lost in thought for a moment; then she looked up at Rich, her face transfigured. 'Allora. I have a wonderful idea. You will give us a picnic. On Sunday.'

It took all Rich's professionalism not to let his horror show. 'I wish I could, Galina, but I have so much to do. For one thing, I have to organise my partner's funeral.'

'Ees not possible on a Sunday,' she said cheerfully. 'Please,

please, Reech. My friend Giovanni Balducci, he told me about a picnic you have. I wish one.'

Their eyes locked. Galina, blithely unconscious of Rich's pain, summoned up her most implacable expression. 'Reech, I do not like to be disappointed.'

Rich's shoulders sagged in defeat. For a moment he looked very old.

'Oh, very well. How many do you want to come? We'd better keep it small.'

Galina frowned, muttered under her breath and counted on her fingers. 'Fabrice, Ahmed, Davina, Alessandro, Karl, you, me — we will be in seven.' She thought again. 'No, eight Reech. You must make Gavs come. Ahmed likes him.'

'You will tell the other students?'

'Oh, yes.'

'I will see you all here at lunchtime on Sunday.' And Rich escaped to go home and continue mourning his friend.

'Rachel, I'm at Heathrow. On stand-by. Should get to you at bedtime.'

'You haven't forgotten I'm working tomorrow?'

'No. But we can have Saturday night and most of Sunday, can't we?'

'Certainly. What a smashing surprise. Have you robbed a bank?'

'No. You'll have to lend me the money.'

'Well, of course it's a gentleman's privilege to change his mind. What brought this about?'

'I've had one of those birthdays.'

15

Amiss felt at peace. He had had a most therapeutic day wandering aimlessly around Paris and had been thrilled to find again, purely by accident, the crêperie near the Sorbonne which he had frequented during the summer after he'd left Oxford. He enjoyed his inexpensive lunch there more than any of the extravagant meals he had had during the previous four days. 'It would have been nicer had you been with me,' he told Rachel when she joined him, much later, at their favourite restaurant. 'But I had a lovely time anyway.'

'You needed it,' she said. 'You badly needed a treat.' She gave him a hug. 'I'm so glad you came.'

'Oh, so am I. I was an idiot not to come before. I don't know why I was so obstinate about not borrowing money from you.'

'Probably hidden anti-semitism. Fear that I'll reveal myself at bottom as a usurer.'

'Idiot. Will you have a drink to start?'

'I certainly will. And can we order straight away? I'm starving. I had no time for lunch between meetings.'

When they had ordered, and a plate of crudités had alleviated the worst pangs of Rachel's hunger, she leaned back gratefully and emitted a long and happy sigh. 'Oh, this is nice. Now divert me. I want to hear all about your BPs. All you managed to tell me last night was that you hated them all.'

'I do, I do. And I feel so guilty about it.'

'Robert, you've got a capacity for guilt that is positively Jewish. Where did you get it?'

'Well I didn't catch it from you, that's for sure. How did you escape without it?'

The waiter arrived and delivered Amiss's garlic mushrooms and Rachel's shellfish. 'That's another anomaly,' she said, sounding slightly muffled through her first mouthful of moules marinière. 'You're the one with the Jewish stomach.'

'I expect we were switched at birth.'

They ate with concentration for a couple of minutes. 'That's better,' she said. 'Now go on. Tell me why you've become a xenophobe.'

Amiss ran his fingers through his hair. 'I really really loathe them and it frightens me. You know how I abhor racial stereotyping, and all that sort of stuff — especially the negative kind.'

'Well . . .'

'Oh, for God's sake, Rachel. I'm being serious. I'm not talking about our yid/goy banter.'

'Sorry, yes of course. You're a fully paid-up nice liberal who keeps an open mind, avoids labelling people and scores very low indeed on racial prejudice.' She finished the last of the moules, mopped some of the broth with the remains of her roll, chewed it enthusiastically, washed it down with a gulp of the house white, smacked her lips and looked enquiringly at Amiss. 'What are you waiting for?'

He looked at her suspiciously.

'I mean it! You're a nice person: it's official.'

'That's good to know. In fact that's what I thought I was. And it was certainly in that spirit that I approached this job.'

'And?'

'They're all living up to the worst of the goddamn stereotypes, and I find myself thinking, "Just like a kraut/frog/wop or whatever."'

'Kike?'

'We don't get any of them — too hardworking for us.'

'I have to say that if you'd spent the whole day arguing with French bureaucrats you'd believe in national stereotypes. When they weren't shrugging and making moues, they were trying to change the rules without telling us.'

'Oh, well, bureaucrats.'

'Balls! It's the French. Nothing like living abroad to make one robust about disliking other nations. Anyway, what makes it all right to disparage bureaucrats? Because you were one? Same way you've a licence to mock the English?'

The waiter reappeared, served up their *pot au feu* and poured them some of the house red. Rachel raised her glass. 'Happy Birthday, Robert. Now, as a favour to me, will you forget your liberal conscience and tell me why you hate them so much. And linger over it. I'm in the mood for unrelieved character assassination. Tell me about them one by one, in all their ghastliness.'

'Starting with the least or most offensive?'

'Oh, please save the worst till last. I always like a treat to finish.'

'OK. I'll save Ahmed until coffee. I think he's the most awful, though of course I concede that it's early days yet. Right. I think on the whole that Gunther is the least offensive, but he's very hard to take nevertheless. Quick, quick. Bad thing about stereotype German? And don't stop to think.'

'Fat, ponderous, humourless.'

'Perfect. Well, Gunther must weigh fifteen stone and tucks into the starchy foods at every opportunity. He carries a large pocket dictionary around with him and oblivious to his waiting audience, he halts mid-sentence to thumb through it for the *mot juste*; it is, he explains often, important to get things right. I said to him once that something wasn't important, and he responded with, "Everything is of importance."

'He has to have every joke explained to him; in fact I truly believe he's only just learning to grasp what jokes are. He can spot them now — they're what has just happened when people laugh.'

'He sounds boring, but not actually objectionable.'

'You don't allow that boring can be objectionable? Well, how about his preoccupation with status? Can you believe that Gunther wanted a conversation about the rank of the stripping WPC? I had to spell out every rank in the Met. In fact,' and in his excitement Amiss dropped his fork on to his plate and spilled gravy on the tablecloth, 'the only time I've ever seen him animated was when we talked about who called whom what in Britain. He was thunderstruck to learn that secretaries often called their bosses by their first names. Produced the response, "But how could this be? The boss he has no honorific? This is incredulous."'

'What does he do for a living?'

'Lives off his inheritance, as far as I can gather. His papa founded a pretty successful pharmaceutical company and he's got a seat on the board. No chance of one not knowing. He's got the company logo on his key-ring, socks, sweaters and probably underpants.'

'And he's in London for what?'

'Gambling clubs.'

'Age?'

'Late forties.'

'What does he look like as well as fat?'

'Almost bald, but those hairs he does have are beautifully coiffed. My guess is he blow dries it daily.'

Rachel frowned. 'What would he have done in the war if he'd been old enough?'

'Good question.' Amiss ate thoughtfully. 'I know. He'd have sat on the board of the company and asked no questions.'

'Redeeming feature?'

'Stolid good humour.'

'You know that party game — what animal does he most resemble? Sounds as if he'd be a warthog.'

'A carnivorous warthog. Gunther doesn't consider it a meal unless he's scoffed a few kilos of red meat.'

She grimaced. 'OK, that's enough Gunther. Next worst?'

Amiss pushed his plate away. 'Coffee?'

'Please.'

He mimed coffee to the waiter.

'Fabrice. Well, you've already done a bit of stereotyping of the French. What was it? Gallic gestures. Duplicitousness. Other negative characteristics?'

'Food snobs, wine snobs, womanisers and think they're God Almighty.'

'Fabrice thinks if you get a good meal in London it's because the chef is French. Therefore, if he doesn't know who's doing the cooking, he demands steak *frites* every time. He refuses to countenance any other than French wines. Californian? Australian? Bulgarian? Italian? All rubbish. He tells me he has a wife and two mistresses exclusively to himself, for all three of whom he's just bought kilts at the Scotch House. *And* he's at it with Galina. Yes, and he also thinks he's God Almighty. And he says "Bof!"'

'What else? Oh yes. Every time he discovers a new quirk in the English language he assures me that "it is not logique", and shows what an inferior language it is to French. All this along with aforementioned shrugs and moues.'

'Is he sexy?'

'Oh, I'd say so. Same age as Gunther, but slim, graceful and with lots of black hair with wings of white at the temples. Mind you, if I had half the money he spends on it I wouldn't need to work. He's bought lots of English clothes which he wears with careless elegance — le sports coat, le cashmere sweater, le Burberry raincoat, that sort of thing.' He began to laugh.

'What is it?'

'Poor old Gunther. I heard from Gavs that they both went shopping separately last weekend and bought Burberrys. Came in on Monday wearing them and of course Gunther looked vile and Fabrice marvellous. Gunther hasn't worn it since.'

'Job?'

'Owns a prosperous vineyard. As far as I can gather his wife actually runs it.'

'Purpose of visit?'

'Learn a bit of English; find a bit of new crumpet; avoid work.'

'Redeeming feature?'

'Honesty. When I asked him what was the essential problem in Anglo-French relations, he said, "We 'ate you."'

'I think I could get to like Fabrice. Animal?'

'Only a camel, I think, could convey his quintessential snottiness.'

'Who's next?'

'Simone, who's Swiss. Well?'

'Obsessed with cleanliness, order and keeping to rules. Boring, unimaginative?'

'Yep. That's our Simone. Eating anywhere she hasn't eaten before is an act of heroism. We went to a Thai restaurant yesterday and she was convinced she would be forced to eat dog. As she goes through the city all she sees are dog turds and litter. Talks about nothing except the bloody germs that lie in wait for her all over London. Yesterday, over lunch, she told us that the previous night she had seen from her taxi something very disturbing.'

'My God, let me guess. A badly rinsed teacup?'

'A dosser asleep in a cardboard box. That shouldn't be allowed, she explained. These people spread disease. Fabrice, to do him justice, said they had to sleep somewhere and what should be done with them. She said they should be put in jail.'

'Yeech!'

'Quite.'

'Looks?'

'Reminds me of nothing so much as a Swiss Doris Day, except her yellow hair is curled. She wears the modern equivalents of Peter Pan collars and gingham dirndl skirts. Expensive ones, mind: lots of lace, embroidery, that sort of thing. Goes in a great deal for pretty little feminine gestures to denote, for example, despair at the hotel's failure to air duvets at the correct times, or whatever sodding thing is on what only another Swiss could call her mind.'

'Source of income?'

'Recently divorced rich husband.'

'Redeeming feature?'

'Stays quiet most of the time.'

'Animal?'

'Persian cat.'

'Hmm. Next?'

'Galina — Italian. Yes?'

'La Dolce Vita stuff, voluptuous, vivacious, lots of gestures, amoral.'

'Spot on. Jesus, what a pain in the ass that woman is. Permanently the life and soul of the party — which means she decides when and where the party is and draws up the guest list. "Ees not clear for me" is what she comes up with every time she feels she isn't getting enough attention. She's got a pout that must have been helped on by a plastic surgeon and she points it in my direction every time she notices I've been looking at someone else for two seconds. Wants to have me looking gooey-eyed and making Fabrice jealous. At that I draw the line.'

'Source of income?'

'Husband. Must be loaded. Even I know she's wearing thousands of pounds worth of clothes and sometimes tens of thousands worth of jewellery.'

'Redeeming feature?'

'Generous with money, I suppose. In fact most of them are. But it's not what I call generosity. It's just that they don't mind how much they pay to buy you. You wouldn't catch any of them giving money to a blind beggar. Unless maybe Gunther, if someone sat him down and explained at length exactly how this beggar had come to this state through no fault of his own and why it was that there were no appropriate authorities for him to go to in order to claim welfare benefits.'

'What animal is Galina?'

'A lynx.'

'And Ahmed?'

'Ah, our *pièce de résistance*. Oh, I can't think of any animal that deserves to be compared with him. Maybe a cross between a shark and a tomcat.'

'Nasty?'

'He is. Nasty young Ahmed ibn Mohammed ibn Abdullah from Saudi Arabia.'

'Don't tell me. Flash clothes, throws money around ostentatiously, thinks all women are potential lays, fast cars, lazy.'

'You've been reading my diary. In fact, of all the lines they trot out, the one that maddens me most is "Insh'allah" — as God wills. Ahmed uses his religion in a way that is insulting both to it and to me. He's always late, and it's always God's will. Anything he doesn't want to do is forbidden by Islam; anything he does isn't. They all think of me as a servant, but Ahmed openly treats me like one.'

'He's swarthy?'

'And cross-eyed. Just on the edge of running to flab and certainly will if he goes on imbibing the way he does. On the three separate occasions I've met him he's been ostentatiously sporting different watches and shades. His clothes are the wrong side of vulgar and curiously chosen. Yesterday he was wearing a pale blue leather jacket which must have cost him several hundred quid, along with a yellow sweater from Marks and Spencer, in which, incidentally — because it is Jewish-owned — Saudis are not supposed to shop.'

'Income?'

'Claims to be a member of the Saudi royal family. It's quite possible, I suppose. I believe there are five thousand princes. In any case, true or false, he is forever boasting about his great connections.'

'Phew. What a menagerie!' Rachel accepted the waiter's offer of more coffee. She thought over the conversation. 'Tell me, do they all stay in the same place together, or what?'

'Mostly. We've got a deal with a local swanky hotel which gives the punters a tiny discount — the rich love those — and us a cut. One of the great advantages of this arrangement is that our students can screw each other without inconvenience. The rooms are pretty palatial, apparently, but Ahmed complains anyway because he'd rather be staying with one of his royal cousins, who, he claims, owns an apartment in Earl's Court with six bedrooms and four bathrooms.'

'What?'

'For wives, children, in-laws and servants. Ahmed said he couldn't stay there because his cousin is in London for a small operation and has brought with him a retinue of seventeen: two wives; six children; one mother-in-law; one father-in-law; two brothers; one brother's brother-in-law; four servants. With the best will in the world, there wasn't room for Ahmed.'

'That does it,' said Rachel. 'I've had it with foreigners for tonight. I'm totally out of touch with cricket. Tell me how Surrey are getting on in the county championship.'

16

Though Rich's mother was long dead, she played an important role in saving her son from being swallowed up by his clients. Most of these came to London for a matter of two or three weeks, having been told by friends to expect a wonderful time with Rich and his jolly young helpers. The more demanding of them expected these up-market equivalents of Butlins Redcoats to be permanently at their beck and call. Had Rich not been able to plead filial duties, he would rarely have had a weekend to himself.

Even with a very small staff, Rich was able to organise extra activities for every night of the week, so many of the punters had no objection to being left to their own devices at the weekends. Shopping took up all of Saturday, and with most of them staying in the same hotel, there was no shortage of company.

Unfortunately for Rich, he and his staff were often victims of their own success. Most of their punters were hedonistic, selfish people who were disinclined to put themselves out for each other. Consequently, they enjoyed themselves far more with a professional escort in attendance. So when one of their number suggested persuading Rich or Gavs or Cath to join them at the weekend, there would be plenty who would concur enthusiastic-ally. They had no qualms about spoiling someone's weekend. In their view, they were conferring favours by taking school staff out and entertaining them lavishly. It was a pity that Jenn, who actually liked being taken out, was the least popular.

Latterly, pressure from Gav's partner was intensifying and Cath had stated firmly that she needed three out of four weekends completely free. Rich found himself fighting to have any weekends at all to himself; without the help of his late mother he would have had none.

At the best of times he would have resented Galina's coercion, while also realising he had little choice but to acquiesce. He knew her type all too well. Thwart them and the grapevine would begin to hum with suggestions that service at the Knightsbridge was no longer what it had been: she and her kind were unforgiving. In such circumstances Rich could do little but shrug and remind himself that every job had its drawbacks. This time was different: he felt very bitter that he could not even be left alone for a few days to grieve. Even allowing that Galina and the others did not know fully the depth of his relationship with Ned, he would have thought that they would realise that the loss of a business partner could hurt.

Before he could relax, he had to talk to Gavs. To his relief, he, rather than Kenneth, answered the phone.

'Gavs, that bitch Galina blackmailed me into having a picnic on Sunday and she was very insistent that you should come as well.'

'Well, I promised to spend the whole weekend at home. We've got a lot of decorating to do.'

'I'd be awfully grateful if you could stretch a point, Gavs. They'll be disappointed if you don't come — particularly Galina and Ahmed.'

'Ahmed?'

'That's what she said.'

'I'll have to ask Kenneth. Is there any reason why he shouldn't come too?'

'You should be the judge of that, Gavs. You've been to picnics before. Is it his sort of thing?'

'Could be. I'll ring you back.'

And to Rich's great relief, Gavs reported within five minutes that they would both be on parade on Sunday.

All Friday evening he sat in his little Georgian house sipping his treasured wine and thinking regretful and loving thoughts about Ned. The neighbourhood odd-job man had already put in a catflap, so Plutarch was let out and stayed away for hours. It was with mixed feelings that Rich saw her return in the late evening. He wanted her safe and with him as a link with Ned, yet he hated her and what she was already doing to his immaculate sanctuary. He was losing hope that she would settle down quickly and stop her campaign of destruction. He could not remember that Ned had ever talked about her chewing or shredding fabrics and furniture. But then, as he recalled with a sigh, Ned would scarcely have noticed.

They ate. Plutarch was given tinned salmon, which Rich hoped might put her in good humour. He made himself a Salade Niçoise and finally felt able to listen to some music. As he lay back in his favourite armchair and closed his eyes, an enormous weight landed squarely on his stomach and winded him. He stayed still, and Plutarch turned round and round until she found a comfortable position. Tentatively Rich tried stroking her, and to his astonishment, then his delight, she began to purr.

He had twelve hours sleep that night, waking eventually because Plutarch, who had chosen his bed as her sleeping quarters, wanted her breakfast. Later on, Rich went out to buy supplies. He always went to Fortnum and Mason for a hamper for these picnics. Most of the participants were too lazy to shop anywhere outside Knightsbridge — indeed some of them never outside Harrods — so Fortnum's had novelty value for them. He took the hamper and the other provisions to the school, put the champagne and white wine in the main refrigerator in the cloakroom and checked in the big cupboard that there was sufficient cutlery and crockery. It had been nearly three months since the last picnic. He wished very much that he did not have to go through with this one.

By the time the picnic began on Sunday, Rich had put in several hours work. He was a great believer in doing things properly. The extra work, the little touches, all added up to class, and it was class that had the punters coming back time and time again and urging their friends to try a wonderful experience.

The garden, to which Amiss had given scarcely a glance during his few days on prefab duty, was very cleverly landscaped. The enclosed area where the garden furniture stood was entirely private, and covered over with an arch of climbing roses. Honeysuckle and virginia creeper assisted in giving it the aura of a green and pink boudoir. Rich spent some time positioning the furniture. The white-painted, wrought-iron dining-table and chairs were placed where the sun would hit them in early afternoon. He pushed slightly to the side the reclining chairs and the swinging two-seaters.

During the next few hours he organised the music, the flowers, the food and the wine. He modelled the layout on a magazine colour spread of a party in the South of France and imitated it so successfully that Galina and Fabrice, the first to arrive, were actually moved to clap. 'Reech, Reech,' cried Galina, rushing over to give him a kiss. 'What genius you 'ave to make a so beautiful picnic.' And then with a merry laugh, 'But what genius I 'ave to order you to make one.'

Rich had had a long apprenticeship with the wealthy and had learned the hard way what gave them pleasure. Early on he had sussed out how you made friends with those who were actually your employers. He modelled himself on those hairdressers and fashion designers of international repute who rubbed shoulders with princesses and the wives of tycoons.

The key was to dress as well as the BPs, have manners that were better than theirs and be such fun that their real friends — their equals — congratulated them on their finds. But what was much more vital was never to presume. If they invited one to their parties one accepted with delight; if they did not, one never showed resentment: one had no rights. In a nutshell, you sang for your supper and knew your place. And you did that while giving the impression that you loved them for themselves and were indifferent to their money. The combination of requirements would have been almost impossible to achieve had it not been that the wealthy were themselves part of the conspiracy. Because they wanted to be loved for themselves or at least to appear to be loved for themselves, they helped the illusion along. Part of his cleverness consisted in knowing how to give them a good time but have them think they contributed to it. Thus after an evening out with Rich, his companions thought they had been hilarious company themselves. And when it came to parties at the school, Rich always made them help with the drinks and encouraged them to help clear up afterwards. He had first had this idea when he read about Queen Elizabeth insisting on herself washing-up after picnics at Balmoral. 'Isn't Rich too awful,' they would scream. 'He makes us work like *slaves*', and he would produce his most manly laugh and urge them on with cries of 'All hands on deck', 'Come on, show a leg', and various other nautical injunctions which they tried to learn to show off with back home.

So now, although he had done all the serious work, he was able to demand that they prepare the picnic. He had left for them the kind of chores they loved: unwrapping the contents of the hamper; fetching the champagne and opening it; later doing the same with the white wine. He even required Galina to cut some bread. By the time most of the others had arrived, Galina was able to fall into a chair calling for others to take on the onerous duties. It was official: she was exhausted from preparing the picnic.

Rich's only qualm was about Gavs's friend Kenneth, who could be surly — a luxury allowed only to paying customers. Fortunately on this occasion his behaviour was impeccable and when Ahmed arrived two hours late and sat beside him he became positively animated.

Towards four, everyone except Rich was slightly drunk and a gentle stupor was descending on all of them. The two-seaters were occupied by embracing couples and Galina and Fabrice had just returned from the house, to which they had retired for half an hour. Galina suddenly fractured the peace by clapping her hands loudly and shouting, 'Reech, next course, please.'

'Everyone's happy, Galina.'

'They will be more happy. Come on Reech. Where ees it?'

So Rich, who only wanted to go home to Plutarch, produced from his pocket the cocaine and the razor blade and started work. As always, he flatly refused to take any himself. 'Not on duty, loves.' The price he paid for this was extreme boredom and sometimes great irritation. This time all went swimmingly for the first hour and then Fabrice started a conversation about dangerous sports.

It began in great good humour, but within ten minutes Ahmed had turned it into a bragging competition. Fabrice had mentioned that he was an enthusiastic skier and Ahmed had said idly that he had always wanted to try it. When it had then emerged that Alessandro, Davina, Marcello and Rich were highly proficient and everyone else competent, Ahmed clearly felt dishonoured. He boasted about the speeds at which he drove; Alessandro mentioned mountain climbing; Davina crewed her husband's racing yacht; Marcello was a wind surfer. Ahmed came in with hang gliding and Marcello capped it with sky diving.

Ahmed thought hard and claimed to fly his own private plane. The others looked unconvinced. Plunging in even deeper, Ahmed began to boast about his strength. Karl said he had boxed for his university; Kenneth was a judo black belt; Fabrice fenced. 'Wallahi!' swore Ahmed. 'Who here kill a man?'

Several of those present were used to Ahmed's melodramatic outbursts and paid little attention to this one, but Davina cried, 'Ahmed, we do not believe you.' As Rich remarked later to Plutarch, if the silly bitch had set out deliberately to enrage an Arab, she could hardly have done a better job.

'You . . . you . . . brostitute,' screamed Ahmed. 'You dirty beef.'

It took Rich, Gavs and the more responsible element the best part of half an hour to restore order. 'Is not allowed to say this,' Ahmed kept shouting. Eventually Alessandro removed the sobbing Davina, and Gavs and Kenneth the still enraged Ahmed, and Galina and Fabrice followed suit almost immediately.

Rich sat alone until the light began to fail. Then he pulled himself together and spent two hours clearing up and restoring the school to the condition in which it must be the following morning. Exhausted and sore at heart, he went home to Plutarch.

17

'They're all rich.'

'I realise that,' said Amiss patiently. 'Now go to sleep.'

'So that's a large part of the reason why you hate them. Of course it's also a large part of the reason why they deserve to be hated — not because they're rich, I mean, but because of what they've let money do to them.'

'Do you mean I'm envious?'

'Of course you are. Anyone would be. Except unworldly people like Ned Nurse. It's the injustice of it all that's getting to you. They're all parasites: not one of them has earned what he's got. You're jealous because they've no more right to it than you have. And you feel puritanical because of the worthless way they use their wealth. All that is much more important than their nationalities: that's just the icing on the cake. So stop worrying about hating them and just enjoy it, whatever form it takes.'

'I'm not quite with you.'

'I mean you hate Galina because she's an undeserving rich bitch. So hate her. She also has many Italian mannerisms. Just hang on to the fact that her hatefulness and her Italianness are coincidental.'

'I think I follow.'

'I'll try once more. Ahmed is an Arab. He has many characteristics associated these days with Arabs from nations that have become Westernised very fast. He's a shit. That doesn't mean Arabs are necessarily shits. Got it?'

'You're talking false syllogisms?'

'Right.'

'Got you.'

'Good-night.' She turned over. He put his arm around her and they fell asleep instantly.

*

'Nice weekend?' Pooley tried not to sound bitter.

'Marvellous. I went to Paris. How about you?'

'It was long.'

'How do you mean?'

'I've just clocked up twenty-four hours overtime, which would be nice if I needed the money, but I don't.'

'It's only recently I've begun to understand the disadvantages under which the rich labour.'

'I'm too tired for this, Robert. Please, just tell me anything you think I should know before tomorrow morning when Doug and I have got to try to turn this into a murder inquiry.'

Amiss was conscience-stricken.

'Nothing that won't keep, Ellis. The important thing is that the police find out officially that he never touched alcohol: that should be easy. Now go to sleep and we'll talk tomorrow.'

'May I invite myself for next Saturday in any case?'

'Of course you may.'

'And by then we may have a murderer?'

'Ees possible. Good-night.'

'Good-night.'

'Reech?'

'Yes.'

'I am Galina.'

'Hello, Galina. Isn't it a little late? Shouldn't you be getting some sleep?'

'I am not sleepy. I 'ad sleep before.'

'Can I help you?'

'I ring up to thank you for a beautiful picnic. Everyone had a very very lovely time.'

Rich was so touched by her thoughtfulness that he forgave her for ringing at midnight. 'That's very nice of you. I appreciate it, Galina.'

'Reech?'

'Yes?'

'I want Bob.'

Rich was mystified. 'You'll be seeing him in the morning, Galina. Can't whatever it is wait till then?'

'You do not understand. I want him. I am bored with

104

Fabrice. Next week, I want Bob. To dance, to laugh, to make love.'

'Bob has five of you to look after, Galina.'

'But I am bored and I want someone young.'

'You must sort this out yourself. Good-night. See you tomorrow.'

As he put down the phone, Rich hoped she was still under the influence of something and would be more circumspect in the morning. He drew the line at forcing his staff to go to bed with punters. Still, no need to worry, he thought. That cocky little devil will cope fine. He'll probably be happy to oblige if the price is right.

Doug Layton and his inspector arrived at the school half-way through Monday morning and saw Rich Rogers. Within a couple of minutes they had established that Ned Nurse and alcohol did not mix.

'He just never drank, Inspector.'

'Do you mean never ever?'

'Not in nearly forty years. The first and last time was when he was on National Service. He got so sick he could never face alcohol again.'

'So how do you explain the alcohol in his bloodstream?'

'I can't.'

'Could it have been an accident?'

'I don't see how,' said Rich helplessly. 'It's not as if we were serving a fruit punch or anything. It was a cocktail party. Everyone had to order what they wanted from the people with the cocktail shakers. Ned and any other non-drinkers would have been drinking from a jug of fruit juice. There couldn't have been any confusion.'

'Who was serving the cocktails?'

'Two of my staff and two students.'

'May we see them?'

'Certainly.' And Rich went off to summon Cath, Jenn, Fabrice and Marcello.

'It's a messy one. I can't make up my mind.'

'Sir, we've got means, motive and opportunity,' said Layton, who had picked up some of Pooley's style. 'His drink must have

105

been spiked. Clearly anyone at that party could have done it, and at least one of them has a real motive.'

'Rich Rogers.'

'Absolutely, sir. Half a million quid is a lot of money.'

'But he was doing perfectly well out of the profits anyway. Why would he kill to get the building?'

'I don't know, sir. But it seems to me we've got to press on. If Nurse didn't take the drink on purpose, which he almost certainly didn't, and he couldn't have been given it by accident, which seems almost certainly the case, then he must have been given it on purpose. Sounds like murder to me.'

'Unless someone did it as a joke.'

'Well, then why wouldn't they own up?'

'In a foreign country?' The inspector chewed his upper lip. 'I don't know, Layton. I just don't know.'

'Well, sir. If you'll forgive me, I —'

'All right, Layton. You're probably right. We'll have to assume murder. I suppose on the evidence that's what the inquest is going to come up with.'

Layton sighed with relief. 'Sir, will I —'

'It's OK, Layton. You get back to those Kensington burglaries. I'm going to ask the boss to get the Yard to take this on. With all these foreigners, Interpol will probably have to be involved. Much better dealt with at the centre. Thanks for your help.'

He left the room oblivious to having broken his DC's heart.

Amiss found his group rather hard work that Monday. Ahmed failed to arrive until noon, which meant he missed the film and could make no contribution to the discussion. He fell asleep for the last half hour and Amiss left him undisturbed until he began to snore.

Fabrice and Galina seemed tired as well and instead of giving each other the customary flirtatious signals, studiously ignored each other. She concentrated on Amiss instead, he presumed in order to make Fabrice jealous. She was wearing a blouse cut so low that it was almost impossible to look at her and avoid staring at her generous breasts. He tried looking her in the eye and caught what seemed terrifyingly like amorous glances. He rang Rachel that night to complain he was being ogled.

'Try looking directly at her nose.'

'I tried that, but then I could see her mouth, and she was running her tongue over her lips until they were so shiny you could see your face in them.'

'This sounds serious.'

'Oh, I'm sure it'll be all right when she and Fabrice make it up. But I'm getting fed up with all this attention. Jenn was after me today to know when I was taking her out again.'

'Do you think it's Ellis's clothes that have turned you into an *homme fatal*?'

'Not at all. I've always had that raw sex appeal. It was just that I had to hide it in the Civil Service: they wouldn't promote raunchy brutes. Now at last I've found the real me.'

'Just be careful you don't excite Ahmed.'

'Judging by his performance today, the only thing that could excite Ahmed at the moment would be a boot up the arse.'

Pooley was in a playful mood. He had had two good pieces of news that day and also a *tête-à-tête* lunch with Pardeep. As he talked to Amiss mid-evening, his toes were curling with well-being. 'Do you want the good news or the bad news?'

'The good news.'

'It's a murder inquiry.'

'Oh, good. What's the bad news?'

'Central say they can't handle the case and have passed it on to the Yard. So after all Layton's efforts, he's been dropped.'

'What rotten luck! Poor sod. Without him there wouldn't be an investigation.'

'Right. Do you want the good news or the bad news?'

'The bad news.'

'The case has been given to Romford.'

'That wally? You're not serious.'

'I am. Now do you want the good news?'

'Oh, Ellis, for fuck's sake get on with it.'

'Oh, all right. Two good things. He'll only be on it for a few days 'cos he's being moved next week. And better still, I'm the DC on the case, or rather — wait a minute — the DS on the case.'

'Ellis! Your promotion hasn't come through at last?'

'Confirmed this morning.'

'I'd suggest opening a bottle of champagne when we next meet, only I'm sick of the stuff. How have your parents taken it?'

'I haven't told them yet. It won't mean anything to my father. He won't think I've got anywhere until I'm a Chief Constable.'

18

Pooley had underestimated quite how frustrating it would be to work on the Nurse case with Romford. To have to pretend that he was starting from a position of equal ignorance was agony. All he was supposed to know was what was contained in the slim folder Romford tossed to him on Tuesday morning. Additionally he had the worry of wondering what would happen when Romford found Amiss *in situ*. Could he really be so unimaginative as not to smell a rat?

'Just act dumb,' he had told Amiss the previous night. 'And bear in mind that he's a sanctimonious prig.'

'What would happen if you told him the truth?'

'He'd try to have me busted back on the beat and he'd probably succeed. The Met's not too keen on private enterprise.'

'My head is beginning to hurt with the strain of remembering what to keep from whom.'

'Just keep everything, but everything, from Romford.'

'Maybe he won't find out I'm here. He's only got a few days.'

'One of the positive things about Romford is his conscientiousness. You'll meet him all right.'

'I look forward to it. I'll make a point of wearing my cloak and dagger.'

'I'd say it's an open and shut case, Pooley. Shouldn't take us long to sort out. It'll be the partner, you mark my words. It's true about money being the root of all evil.'

Pooley assumed a respectful look. 'What do you think happened, sir?'

'Maybe he was afraid Nurse would change his will. Who knows? Or he just got greedy. Couldn't bear to share the profits. Anyway he slips the alcohol into his drink, hoping he'll have an accident. If that hadn't worked, he'd probably have staged another mugging, only this one would have been fatal.'

They walked past Harrods. Romford stopped and gazed at a simulated drawing-room containing about fifty thousand pounds worth of furniture and inhabited by male and female dummies clad in equal splendour. 'Take my advice, Pooley. Always remember that money doesn't buy happiness. Nowadays . . . I don't know. There's all this materialism, not like when I was young . . .'

To Pooley's relief, Romford recollected he was not supposed to preach during working hours. He still smarted at the memory of the ticking off Milton had given him when he found him enjoining on three probationers the reading of the Bible. They walked on and took the first left.

'Do you think he murdered Armstrong as well, sir?'

'Oh, I doubt if there's anything in that. No money involved. That was almost certainly an accident. No, as I say, this is a straightforward case.'

'Just one thing worries me, sir.'

Romford wondered if this boy were going to relapse into fancifulness. He'd thought him cured. 'What?'

'Why was he so insistent to Inspector Clarke that the alcohol couldn't have got into Nurse's drink accidentally? I'd have thought if he had any sense he'd have set up a party where a mistake could easily be made.'

Romford was essentially a kind man. 'Pooley, you're still very new. When you've been in the force as long as I have, you'll know that criminals are mostly very stupid. You've got the wrong idea from all those detective stories you used to read. You have given them up, haven't you, son?'

Mischief got the better of Pooley. 'Yes, sir. "When I became a man, I put away childish things."'

Romford looked at him in open-mouthed delight. 'I didn't realise you knew your Bible, Pooley.'

'Oh, yes sir. They were very strong on it at school.'

'Ah, yes. That was the grammar schools for you. Now these modern comprehensives . . .'

Within a few moments, to Pooley's mingled relief and apprehension, they saw ahead of them the Knightsbridge School of English.

Pooley identified the dapper little man with the black tie straight away: he seemed very subdued.

'Here are two copies of the list you asked for of everyone who was at the party, Inspector. And here's my office. I hope you and the sergeant will be comfortable here.'

'This will do nicely thank you, Mr Rogers.'

'You want to interview all these people?'

'That is correct.'

'Separately or together?'

'Separately.'

'Well, they're all here at the moment, hard at it. The list is broken down according to the group they study in. It would make things easier if you took people as far as possible in the order in which they appear on the list. There'll be havoc at lunchtime otherwise. They like to hunt in packs,' he guffawed.

'That seems satisfactory, Mr Rogers.'

'Jenn, my secretary, will be out there in the lounge and will fetch people as you want them. She can also go out and get you sandwiches at lunchtime. But for now can she get you some coffee?'

'How very kind. Yes, please.'

'Goodbye, Inspector. I'll see you later, then.'

'Yes, Mr Rogers. We would like to see you last of all.'

Romford read slowly down the list. 'Do you speak any foreign languages, Pooley?'

'French and German not very well, sir.'

'Hmm . . . we'll see. Pooley, I hadn't realised what a classy place this was; there are two countesses and a princess on this list.'

'So I see, sir.'

'Well, don't let them intimidate you, Pooley. Simple faith is better than Norman blood, isn't that so?'

'Absolutely.'

'Ah, here's the coffee. Thank you, my dear. Now, could you ask Miss Cath Taylor to come and see us.'

Romford had little experience of talking to non-English speakers. He had never been abroad except to Germany on National Service, and since he avoided alcohol and disliked dancing, his exposure to the natives there had been mostly limited to canteen staff who spoke English. His inexperience was matched only by his lack of linguistic talent. Interviews that would have taken Pooley ten minutes took Romford forty: the foreigners and Romford floundered in a bog of malcommunication. A couple of times he speeded things up by asking Pooley to break a deadlock by explaining something in French, but for the most part he conducted the proceedings himself. While he seemed to be getting the facts they needed, the process took a terrible toll on everyone.

By four o'clock there were still Rich, Jenn, Amiss and six more students to see. Romford mopped his brow and loosened his tie a little more. 'I don't know when I've been so exhausted. All that jabber, jabber. We'll have to come back tomorrow, Pooley.' He checked his watch. 'We've time for three more, I'd say. Let's finish off Miss Taylor's group by seeing that Jap and then see the English ones. They'll be a welcome change.'

As they waited, Romford plunged into deep thought, pursed his lips and then pronounced, 'I don't think I can shake hands with this one, Pooley. Not after what our lads went through as prisoners-of-war.'

'It's a long time ago, Inspector. Yamaguchi can hardly have been involved.'

'I'm afraid it's not that simple. The sins of the fathers and all that, Pooley. These nips. They haven't learned anything. Coming in and taking over our factories.'

'They seem to be very good managers of people, sir. Very popular with their workforces in Britain, I hear.'

Romford shook his head reprovingly. 'Pooley, you mark my words: leopards don't change their spots.'

The leopard's arrival coincided with Jenn's delivery of tea for three, so to Pooley's relief the absence of handshakes was unnoticed in the general flurry. He was most impressed at the attention to detail evident in the provision of two kinds of tea: Romford was made happy with strong Indian; Yamaguchi content with weak China. On the downside was Romford's disgust at the way his interviewee slurped the liquid.

The conversation ran true to form. On the frequent occasions when Yamaguchi failed to understand a question, Romford raised his voice. When that did not succeed, he made inept attempts at miming. Thus a question about how long Yamaguchi had stayed at the party involved Romford in stabbing his finger at his watch and repeating loudly, 'How long, how long?' It fascinated Pooley how his boss failed to learn by experience. Mr Yamaguchi, like several other students, maddened Romford by coming up with the helpful information that it was now four thirty-six.

Just when Romford had about wrung his victim dry, he had a sneezing fit. Pooley and the Japanese gazed at him while he sneezed and sneezed and choked and sneezed some more. When the paroxysms wore off, Romford blew his nose furiously and said goodbye from behind his handkerchief. Pooley, out of Romford's line of sight, bowed slightly. Yamaguchi reciprocated and left, but unfortunately for Romford's peace of mind, he left the door slightly ajar. They heard Jenn's piercing south London voice ask 'How did you get on?'

'Quite lewd man, Mr Lomufolu.'

'What does he mean "lewd"?' Romford was outraged. 'I've never heard of such a thing. What's he talking about?'

'Er . . . I think he means "rude".'

'Ridiculous. I was politeness itself.'

'The way you blew your nose, sir, I'm afraid. They tend to be rather more delicate about it. To his sensitivities it was as if you'd . . . well —'

'"Well", what?'

'Excreted, sir.'

Romford's eyes flicked towards the pocket where he had stowed his handkerchief. 'He's not in Japan now. I've a good mind to tell him what I thought of the way he drank his tea. Noisy brute.' He sulked for a couple of minutes, then brightened up. 'We'll have someone English now.'

He looked down his list. 'Bob Amiss. Amiss? I don't suppose this could be the Robert Amiss who was at the BCC. Surely not. He had a good job.'

'Couldn't tell you, sir.'

'It'd be a stroke of luck, wouldn't it,' said Romford unexpectedly. 'He might be able to help a bit.'

Pooley was astounded. He still remembered vividly Romford's insistence in the teeth of the evidence that Amiss had to be taken seriously as a possible mass murderer.

'Let's see. Ask Jenn to bring him in.'

Amiss entered wearing an expression that reminded Pooley of an amateur actor desperately trying to remember his lines.

'Good-evening, Inspector Romford. I'm Robert Amiss. We talked on the telephone a few times when you were on the BCC case. And Constable Pooley. We met the night Superintendent Milton made the arrest. How nice to see you again. And goodness me, what a coincidence.' Pooley felt a sense of almost paternal pride: his boy was word perfect.

'Indeed it is, Mr Amiss. And I may say it's a pleasure to meet you. I know you gave us some help with that terrible business. Dear me, the wickedness there is in this world.'

'Shocking, shocking, Inspector. We must pray that there has been no wrongdoing on this occasion.'

One of Robert's problems, thought Pooley, was that he tended to throw himself over-enthusiastically into his roles. How would he manage if he had to talk to Rich and Romford simultaneously?

'I fear there has been, Mr Amiss. It certainly appears that Mr Nurse's drink was deliberately spiked.'

'Dear me.' Amiss shook his head. 'It seems almost impossible to believe. Now how can I help you?'

Romford took him through the key questions efficiently enough. It was clear that Amiss was an almost useless witness as far as the party was concerned, having known virtually no one there and been involved in conversation with a group by the bar for almost the whole time. 'So you didn't talk to Mr Nurse at all?' Romford's disappointment was almost palpable. Here was a witness he could both understand and trust, and he had seen nothing.

'Hardly at all. He waved at me when he came in and called something like "Enjoying yourself, dear boy?" and I had the briefest of exchanges half-way through when I went over to the table near him to get some olives. But I don't think he ever came over to our side of the room. I did see him gesticulating a couple of times.'

'Was that normal behaviour for him?'

'Don't know, I'm afraid. I'm very new here.'

'Thank you, Mr Amiss. I'm sure we'll see you again.'

'Goodbye, Inspector. And good luck.'

As Amiss rose, the door was flung open and in came a scantily-clad woman crying, 'Bob, Bob, you come with me now.'

'Excuse me, Inspector,' said Amiss. 'Galina, let me introduce Inspector Romford and Constable Pooley. Gentlemen, this is the Contessa Galina Domani.' Barely glancing at them, she tugged Amiss vigorously by the sleeve and pulled him out of the room. 'Come on, Bobby, come on. You come with me. We go somewhere nice, just us. I am tired of the others . . . so vulgar . . . so boring . . .' Her voice receded into the distance.

Pooley dared not look at Romford; he doubted his ability to keep a straight face. Eventually Romford said, 'Well, so that's a countess. Did you see what she was wearing? Or rather not wearing? And old enough to know better. I don't know what the world is coming to.'

This favourite refrain of Romford's was more apposite than usual, thought Pooley, for if ever a man had no idea what was going on, it was he.

It was a new experience for Pooley to feel sorry for Romford, but only a very hard heart could have withheld pity from the crumpled and pathetic figure who left the school at six. His interview with Jenn had produced what seemed like strong evidence that one of the few people at the party who could definitely not have spiked Ned's drink was Rich. And from Rich he had got proof that his finances were in such an excellent state as to make his inheritance from Ned unimportant. 'And there's still all those other foreigners to interview,' he said in the back of a taxi, itself an unheard of extravagance of Romford's, who had strong views on saving public money. 'I don't know if I'm coming or going, to be truthful. I don't see how that Rogers fellow could have done it but I can't see who else would have wanted to. And anyway how are we to find out about what motives all those foreigners might have?'

Pooley recognised the question was rhetorical. 'Maybe it'll all fall into place tomorrow, sir.'

'And maybe not.' And a chastened Romford left the taxi at Leicester Square and set off for the tube to Tooting.

'Have you a minute, Rich?'
'Always for you, Cath. How are things going?'

'Bit tiring. The nip's really hard going. Seems to be more keen on English than on enjoying himself, and of course that causes tensions within the group.'

'I'm sure you handle it magnificently, my dear.'

'Rich, I know this isn't the best time for you, but I want to talk about my future.'

'Can't it wait? I'm very shaky at the moment.'

'Yes, I know. It's just that I want to get in before Gavs does. I don't want to lose out by holding off.'

'I'm not with you, Cath. Hold off on what?'

'Buying into the business. You remember when the profit-sharing started we asked about the possibilities of becoming partners and you said no, because you were a two-man show.'

'And it's not a two-man show any longer, you mean,' said Rich slowly.

'That's right, Rich. I'm really sorry, but I had to get my bid in. Just because Gavs has been here longer doesn't mean it should be him rather than me.'

'Very well. You've made your bid. I'll think about it.'

'Do.'

'It would cost a lot to buy your way in.'

'I'd get it somehow. My parents would help.'

'All right, Cath. Leave it for now. We'll talk again soon.'

'I'm relieved to get you. I kept trying until after midnight and then assumed the contessa had kidnapped you.'

'Sweet Jesus, I've never been through anything like it. I could have her up for sexual harassment. If this is what women have to go through with randy chaps, they have my deepest sympathy. She kept feeling me up on the dance floor. I can't imagine what we looked like, with her advancing, me retreating, while all the time I kept a bright smile as if I didn't know what was going on. Then she got going on bribes. Things were said about presents, yachts, holidays in the West Indies. Then came threats. What she'd have to tell Reech if I wasn't nice to her. Christ, I never came so close to smacking a woman round the chops.'

'Well, well. Just the two of you?'

'No. I told Galina my job required me to ask the rest of the group. I was terrified, because they were all supposed to be going

116

to the theatre with Gavs. But Ahmed decided he preferred dancing and he brought Jenn. Things have come to a pretty pass when I'm grateful for the company of those two.'

'Did you escape without a fight?'

'Sort of. Produced an up-market version of the line I used on Jenn. Told her my fiancée was so jealous she was having me watched by private detectives.'

'Rich girl, is she?'

'Loaded. Galina therefore quite understands why I can't take the risk of losing her.'

'How could she seriously believe such garbage?'

'Her self-esteem requires it. She's just like Jenn. Can't imagine anyone wouldn't be mad keen to go to bed with her. They really think "No" means "Yes". So she has to believe any half-way reasonable excuse. I'm hoping she'll give up now. God knows whom she'll go after. Are you interested?'

'No, but I'll ask Romford if he'd like to help out.'

19

'The Super's in. Dunno what's going on. He wasn't supposed to be back for several weeks, was he?' Pooley found Pardeep's gorgeous eyes so distracting that he almost missed the astonishing news she bore.

'No, he wasn't. Maybe there's a crisis.'

'Don't think they get called back from Bramshill unless there's a world war. See you.'

Pooley sat at his desk longing to be sufficiently senior to be able to stroll into Milton's room and casually enquire what had happened.

'Ellis.' It was Milton. 'Will you come in for a moment?'

Pooley's heart leaped.

'Coming, sir.'

'Inspector Romford not in yet?'

'No, sir.'

'Well, perhaps you can help me. Do you know of anything going on on your patch that you think I might be gainfully employed on for a couple of days? No one else has anything that fits the bill.'

'Sorry, sir?' Milton tended to be a bit unorthodox, but this approach really floored Pooley.

'Oh, sorry, Ellis. Bramshill's had an outbreak of salmonella, so the course is suspended until Monday. I was one of the lucky ones; I refused the Scotch eggs. So I'm really extra to strength here and am looking for a specific job to do.'

Pooley looked over his shoulder. 'We badly need you at the Knightsbridge School of English, sir.'

'Is Robert all right?' Milton sounded so seriously alarmed that Pooley had one of his occasional stabs of envy about their friendship.

'Oh, he's fine, but Ned Nurse is dead and was probably murdered.'

Romford came crashing in, wreathed in profuse apologies about late trains. 'Don't worry, don't worry. Sit down and bring me up to date. Thanks, Ellis.' He gave Pooley a distant nod of dismissal. Pooley trailed out dejectedly, anathematising whoever had finally got Romford to his destination. Had the Super got the message? If he had, how could he squeeze out Romford? Moodily, he got down to typing out statements from his own shorthand.

He had been at the job for only ten minutes when he was called into Milton's office again. 'Ellis, Inspector Romford suggests I might take over from him on this English school business. He has a great deal to clear up before leaving us, so I think the least I can do is give him time to do it. You'll be able to brief me, won't you? I don't want to waste any of the inspector's time.' Pooley nodded: he felt unable to speak.

Romford was silently extolling the power of prayer. What else could have sent the Super out of the blue to release him from another day with these awful people? He congratulated himself on the skill with which he had manipulated him into taking it on.

'I feel as if I'm having a half holiday from school,' remarked Milton. 'Of course I'm terribly sorry for my stricken colleagues, but it's an ill wind . . .'

'It certainly is, sir,' said Pooley fervently.

They were taking a detour through St James's Park. 'Now, Ellis, I've told the school that we won't be along for about an hour, so just to increase my holiday feeling, we'll have a cup of coffee somewhere near by and you can tell me the full story. It goes without saying that you must omit no detail, however slight.'

'Are you sure you mean that, sir?'

'Oh, certainly, Ellis. If you mean should you leave out any of the absurdities, please don't. I'm sure with Robert involved there must be some.'

Pooley collected his thoughts and, over coffee, he managed to produce a coherent narrative. He was much encouraged by Milton's reaction, which seemed to his besotted protégé to be a model mixture of quick understanding, intelligent questioning and well-placed laughter. 'I can't wait to meet Robert's students. Can you, Ellis?'

'We'd better not leave each other alone with the contessa, sir.'

'Oh, I don't know. I'm in the mood to live dangerously.'

Milton checked himself as he realised Pooley was looking disconcerted. 'Sorry, Ellis, but for some weeks I've been immersed in policy and strategy. I'm aching to deal with something practical, immediate and with a bit of fun in it. It can get very dull being a senior policeman. This is a wonderful break.'

He called for the bill. 'Now, let's get this business sorted out. Here's how we proceed. When we get to the school, you get from Jenn the names and addresses of all the students who attended the party. Ring the local station and ask for a PC. I'll talk to Interpol and tell them to see if any of them have a form. Then you give the list to the PC to fax across to them.' He paid the bill and they left the café.

'Then I sort out Central. They can't just abandon all responsibility for this. I want someone to come up fast with that information you asked your friend Layton for unofficially. It's high time we talked to someone outside the school about Armstrong. With a bit of luck they'll put DC Layton on to the job.'

They walked along Piccadilly towards Green Park. 'Then I want a plan of the room, with furniture location marked: a visual aid should improve communication. We'll process the information you got yesterday with a view to eliminating as many of the possibles as we can. When we've got a shortlist we can get Interpol to make more thorough checks.'

They went downstairs to the ticket hall. 'Have you a travel card, Ellis?'

'Yes, sir.'

Milton scrabbled among his change and found the right coins. 'And when all that's sorted out,' he said as he took his ticket, 'we'll settle down to whatever interviews need to be done.'

They travelled down the escalator to the sound of 'These Foolish Things' played on a saxophone. Milton threw some coins into the wide-brimmed hat that lay at the feet of the dreadlocked musician. 'Lunatic, the laws against buskers. They're the only cheerful thing about the underground.'

They caught a train immediately and got off at Knights-bridge. When they reached street level and began the walk to the school Milton said, 'OK, Ellis. What have I forgotten?'

There was silence. He looked at Pooley. 'You've been knitting your brows for the past five minutes. What is it?'

'I don't know how to say this, sir. I don't wish to appear critical of Inspector Romford.'

'Quite right too, Ellis. You don't want to be the school sneak. It does you credit. But this isn't school. If there's something important, spit it out.'

'He mentioned to Rich Rogers that we knew Robert. "Had dealings with him a few months back" were his exact words.'

'Shit,' said Milton inadvertently. 'Did he elaborate?'

'Frankly, sir, I think he was about to explain the connection, but I interrupted him.'

'Well, thank Christ for that.'

'It wasn't his fault, sir. He had no reason to keep it quiet.'

'Don't say anything for a while. I'm thinking.'

The silence lasted for as long as it took to walk the length of the front of Harrods. 'OK, Ellis. It's damage limitation time. I've an idea that may work. I'll try it on both of you when we get in.'

'Oh, and sir, I told Robert about this when I spoke to him this morning.'

'What was he going to say if Rogers asked him about it?'

'As little as possible. We were to confer later. I was trying to think of a way of talking to the inspector about it.'

'Just as well I don't like Scotch eggs.'

'You can say that again, sir.'

'Introduce us, Ellis.' Milton gave Jenn his best smile and was gratified to see her thrust out her chest and pat her hair in response. 'So you're looking after us. Don't normally get this sort of treatment.'

She installed them and took orders for coffee. 'Oh, Jenn!'

'Yes?'

'Could you get me Bob Amiss? There are a couple of

questions the inspector says he forgot to ask him yesterday. Tell him we won't keep him long.'

'Your word is my command.' She flashed him a radiant smile.

'Now don't give me ideas, Jenn.'

She swung her hips out the door and went off tittering.

'You've certainly got a fan there, sir. She didn't take so well to Inspector Romford: doesn't seem to like people being paternal.'

'Unless they've got incest in mind, I expect,' said Milton absently. He shut the door, checked a number in his diary and punched it in. 'Romford? Milton . . . Yes, thanks . . . Fine. One small matter. If by any chance Rich Rogers — or indeed anyone from the Knightsbridge school asks you about Robert Amiss — What! He did? . . . Oh, thank God . . . Tell him you can't speak about it . . . Say it's private . . . Just clam up . . . No, sorry . . . I can't talk now. Goodbye.'

'He had a message on his desk asking him to ring Rogers.'

'Phew!'

A step sounded outside. Milton strode to the door, threw it open and said loudly, 'Mr Amiss, I presume.' He had the satisfaction of seeing Amiss's jaw drop before he said, 'Yes. Hello.'

'I'm Superintendent Milton, Mr Amiss.' They shook hands. 'Please come in and sit down.'

'What the hell are you doing here? All Jenn said was that there was a new one who wasn't such a stuffed shirt.'

'I'm touched that she noticed.' Milton filled him in rapidly. 'Now, Robert. It's time for a pre-emptive strike. Unless you or Ellis have a better idea, this is what you've got to do.'

20

Cath and Gavs had already disappeared with their groups when Rich and Amiss met by prearrangement in the lounge with theirs.

'Could you spare me a couple of minutes in private, Rich?'

'Certainly, old man.' Amiss could not tell if it was his imagination or his guilty conscience that made him detect a heartiness false even by Rich's standards. 'I'll send them all off to the winebar ahead of us.' He clapped his hands. 'Everybody! Everybody! Stop chattering and listen. Off you all go with Jenn. Bob and I will be after you in a tiny minute.'

The token protests from Galina and Davina were dealt with by the usual badinage, various students were helped on with their jackets and they all straggled off with Jenn. 'You must come soon,' were Galina's last words, to which Rich replied rather wearily, 'You couldn't keep us away, dear lady.'

'Funny,' said Amiss, as they sat down. 'I started off teaching tarts and waiters and now I've become both.'

'Oh, har . . . har . . . har . . . Very amusing, Bob. Now what's the problem?'

'I've got to come clean with you, Rich. I wasn't quite straight about why I left the Civil Service.'

'What's brought on the confession, old man?'

'The police, of course. I had a spot of bother and that twat Inspector Romford was vaguely involved.'

'So you think he might have said something to me. Is that it?'

'Frankly, yes.'

There was a silence. 'Did he?'

'That would be telling, Bob. Why don't you just tell me the story?'

'I wasn't actually a diplomat. I worked in the Department of Conservation. Last year I was seconded to the FO to work on a conservation conference in Paris.'

'Go on.'

'And there was trouble over my use of the diplomatic bag. A real balls-aching fuss. And all over a bit of hash I sent a friend.'

'And they brought in the police?'

'Yes . . . Well . . . To cut a long story short, I'd got a few ounces of some really terrific Moroccan black. Very hard to get here. I didn't want to run the risk of bringing it through customs, so I tried to send it by diplomatic bag. By a real stroke of bum luck, the day I sent it down to the post room at the Paris embassy was a day when they made one of their routine checks that no improper use was being made of the bag.'

'That was certainly rough luck, Bob.'

Amiss could hear the doubt in Rich's voice.

'I'd gone back to London that same day so I got hauled up back in the department and of course I had to deny I knew what was in the parcel. Produced the usual line: I'd been given it by a girl I met at a party. And obviously my friend denied all knowledge of it or me. But the police were brought in and I had a bit of a hard time. They couldn't prove anything so the case was dropped. I got a nasty turn when I realised yesterday who that pair were. Still, they were friendly enough. Maybe they really do believe you're innocent until proved guilty.'

'But why did you leave your job?'

'It was made clear to me it would be wiser to resign. After all they could have disciplined me on the technicality of improperly using the diplomatic bag. So I got out before I was pushed and here I am.'

'I'm glad you've got it off your chest, Bob. You needn't have worried about the police. Funnily enough, Romford mentioned he knew you, but the young fellow broke in and quite rightly stopped him saying any more. Still, frankly it did make me wonder.'

'I wouldn't want you to think I'm a drug smuggler or anything. The stuff was only for me and my friends.' He looked anxiously at Rich. 'You're not down on soft drugs, are you?'

'No, Bob. I'm not down on soft drugs. I'm not a believer in the nanny state. Now come on, let's go and join the BPs. And don't worry any more. Your secret is safe with me.'

*

'Personnel Department, please. Hello, I want to enquire about a past employee of yours who has applied for a job with me.'

'What was his name and rank?'

'Robert Amiss. Don't know his rank.'

'Well, was he clerical? Or scientific and professional? Or administrative?' The voice was impatient.

'He has an Arts degree I think.'

'Hold on.'

It took only another five minutes for someone to be found who knew about Amiss. 'Yes. We did have an employee of that name. Left in May.'

'Why did he leave?'

'He resigned. You'll have to ask him the reason.'

'Look, I have to check what he told me.'

'Which was?'

'That he left under a slight cloud.'

'I won't argue with that. Anything else you wish to know? No? Goodbye.'

The head of Personnel put down the receiver. What the devil was young Amiss up to, he wondered? The police superintendent had been very vague. And when would the young idiot get some sense and come back to the place where he belonged?

Rich was relieved that his fears about Amiss had not been realised. On the make he might be, but nothing wrong with that, and he was likeable: except for Gavs, he had been the only one to show any sympathy over Ned.

He rebuked himself for paranoia. After all, had Amiss been a police spy Romford wouldn't have acknowledged him. And how absurd to think they would want to stake out the school anyway. No. He must watch himself and not let the stress get to him. His job was to go on running his successful business as well as ever.

He looked at his watch. Twenty minutes more before Jenn brought his group down for tea. He signed a few cheques for the part-timers, made two routine phone calls and was interrupted by Galina.

'What are you doing out of class?'

'I tell Bôb I have important call. I wish to speak with you, Reech. I wish another picnic Sunday.'

Rich came close to exploding. Were there absolutely no limits to the demands of this horrible bitch?

'I'm sorry, Galina, but no. My mother —'

'Stop about your mother, Reech. Look.' She took from her handbag a diamond tie-pin. 'You like this?' She held it out.

Christ, he thought, it must be worth thousands. 'It's very nice, Galina.'

'A picnic, Reech?'

Greed fought with self-disgust and won. Hating himself, Rich put out his hand. Galina smiled. 'Good. I am pleased. But there is a condition.'

'Which is?'

'I wish Bob at the picnic.'

'I can't force him to come, Galina.'

'You are clever. You will do it.'

And putting the tie-pin back in her bag, she went back to join her class.

Milton put the phone down.

'I think we're just about ready to start the interviews, Ellis. You've done a first-rate job on the reconstruction of the party. We just need to check it with the remaining people.'

'Any news from Central, sir?'

'I'm told Layton is making excellent progress. Which reminds me. Now that you're a sergeant, there's a vacancy for a DC with us. Would your friend Layton be interested?'

'I'm positive he'd jump at it, sir. Doesn't get a lot of encouragement where he is.'

'Now there's no guarantee he'd get it, but if he wants it he'd be in with a strong chance. I'm impressed by his dedication. Too many coppers look for opportunities to up the solved crime rate rather than insisting on making the figures worse because they are concerned with truth. I leave it to you. Speak to him if you think it a good idea.'

Pooley's heart was full. 'Oh, sir,' was all he could say.

Milton looked at him in momentary alarm. This lad is too devoted, he said to himself. He watched Pooley as he returned to his labours and felt sad that one could inspire hero worship just by giving someone junior a bit of scope. 'Right, Ellis. Off we go. Let's be brave. Find Jenn and ask her to fetch the contessa. And may the Lord have mercy on our souls.'

21

Somewhat to Pooley's disappointment, Galina gave her evidence crisply.

'Surprisingly straightforward,' mused Milton. 'She seemed preoccupied. Still trying to think of a way of getting her hands on Robert, perhaps.' He sneezed. 'Dreadful pong in here, Ellis. She certainly puts on enough perfume.'

'It's not just perfume, sir.' Pooley prided himself on his discriminating sense of smell. 'It's the additional smells from all those cosmetics, not to speak of the hair spray.'

'Well, I hope our next client doesn't think *we*'re generating them. Ask for Ahmed, Ellis, will you?'

It was an unwise move, for Ahmed also moved in a cloud of perfume — one of the macho brands, the sufferers assumed. He confirmed having had a brief conversation with Ned. 'He is old,' he said helpfully.

'What did you talk about?'

'My family. I tell him I am brince.' He waved his hand in a lordly fashion and the stones glittered in the evening sunlight.

'Brince?' Milton was momentarily mystified. 'Oh, I beg your pardon. You are a prince?'

'I am.' Ahmed nodded. 'I am brince of the royal house of Saud. Some trouble — the embassy come.'

Milton felt an urge to congratulate him on his good fortune. Instead he assumed an expression of great gravitas. 'There is no trouble, sir. We simply wish your help in finding out who put alcohol in Mr Nurse's drink.'

Ahmed gave a massive shrug. 'Why? He is dead. Insh'allah.'

'This is how we do things in this country,' said Milton, rather stiffly. He observed that Ahmed was scarcely listening, but because his eyes seemed focused in opposite directions, he could not detect whether he was looking at him either.

'Sir,' he said more loudly, 'I must ask you did you see anyone put any liquid into Mr Nurse's drink?'

Ahmed shook his head.

'Did you see anyone put any liquid into the blue and white jug?'

'No. Now I go.' He jumped up and began to put on the red leather jacket he had brought in with him.

'Wait please, sir.'

'I go. I am sick. I see doctor.'

'Very well, sir. But I may need to see you again.'

Ahmed's indifference was clear. 'Insh'allah,' he said, and slouched out of the room.

'What a prick!' said Milton.

Pooley looked at him in slight surprise. Then he smiled. 'Don't you mean "brick", sir? Shall I call the next one?'

Milton felt pleased. Pooley was learning to relax with him at last.

By the time Milton and Pooley finished interviewing Amiss's group, they were able to put together a reasonably full account of Ned Nurse's last few hours. He had finished prefab duties at five and gone to his and Rich's office to mess around with some papers. Jenn had laid out all the alcoholic drinks for the party by four forty-five, but had not brought in the mixers and soft drinks until just before five. Most of the drinks were on the table beside the window, which was referred to as the bar. Since the drinks were cocktails, they had to be ordered at the bar, not as usual left for people to help themselves. So the only drinks on the table at the other end of the room were soft.

Jenn stated that just before five she had taken from the refrigerator two unopened cartons of mango and kiwi juice and had decanted them into a large blue and white pottery jug that was always used for this purpose.

Three people confirmed that Ned had come in about five thirty and had helped himself from this jug; two of them had understood him to say he had never tasted anything like it before.

Everyone who had noticed Ned agreed that he had never moved from the far end of the room. That was typical, Cath and Jenn had confirmed. He was very shy of the BPs and tended to wait for them to approach him rather than initiating contact. The concern of the police was to eliminate anyone who was never near enough to the jug or Ned's glass to spike his drink.

Gavs and his group had been out for the whole day in Oxford, so there were only fifteen students at the party. Fabrice and Marcello, the volunteer cocktail-makers, had gone straight to the bar as soon as they arrived in the lounge and had stayed at it until the end.

Of the remaining thirteen, there were five who would swear that they had been together from the very beginning, had stuck together throughout and never moved from the window area. Neither had Cath, who was also making cocktails.

Davina had come in with Rich and had then latched on to Amiss. She had never been alone between five and seven.

Rich had been seen greeting Ned when he arrived at about five thirty, but immediately afterwards had gone to the other end of the room and not left it until after Ned's departure. According to the four people who saw them together, for him to have administered the alcohol would have been a mighty feat of prestidigitation.

That left eight possibles among the students: Ahmed, Galina, Gunther, Karl, Alessandro, Simone and Mr Yamaguchi. Among the staff there was only Jenn.

There was, of course, the slight possibility that someone had given Ned alcohol before or after the party, but it was so remote that Milton decided to ignore it. This was not the time to worry about such long shots.

'OK, Ellis, let's pack it in for tonight. The school's shut tomorrow morning, and I think we'd better not come back until Friday. Until then, you sort out the paperwork while I talk to Interpol and Central and clear a bit of other work. If Layton has lined up any interviews relating to Wally Armstrong, we'll start them in the afternoon.'

'Sorry, sir, but weren't you going to see Rich Rogers?'

'I want a bit more information on his finances first, and I really don't want to bother him on the day of the funeral.'

They gathered up their papers. 'I'm anxious to talk to Robert about how things went with Rich,' said Milton, 'but I daren't call him in again. Have you any idea what he's up to tonight?'

'Jenn mentioned that Gunther's taking them gambling.'

'Robert's appetite for pleasure seems insatiable,' said Milton.

He shook his head. 'Poor devil. I hope he'll be able to get some sleep at the weekend.'

'Robert!' Rich's tone was so friendly that Amiss decided the danger was over.

'Yes, Rich.'

'Do me a favour, old love?'

'Of course.'

'Help me out on Sunday with an extra activity? I really need a man to balance the numbers and Gavs did it last weekend.'

'The whole of Sunday?'

'Best part of it, I'm afraid.' Rich reflected on what Galina was requiring of Bob and added, 'In fact, I'd write off the afternoon and evening. Sorry, but that's the way it goes.'

Amiss would have tried to get out of it, but he felt so anxious to get back on easy terms with Rich that he was prepared to put himself out considerably.

'OK. What's it involve?'

'A picnic here at lunchtime.'

Amiss was surprised at the modesty of this activity. Then he shrugged. Whatever turned them on.

'Good-morning, Robert. This is Jim. How are you feeling?'

'Atrabilious.'

'I don't know what the word means, but it certainly sounds unpleasant.'

'It means full of bile, which is about what I am mentally and physically at the moment. I found the spectacle of very rich people frantically scrabbling to get richer very depressing and drank too much to compensate. Puts me in the right mood for a funeral, I suppose. How are you? How's it going?'

They exchanged news. 'You did well with Rich. Congratulations.'

'Thanks. About Ahmed by the way. He really did think he's sick. He's gone off to see the school's tame doctor. Gavs tells me his speciality is giving hypochondriacs what they want.'

'When can we meet, Robert?'

'This evening for a quick drink? Then I've got to go home and sleep.'

'OK. Where's safe from civil servants, police, BPs and whoever else I've forgotten?'

Amiss nominated a pub in Pimlico, off the beaten track.

'I'll be there at seven. Perhaps we can manage something longer over the weekend?'

'Well, I've got Ellis coming to dinner on Saturday night, Jim. How would you feel about joining us?'

'Good question. I'd like it very much but I'm not sure that I should do it.'

'The three of us really need to talk things over sometime, don't we?'

'Yes. We do. But I had assumed we'd be in more formal territory.'

'You know all this officers and gentlemen stuff is very difficult for me to accept, Jim. I think I understand why the police have to be run on quasi-military lines. But I find it hard to believe that I can't invite two friends to dinner because one of them has the power of life and death over the other.'

'You're right, Robert. I'm being ultra-cautious. It's really Ellis I'm trying to protect.'

'And Ellis is trying to protect you. Do you know he always refers to you as the Super even when he's talking to me in private? He's terrified that if he thought of you as Jim he'd let it out some day in public and your career would be compromised.'

'It is ridiculous, really, when you look at it from the perspective of outside. Bugger it. Of course I'd like to come. And Ellis is just going to have to learn two modes: public and private.'

22

There were very few English people at Ned's funeral: apart from Amiss, Gavs and Rich, there were no more than a dozen. The only BP to turn up was Gunther, who explained to Amiss that it was proper to pay respect to the principal. What was heartening was the sight of a substantial contingent of the tarts and waiters: clearly Ned's gift for inspiring affection penetrated the language barrier.

The church was small and elegant; the flowers discreet but exquisite; the organ music — mainly Bach — was splendid; the hymns were nobly sung, for Rich, perhaps anticipating a small turn-out, had hired a quartet of singers; and the vicar was well-briefed and talked about a Ned that Amiss recognised. Above all, Rich read with great dignity a lesson that suited gentle Ned Nurse very well, the passage from St Paul to the Corinthians that ends, 'So faith, hope, love abide, these three; but the greatest of these is love.'

The entire congregation melted away after the service and Rich went off alone with the vicar to bury Ned. Amiss and Gavs walked together towards the tube.

'What are you doing for lunch, Gavs?'

'Hadn't thought. And you?'

'Same. How about trying the pub beside the station?'

'Sure.'

It was a theme pub, a phenomenon of the 1980s that Amiss particularly deplored. This one had a library theme, which meant that a corner of it had subdued lighting, darkish wallpaper, a couple of button-back leatherette sofas, two similar armchairs and four rows of books that looked as though they were a job lot from a jumble sale. The rest of the pub was laid out more like an aircraft hangar; under strong white lights, ten people occupied a space that could have fitted a hundred with ease.

'What's yours?'

'Gin and tonic, please, Bob. I'll get a table, shall I?'

Amiss brought the drinks over to Gavs, who had commandeered the whole library corner by cleverly strewing his raincoat, briefcase and newspaper over all available surfaces.

'Cheers,' said Amiss, raising his pint of bitter. 'To Ned.'

'Ned.'

'Lunch?' Amiss inclined his head towards the glass and plastic food counter positioned what seemed like fifty feet away. They walked across and silently surveyed a display that gave pride of place to slices of processed cheese and rubbery ham. Around these were scattered lettuce, parsley, green and red peppers and tomatoes, all constructed out of plastic.

'Can I help yew?' The girl looked impatient.

'Er . . . is this it?'

Her irritation at their ignorance was barely contained. 'There's a menew.' She pushed over a red plastic folder. 'Everything hot's off except the sausage.'

'I'll have two Scotch eggs with chips,' said Gavs.

Amiss stifled a grin. 'And I'll have the sausages and beans.'

They paid and returned to their drinks.

'Progress!' said Gavs. 'I can't wait to get out of this fucking country.'

'Where to?'

'Kenneth — that's my partner — and I, we're buying a place in Morocco. We'll run it as a small high-class hotel.'

'Do you know Morocco well?'

'Sure. Been two or three times a year for the last four or five. Kenneth can't stay away from Arabs.'

Amiss was rather nonplussed by Gavs's directness. 'Oh, really?' was the only response he could think of.

'Yes. Fortunately I don't mind. If he wants to bring them along to join us now and again that's all right with me. The important thing is having no hanky-panky on the side.'

'You're happy with troikas, you mean,' said Amiss, trying to sound like a man of the world.

'Well, I can take them or leave them, but it's important to keep Kenneth happy.'

'Oh, yes, of course. Absolutely.' As the girl arrived and slammed down their plates, Amiss speculated on how Rachel

134

would react if he asked her if she would mind the occasional threesome. His imagination was not up to it.

'Mind you, I wish it didn't always have to be Arabs. The Moroccans are all right, but I don't like the Saudis.'

Amiss murmured sympathetically as he tucked into his baked beans.

'Ahmed was really rough.'

'Ahmed!'

'Oh, I thought you'd have known.'

'But I've seen him all over women several times. And I'm sure he's had his leg over with Jenn.'

'Yeh, sure. He's AC/DC. Probably does it with camels too. That boy just likes sensation.'

Amiss ate some more beans. He felt too dazed to think clearly about what other information Gavs might be able to give him. Finally he asked, 'Lot of sex goes on with the students?'

'Oh, sure. With and among. Most of them are in the mood and we're pretty cooperative. A romance every second group would be about the size of it. AIDS is cutting down the fun more and more, mind you. Though you'd be surprised how many of them still don't believe it can happen to them.'

'I hadn't thought Cath —'

'Oh, very selective, very, very. Nobody gets that baby cheaply. In fact, I don't know if anyone has in the last six months or so. She says she's got a steady. You had much action yet?'

Amiss swung into the account of his rich, jealous girlfriend. 'Cramps my style a bit, I can tell you. Galina's not too pleased.'

'I've heard. Another?'

'Yes, please.'

Amiss collected his thoughts. He remembered he was supposed to be focusing on the supposed murders rather than getting lost in details of other people's sex lives. When Gavs returned, he asked, 'Will Rich manage OK without Ned?'

'I don't know. I think Ned was a lot more important to Rich than the others realise. But then I understand about partnerships. And even though I don't think they were what I mean by gay, they were more than just friends.'

'What do you think happened to Ned?'

'Search me. The only thing I can think of is that one of the students played a joke that misfired. Or Jenn. It'd be just the sort of idiotic thing she'd do. But I doubt if she'd ever admit to it.'

'One of the fuzz asked me if I'd heard anything about Wally Armstrong's death. All I knew was what I'd heard from you and Jenn.'

'Well now, if you were looking for someone to murder, Wally would have been a serious proposition. I couldn't stick him. It was a mercy Rich kept him out of things as much as he did. Wally would definitely not have approved of some of our goings on. Fortunately, he was too thick to see anything that wasn't handed to him on a platter.' He took another sip. 'Mind you, people don't usually get murdered just for being annoying, do they? It must have been an accident.'

'How did he get on with Rich?'

'I think he resented him. I came after Rich took over, so I don't really know how things were before. But certainly Wally's nose seemed out of joint. Mind you, Rich was very generous to him. Cut him in on the BP profits even though he made no contribution to them.' He looked at his watch. 'Drink up. We're due back at base in half an hour.'

In the tube Gavs asked casually, 'Have you a heavy load of extra activities?'

'Pretty bad. Three nights this week. And Sunday. It's a bit much, but Rich seemed desperate.'

'He's having another picnic so soon? That's unusual.'

'I suppose it's because of the nice weather.'

Gavs looked at him curiously. 'I suppose it is.'

They got out at Knightsbridge and began the walk to the school.

'Expecting Galina on Sunday, are you?'

'God, I suppose so. She turns up everywhere.'

'Well, if you want my advice, I'd be prepared.'

Amiss weighed up the importance of keeping up a cool façade against his urgent desire to know what the hell Gavs meant. The façade won.

'*Che sera, sera*,' he said carelessly.

'You knew him well?'

'I'd say as well as anyone. I lived beside them from the day they got married till the day they separated. More coffee?'

'Thanks.'

Mrs Clarke topped up the three cups. She leaned back in her armchair, crossed her elegant legs and lit a cigarette.

'Tell me about Wally.'

'The trouble with Wally was that when he saw anyone doing anything, he knew he could do it better. That included running the country, the London Zoo, the local newspaper shop and obviously, most of all, the place where he worked. People didn't have the heart to ask the simple question: why, if he was so bloody smart, was he working in a tenth-rate, two-man language school as the second in command?

'Celia put up with his self-importance for all those years when she was bringing up the children and then she went back to work. Her new perspective helped her to see that she was suffering the double disadvantage of being married to a failure who behaved as if he were a success.'

'You liked her?'

'Very much. Still do. Mind you, I think she bears a lot of the responsibility for the way Wally carried on. Through a combination of sheer good nature and naïvety, she took him at his face value for years. It was 'Wally this' and 'Wally that'. If Wally pronounced on monetarism, the space race, the right colours for a bedroom or whether women should breastfeed in public, Mrs Wally quoted him. No wonder he came to believe he was right about everything. When he talked about his boss's inadequacies as a businessman, she took him as seriously as if he were a senior Cabinet minister shaking his head over the Prime Minister's latest errors of judgement. Some women make fools of their husbands, and she was one of them. But then she had the right material to work on.'

'It must have been a shock to him when she changed her tune.'

'It was, but he managed to rationalise it easily enough. Decided she had fallen in with feminists who had addled her brain. Wally had a very thick hide.'

'Did he talk about Rich Rogers, the fellow who became Ned Nurse's partner?'

'Sorry, I can't help you there. He left next door before that happened and I never heard from him afterwards. I think he'd put me down as one of the wicked feminists.'

'From what you've said, Mrs Clarke, would it have been in character for Armstrong to have decided to pre-empt the electrician?'

'Completely.'

'And also in character to have succeeded in electrocuting himself?'

She leaned her cheek on her hand and gazed at the floor for a full minute. 'I'm sorry, Superintendent. I can't give you a clear opinion. You see it's my vague impression that he was less bad at dealing with electrical matters than he was at a lot of other things. I've known their house flooded out because Wally did something stupid with the plumbing. But I can't remember any electrical disasters. Have you checked with Celia?'

'She was asked that after he died. Said he might have mucked it up, but it would be slightly surprising.'

'That's about the size of it. Good luck. If he was murdered, I hope you get whoever did it. For all I've said about Wally, he was essentially on the side of decency. He wouldn't walk away if he saw someone in trouble.'

'What was he like as a colleague?'

'Superior. Wally was the original tuppence ha'penny looking down on tuppence. You were a part-timer: he was the deputy principal, a man worn down with the weight of his responsibilities. I swear to God if the Vice Chancellor of Oxford carried on the way Wally did, people would say he had got too big for his boots.'

'He had no natural talent for the job, but he was very conscientious with the students, I'll give him that. Worked hard preparing lessons and would help with questions after hours. He was a kind man. Sadly, half the things that maddened one most were caused by kindness. It was his efforts to help me and turn me into a teacher like him that caused me to leave. He couldn't help me become a better version of me; he had to try to make me in his image.'

'Was he right in his criticisms of the school the way Ned ran it?'

138

'Yes and no. Under Ned the teachers got paid and the students got taught. Of course as Rich saw later, the building and its location had lots of unrealised potential. But Wally never had any ideas for increasing profits that went further than increasing fees by four per cent or slightly reducing the length of classes and hence the fees of teachers.'

'So how did he respond to Rich?'

'Couldn't believe what was happening. This little upstart, "the pipsqueak", Wally always called him. He was inordinately proud of being tall; indeed he appeared to be proud of being fat. The pipsqueak just appeared one day and turned everything upside down with Ned's full endorsement. And worse than that, it worked. And worse again, Rich wouldn't let Wally come in on the BPs. He tried to be tactful, but he was firm. Wally kept pushing at the door and it was always shut. Rich even rationed his attendance at parties to the big end-of-course ones. "Sorry," Rich said, "it's a young man's game, Wally." And when Wally pointed out he was the same age as Rich, Rich laughed that funny laugh of his and said, "I'm the exception that proves the rule."'

'Did he come to terms with this?'

'Only by the Cassandra method. You know. "There's something not quite right about it. It'll come to no good." That sort of helpful comment.'

'Did he hate Rich?'

'Probably in a grumblingly resentful sort of way rather than with a white heat. He'd certainly have liked to see him come a cropper. Let's say that if Rich had been murdered, I'd have put Wally high up, but not necessarily at the top, of any list of suspects.'

'Mr Rogers, why didn't you sack Wally Armstrong?'

'Because of Ned. Anyone else would have got rid of him years ago, but not Ned. "Poor fellow, poor fellow. Where else could he go?" That's what he would have said if I'd suggested it. I never upset Ned if I could avoid it, so Wally stayed. Anyway, he did a perfectly good job in the prefabs.'

'But he was a thorn in your flesh.'

'Only a small one. Into each life a little rain must fall, and all that, Superintendent. I'm a realist, been around, you know.'

139

'He was an embarrassment with the students — those you call the BPs, I mean — wasn't he?'

'Quite frankly, Superintendent, so was Ned, but I didn't murder him either. These were minor headaches that I had well under control.'

'It's been suggested to me that Mr Armstrong would have liked to see you fail.'

'He'd have been a fool to welcome that. He'd have lost several thousand a year out of the profit-sharing scheme.'

'A price he might have been prepared to pay.'

Rich shrugged. 'Perhaps. It's all the same now, isn't it?'

'It's not really, Mr Rogers. It was an open verdict on Mr Armstrong, you remember. In view of what happened to Mr Nurse, the balance of probability tips towards murder.'

'You're quite right, Superintendent. Forgive me, I'm not myself. What else do you want to know?'

'Well, if you don't mind, I'd like you to give me a complete rundown on the finances of the school.'

'Certainly, Superintendent. Where shall we begin?'

23

'Got absolutely nowhere with Rich Rogers about Armstrong. -Wouldn't you agree, Ellis?'

''Fraid so, sir.'

'Ellis, if you persist in calling me "sir" tonight, I'll have you transferred after Romford to Stolen Vehicles. Come on, practise. "'Fraid so, Jim." Let's hear it.'

Pooley gulped. ''Fraid so, Jim.'

'Who am I?'

'A friend of Robert's.'

'Good. Now where were we?'

'Drawing a blank,' said Amiss. 'Have another drink and tell me all about it.'

Amiss watched the pair of them attentively throughout the meal. He had felt apprehensive before their arrival, fearful that he had been wrong in putting pressure on them to meet off-duty. Milton had been in excellent form when he arrived, but Pooley began the evening obviously very tense. Amiss admired the way in which Milton had met the problem head-on: it was the right way to deal with Pooley. Obediently, he had applied himself to relaxing, and to Amiss's delight, after two or three glasses of wine, Pooley actually criticised Milton without tying himself in knots of embarrassment.

'There's something important you forgot to do last week, Jim.'

'What?'

'I only realised it on my way here tonight. In fact we've both been downright stupid.'

'Well, get on with it, for God's sake.'

'It's less than a month since someone assaulted Ned Nurse, and we completely forgot about it.'

'So we did.' Milton chewed meditatively on his steak. 'How in God's name did we manage to do that?' He took a sip of wine, set down his glass, shrugged and said, 'Well, sod it. I always knew I wasn't infallible; I'm relieved to learn that you aren't either, Ellis.'

'So what'll we do?'

'Pick it up on Monday, obviously. We'll have to interview all those buggers again looking for alibis for whenever it was.'

'We?'

'You and me. I just had a call to say the course is suspended for another week. Those were some Scotch eggs.'

Pooley's face lit up. 'We should crack it in that time.'

'Let's hope we do, Ellis. Let's hope we do.'

'I've got news as well, chaps.' Amiss began to open another bottle of burgundy. The cork broke and he swore.

'Give it to me, please,' said Pooley. 'I can't bear watching you. You open bottles like a teetotaller, not an ex-barman.'

'I wasn't working in your sort of pub, Ellis. It wasn't a "Dry white wine and my friend will have a Campari" kind of establishment.'

Pooley inserted the corkscrew in the remains, gave a fluid twist of the wrist, and extracted the half-cork with a triumphant flourish. 'Smartass,' said Amiss, holding out his glass for a refill. 'I suppose you learned how to do that on the playing fields of Eton.'

Pooley looked at him in alarm.

'Don't panic, Ellis. Jim knew anyway: he told me the other evening.'

'How long have you known?'

'Don't know. Ages ago. Saw your personnel file. I've kept it quiet. I may not be an inverted snob, but there's lots of them about.'

'They still go on about toffs in the canteen. Toffs and snobs. Toffs are people from my kind of background. Snobs are those who had a good education. It's been bad enough getting accepted despite having been at Cambridge. The thought of the puerile jokes if they knew about Eton . . .' He shook his head.

'Sometimes I wish I'd been to university,' remarked Milton suddenly.

'Why didn't you?' asked Amiss.

'My school head didn't know much about universities: only two or three boys a year went. He advised me to apply to new universities. I loathed all of them on sight when I went for the interview, so though I was offered places at two of them, I turned them down. I just couldn't face spending three years living in the middle of a wasteland.'

'You old aesthete,' said Amiss. 'I never realised what a traditionalist you were.'

'Anyway, all that's by the way. What's your news?'

'I'm leaving on Monday morning with Ahmed to spend a week on a health farm.'

'You're what?' Milton and Pooley asked in unison.

Amiss was enjoying their reaction. 'You heard. Health farm. Rich rang me just before you came. Apparently the school doctor has put the fear of Allah into Ahmed. Told him he's got to get away from London and be looked after properly for a week.'

'What's wrong with him anyway?'

'He's having heart palpitations and pains in his stomach. He was convinced he needed surgery. Doctor Moskal reckons it's over-indulgence in the fleshpots, not that he'd have put it that way to Ahmed. I imagine he's told him his condition has been caught in time and that complete rest in luxurious and expensive surroundings will cure him.'

'So where do you come in?'

'He can't possibly go alone. His English isn't bad but he'd never be able to handle an institution full of strangers. He needs a minder. And who is there to go with him except me? It's got to be a man. Kenneth won't let Gavs go alone and Rich can't leave the school. So it's me. I couldn't say no.'

'So we'll be without our snoop next week, Ellis. It's all down to you and me.'

'Ahmed's still on the list, dammit. I'll go on snooping, but in a more specialist way than usual.'

'He's paying for you, of course?'

'Certainly. From what Rich says, it's going to cost something in the region of a couple of thousand quid, apart from what he's paying for the course anyway. The place the doctor uses is right at the top of the market. You must have heard of it — Marriners.'

Pooley looked impressed. 'I certainly have. It's for the fattest of fat cats, literally and metaphorically.'

'I'm actually looking forward to it a lot. I've always been curious to see inside one of those places, but I was never likely to be able to go.'

'Speaking of money, Jim, we haven't told Robert about Rich's finances.'

'Quite right. You tell him.'

'The school's turnover last year was close on two million pounds.'

'You're kidding.' Amiss did a rapid calculation. 'No, you're not.'

'Clear profit last year was three hundred thousand. Rich and Ned had about three-quarters of that between them.'

'You mean over a hundred thousand each?'

'That's right. And the year before they'd made nearly as much.'

'Good God.' Amiss remembered Ned Nurse's squalid house with incredulity.

'They each owned fifty per cent of the business.'

'When was the partnership set up?'

'Surprisingly not until two years ago,' said Milton. 'Rogers says he wasn't prepared to take a share of Ned's property until he'd earned it.'

'Ned got a very good deal, then, didn't he?'

'Certainly did,' said Pooley. 'In fact Rogers seems to have behaved very well. From everything that's said about him, it would have been child's play to persuade Ned to settle for a much smaller share.'

'What did he do with his money?'

'Gave a lot to some Greek archaeological trust, according to Rich. Otherwise left it in the bank. His current account stood at a hundred and thirty-five thousand pounds. Can you believe it?'

'Of Ned, yes.'

'And he's left everything to Rich.'

'Who's loaded already.'

'Exactly. And he hasn't gambled it away or anything. We have corroboration that he's very comfortably off.'

'When was the will made?'

'When the partnership was set up.'

'Sensible.'

'Precisely.'

'And what's more,' interjected Milton, 'Rogers says he's going to spend most of what he gets from Ned's estate on setting up scholarships in his name.'

'It's all cul-de-sacs, this case,' said Amiss moodily. 'It would be quite nice to be sure anyone was murdered. Sometimes I think we're just wasting our time.'

'We're not,' said Pooley, 'I know we're not. I'm certain Nurse was murdered.'

'But why?'

'Don't know. Maybe because he found out something he shouldn't. There's something funny about that place.'

'We know that. But nothing worth murdering to cover up.'

'That remains to be seen,' said Milton. 'Now stop upsetting Ellis and go and make us some coffee.'

'Goodnight, my children.' Amiss put his arms round the shoulders of both his departing guests.

'Let us know how the picnic goes,' said Milton.

'Sure, but I expect it to be uneventful. I think Galina's stymied.' Amiss opened the door.

'And enjoy Marriners. Take a good book or three.'

'I will. That too should be uneventful. But I'll keep you posted. You'll do the same for me, won't you?'

'Of course.'

'Oh, Ellis, one last thing.'

'Yes, Robert?'

'Remember not to call Jim "Jim" when you're on duty.'

'If he does, I'll have the whole canteen singing the Eton Boating Song.'

24

Amiss was staggered by how much work went into creating a picnic that met Rich's standards.

'Not your sort of thing this, old man, is it?'

''Fraid I was never much good in the house. The mater despaired of me a long time ago.'

'Tell you what, you just do the fetching and carrying. I'll provide the little feminine touches.'

Since it was those that were the most time-consuming, Amiss had finished his part of the work long before Rich. He sat in the sun and had a welcome half hour with the Sunday newspapers. Rich joined him shortly after midday.

'Any advice for me, Rich, on how to handle Ahmed?'

'Keep your temper, that's the most important thing. And expect trouble round every corner. Won't be a rest-cure, this, I can tell you. Don't think Ahmed's cut out for the quiet life.'

'Should I take him on country walks, that sort of thing.'

'Some hope. Have you a car?'

'No. It's not worth keeping one in London.'

'But you drive?'

'Yes.'

'Then hire a car tomorrow morning at the school's expense, Bob. That way you'll at least be able to get him out of Marriners' hair if he gets fractious.'

'Thanks, Rich. Sounds like a good idea.' Amiss reached across and plucked a few hairs from the shoulder of Rich's jacket. 'Plutarch, I presume.'

'Little devil. She's moulting and her hairs get everywhere. I spend ages brushing them off my clothes.'

'I've noticed the odd one still lingering: they're very bright orange. Getting on well then, are you?'

'We rub along, you know.' Rich smiled. 'I never thought I'd get fond of a cat, let alone that cat.'

The doorbell shrilled.

The company was different from the previous Sunday. Galina had decided against inviting Alessandro, Davina or Fabrice: Gavs and Kenneth had had enough of Ahmed, so had refused to come again. For the first couple of hours Galina, Karl and Marcello were supplemented by Amiss and three comely, bright and good humoured young women who had come at Rich's request. It was not until Ahmed arrived and began to haggle with one of them over a price for the evening that Amiss realised they were call-girls.

To begin with Amiss put up such a popular performance as the life and soul of the party that he managed to deny Galina any opportunity to get him alone. Then, to his dismay, cocaine made its appearance. Amiss speculated frantically about whether his image allowed him to say he did not take hard drugs: he concluded it did not. Galina had the first snort and then took command. 'Come on, Bobby. You must 'ave some. It ees very wonderful.'

'Sorry, Galina, I'm on duty.'

'Nonsense, Bob. One of us is quite enough. Go on, enjoy yourself.' Amiss could have killed Rich.

'Sorry, I really can't. I had to stop doing coke: it has a funny effect on me — makes me very violent.' I put that badly, he thought. Probably turns her on. 'And then I always get sick.' Lest she had failed to understand him, he vigorously mimed vomiting.

Her face fell. 'You are disappointing, Bobby.'

'Perhaps I can help,' said Rich. He fetched from his pocket another small plastic container and took from it a lump of cannabis and some cigarette papers. 'Here you are. Have some of this, Bob, I know you like it. Go on, roll yourself a joint.'

'Then what happened?'

'I rolled a joint, of course. What option did I have?'

'I didn't realise you could. I'd have expected you to make a pig's ear of it.'

'I didn't go to university for nothing, you know. Mind you, I'm not much good at it. It's been six or seven years since I last tried.

But fortunately Galina was so determined to help me that any clumsiness I might have shown was obscured.'

'Did you get stoned?'

'Well obviously I tried very hard not to. It was hardly the company in which to let oneself go. I pretended to, of course, but in fact I did quite well on expelling the smoke rather than ingesting it. Dope never did much for me anyway. It used to put me to sleep while my hop-head friends took off on obscure paths of mental exploration.

'However, I digress. So there I am, forced to sit beside her on the swing, and she says, "Bobby, come inside, I wish to make love with you."

'I looked around and saw no vantage point where I might claim a private detective was lurking. The bloody woman had outsmarted my fiancée: ostensibly I was on school premises presumably doing school business.'

'Surely the private detectives I hired have infra-red lenses, or whatever it is the paparazzi use.'

'They'd have had to be on the roof to get us in their line of fire. And remember, we were going inside, to a room overlooking the garden.'

'A tight corner, all right,' said Rachel, who was feeling decidedly less insouciant than she sounded. 'What did you do?'

'Guess.'

'You seem to have had only four options: give in; refuse; pass out or run away. What else is there?'

'You won't like this.'

He couldn't have, thought Rachel. She felt suddenly very cold. He couldn't be about to tell me he actually did it with that whore.

'I told her I'd just discovered I had VD.'

Relief made her burst out laughing. 'Did it work?'

'Christ, did it work? She let out a scream that attracted the attention of the whole gathering, snatched up her handbag and marched out. When the others had gone, Rich asked me what had happened. When I told him he said, "Congratulations, my boy. Most inventive."'

'Wouldn't it have been easier just to say no?'

'I didn't know how to do that and still keep on as the Good

148

Time Boy. Perhaps when all this is over I'll invest in some assertiveness training.'

'Robert.'

'Yes?'

'I should hate to seem self-centred or less than supportive, but I'm getting the tiniest bit concerned about my image. I mean, I had accepted being insanely jealous happily enough, but now I have to assume I've got VD too. It won't go down big with my next promotion board.'

'It's entirely your own fault, my dear. If you'd married me when I asked you to, none of this would have arisen.'

'Your strategy is to continue blackening my name until I yield.'

'Certainly not. I'll blacken it until I know no one else will have you. Then I'll throw you aside like a soiled glove and marry Galina.'

'I need to clarify something, Jim.'

'Go on.'

'I'm at the school to help solve what might be two murders.'

'Right.'

'Not to report on minor misdemeanours.'

'Wrong. You don't necessarily know the significance of minor misdemeanours, so you do need to report them. They might be the cause of major ones.'

'What I mean is I don't want any part in having Rich done for a minor offence if he hasn't committed a major one.'

Milton tried to suppress his rising irritation. 'Robert!'

'What?'

'Do you trust me?'

'Yes.'

'Then explain to me what you're talking about, for Christ's sake, and stop drivelling. I promise you, my interest in Rich Rogers has to do with his murderous potential. If he's been shop-lifting or propositioning on the Earl's Court Road, he may continue to do so with impunity as far as I'm concerned. You know the score perfectly well. What's got into you?'

'Marijuana, I expect. Sorry, Jim. I must still be stoned.'

'Ahmed ibn Mohammed ibn Abdullah, please.'

'Putting you through.'

'Room twenty-three. Hello,' said a female voice.

'May I speak to Ahmed, please.'

'Who is it?'

'Bob Amiss. I think we may have met at lunchtime.'

'Oh, we did. This is Di.' She went off into peals of laughter. 'You certainly upset that countess.'

'Very excitable, Italians. Is Ahmed there?'

'Sort of. He's asleep and snoring hard.'

'Will you be staying?'

'I think so. He'll probably wake up soon.'

'Could you give him a message?'

'Sure.'

'Tell him we have to be at Marriners by three. It'll take three hours to get there, so I'll pick him up at the hotel at twelve.'

'OK.'

'And Di?'

'Yes.'

'Can you please tell him they were very insistent that we have to be there on time.'

'Sure, honey. But don't count on him listening.'

'Do your best. Thanks, Di.'

'Good-night.'

Amiss replaced the receiver and lay back on the bed. His head still felt rather fuzzy from the alcohol and dope. He kicked off his shoes and fell fast asleep. Half an hour later, he was woken by the phone.

'Robert?'

'Yes. Rich?'

'I've been thinking. I should come clean with you.'

'About what?'

'This health farm business. It's not as straightforward as it looks. I think part of the reason Ahmed's been under the weather is because he's been getting death threats.'

Amiss felt suddenly very awake. 'Any idea why?'

'Not really, unless they're connected with some stuff he was going on with last week about having killed someone. When he was low, when the coke was wearing off, he muttered something about blood demanding blood.'

'Has he told you the details?'

'No. He doesn't really want to talk about it at all. I only discovered it because the hotel manager keeps an eye on our people and tips me off when there's something funny going on. Apparently the switchboard operator is a Muslim and can speak some Arabic. She overheard Ahmed being told that Mahmout's death would be avenged by his brothers.'

'So you taxed Ahmed with it?'

'Yes, but for all the information I got, I needn't have bothered. He just came out with slogans: "Nobody frightens Ahmed ibn Mohammed ibn Abdullah"; "I am ibn Saud"; all that sort of stuff.'

'Have you told the police?'

'Ahmed was very insistent that no one should be told.'

'Rich, you've got to tell them. Supposing something does happen to him? You'd be blamed if you'd done nothing.'

'I suppose you're right. I get too used to doing what the BPs want.'

'Does this mean that we're going to be followed to Marriners by a horde of Islamic assassins?'

'I doubt it. I really can't take this at all seriously. But he'll be safer at a health farm than in London. I've told him not to leave a forwarding address.'

'What do you make of it, Jim?'

'I wish you weren't going.'

'I'm not going to back out now. No one frightens Robert ibn Amiss.'

'I'll give Rogers an opportunity to tell me all this first thing in the morning. Then I'll have a word with the local force and ask them to keep an eye on Marriners. For heaven's sake, be careful, Robert. Take precautions like checking under your car.'

'OK. I'll think paranoid.'

'And do try to enjoy yourself. Maybe you'll come back with your VD cured.'

'Not if Galina's still in the school, I won't.'

25

At eleven forty-five Amiss parked the hired Renault in the car-park and walked into the hotel which for a week Galina had been urging him to visit. He was impressed. The lobby was large and luxurious; the carpet was deep; the sofas were leather; the flowers were lavish; the porter was alert; and the receptionist was pretty and competent.

'Mr Abdullah, sir. Just a moment, I'll ring his room.'

After a minute or two she shook her head. 'He's gone out or not answering, sir.'

'Try again,' said Amiss grimly. 'He's probably still asleep.'

Ahmed answered after another minute.

'Ahmed, it's Bob. Are you ready?'

There was a brief silence. 'Hello, Bob. No.'

'Are you up?'

'I do not understand.'

Preposterous oaf, thought Amiss. Who does he think he's kidding? 'Have you risen, Ahmed?'

'Yes. I have risen.'

'I'm coming up.' He put down the phone before Ahmed could object.

'You're from the school?'

'Yes. I'm representing Mr Rogers.'

'Right, sir. You may go up. Second floor, room twenty-three.'

Ahmed opened the door reluctantly and barely awake. Mindful of Rich's advice, Amiss concentrated on keeping his temper.

'We must hurry, Ahmed. We have a long way to go.'

'I do much. I eat. I wash. I dress. I back.'

'Wash. Dress. I will pack. We can buy something to eat on the way. We should be off in fifteen minutes.' As he spoke, he knew he was talking nonsense. Ahmed would be ready in his own sweet time.

He was ready by one thirty, but insisted on having lunch before leaving. In the hotel dining-room, Amiss fretted through his omelette while Ahmed addressed himself stolidly to the three-course table d'hôte. At one fifty Amiss excused himself and rang Marriners to explain that they would be about two hours late. The response was extremely chilly.

They left at two thirty. By dint of exercising all his skill and quite a lot of his nerve, Amiss managed to reach their destination by five fifteen. It had taken all his reserves of patience not to lose his temper on the journey. As soon as they got out of London, Ahmed demanded to drive. Amiss explained about insurance. Ahmed said it did not matter. Amiss said it did. Ahmed then began to shout a lot and throw his arms about. As far as Amiss could gather, the gist of his argument was that a prince did not need insurance because he could do what he liked. Amiss explained that things were otherwise in England. He proffered the example of Princess Anne's husband being fined for exceeding the speed limit. Ahmed thought about that and said it was stupid. Amiss said that never-theless, that was how it was. Ahmed said he was so rich he could pay any fine. Amiss said mendaciously that he would probably be imprisoned. Ahmed shouted a lot more at that. He then pointed out that as a prince he would have diplomatic immunity. Amiss said not in Britain, he wouldn't. Ahmed shouted some more.

In view of the language difficulties, and the fact that Ahmed interspersed his various tirades with abuse about Amiss's driving and a great deal of rodomontade about his own, all this took a great deal of time. It was followed by a long period of silence, relieved on Amiss's part and sullen on Ahmed's. Then, when they were within a few miles of Marriners, he electrified Amiss with a new topic of conversation. 'What day are executions?'

'What are you talking about, Ahmed?'

'What day you execute bad people?'

'This is not Saudi Arabia, Ahmed. We execute nobody in this country.'

'Someone kill someone. What happen?'

'They go to prison.'

'But for blood there must be blood.'

Amiss dimly recalled a magazine article of a few months previously. 'But in your country don't murderers sometimes pay money to the relatives of the person they've killed instead of being executed?'

That foxed Ahmed, but after Amiss rephrased it a couple of times he got it. 'Yes, if relatives want money not blood.'

'Ah, I see. It's the choice of the relatives.'

'Yes. But much times the relatives kill.'

Amiss felt slightly faint when his painstaking enquiries elicited the information that public beheadings were carried out by the relatives of the murderees if they so wished. Executions, he felt, were definitely an area where amateurs were to be discouraged.

As they finished their bloody conversation, they drove through the gates of Marriners and up a tree-lined, half-mile drive to the car-park beside the entrance. Amiss, who hated being unpunctual, took only the most cursory glance at the enormous Gothic façade. He jumped from the car, snatched his bag and two of Ahmed's from the back, and ran up the steps, leaving his charge to carry the other two.

The door was opened by a liveried porter with a stern expression and a broad Glaswegian accent, who whisked their bags out of their hands. 'I'll take these upstairs, gentlemen, when I've shown you to the office. Mrs Cowley-Bawdon is expecting you and you are already very late.'

He led them through an enormous hall, lavishly furnished with velvet-upholstered sofas and easy chairs, which to Amiss's fevered gaze seemed crammed to capacity with women in dressing-gowns drinking tea. They were led into an ante-room and waved to two straight chairs. The porter knocked at a door in the corner, entered and reported, 'The two gentlemen are here, ma'am.'

'Thank you, McIver,' called an American voice. 'Tell them to wait a moment while I finish my telephone call.'

McIver relayed the message ceremoniously and left. Amiss wondered if he should give Ahmed a warning about how he should behave, but concluded that an injunction to conduct himself like a civilised human being would hardly help matters. Ahmed took out his worry beads and clicked away busily: Amiss buried himself in a magazine about organic farming.

After five minutes, Mrs Cowley-Bawdon emerged. Slim to the point of emaciation, she was certainly a good advertisement for a fat-farm. Her hair was bright gold; her blue eyes glittered; her nails were long and enamelled crimson to match her lipstick. Her handshake was of the dried fish variety.

'Very well, gentlemen. We mustn't waste any more time. Which of you shall I take first?'

'It might be advisable to take us together.'

'That is not how we do things at Marriners, Mr Amiss. It is important that patients be able to discuss their condition in private.'

Amiss wilted. 'Er . . . it's just that my friend's English isn't too good.'

She smiled tolerantly. 'You will find that this is a cosmopolitan establishment, Mr Amiss. We are well used to dealing with foreigners. I myself speak five languages.'

Amiss tried and failed to summon up his arrogant alter ego. Mrs Cowley-Bawdon beckoned to Ahmed and led him into her office. Amiss kept his ear cocked as he half-read an article on interesting things to do with pig-shit, but apart from one relatively subdued roar there was nothing to be heard.

She reappeared within ten minutes. 'Come in, Mr Amiss. Mr Ahmed is now with Sister.'

Her office was clinical, her desk furnished only with a Filofax bound in crimson leather, a large vase of crimson roses and a form on which she began to record Amiss's answers to her questions. They had covered name, address, age, marital status and methods of paying the bill when Ahmed's voice came through the door behind her head bellowing, 'No, no, no, no. I am not. I am not. Not true. Not true. Bad woman.'

Amiss enjoyed the spectacle of Mrs Cowley-Bawdon leaping to her feet and rushing in next door. 'Sister, Sister, whatever is the matter. Goodness me, Mr Abdullah. Calm down, please.'

'He's gone berserk,' said a clipped female voice, raised to be heard above Ahmed's, 'just because I told him he was a little overweight. Well, I had to say fat to make him understand.'

'Calm down, Mr Abdullah.' The chatelaine's commanding tones had their effect and Ahmed shut up. The sister went on aggrievedly: 'He's twelve stone and only five feet seven inches

155

and he's got rolls of fat around his middle. If he thinks that by abusing me he can make me say he's thin, he's got another think coming.'

Mrs Cowley-Bawdon spoke soothingly to both of them and returned to Amiss.

'Congratulations,' he said.

Her complacent smile annoyed him. 'Experience, Mr Amiss. I've been running this establishment for a very, very long time. Now tell me, have you a sedentary job?'

A few minutes later the sister came out with Ahmed, had a whispered consultation with her boss and beckoned Amiss to follow her. After a few enquiries about his medical history, she took his blood pressure and weighed and measured him briskly.

'Eleven stone two pounds, Mr Amiss. You don't need to lose any weight, so there's no need for you to fast. You can go on the light diet.'

'What's that?'

'Essentially fruit and salads.'

'What's the next up from that?'

'Nothing, Mr Amiss. There's only fasting or the light diet. Clear out the system, that's the important thing. Get rid of all those toxins that come from all that smoking and drinking you do. And by the way, if you don't manage to stop smoking here, please remember to do it only in your own bedroom. And I recommend you to take plenty of exercise. Thank you, we're finished now. Please return to Mrs Cowley-Bawdon.'

'Just one thing, Sister.'

'Yes?'

'In case my friend is a little confused about what he's supposed to be doing, can you tell me what his regime will be?'

Her lips tightened. 'He is to fast, Mr Amiss.'

'And you're sure he realises that?'

'If he doesn't, I'm sure Mrs Cowley-Bawdon will have explained it to him.'

Amiss was escorted next door. The sister handed over a form and withdrew. 'Right, Mr Amiss. Now let's see. Yes, light diet and you're cleared to take any treatments you wish. Look at this, please, and tell me which you'd like.'

Amiss looked down the long list. 'I'll try the massage, sauna and the Turkish bath for now.'

'Fine. If you want any of the others, make up your mind tomorrow and let reception know.'

'Any problems with Ahmed?'

'No, no. Not at all. He's perfectly happy. Really entering into the spirit of the thing.'

'He understands about fasting?'

'He doesn't just understand, Mr Amiss. He's enthusiastic about it. Pointed out that he's well used to it.' She laughed a tinny laugh. 'After all, as he said, Ramadan goes on for a month.'

'But one can eat at the end of each day.'

'Oh, really, Mr Amiss, I think you're making a mountain out of a molehill. That little kerfuffle with Sister was just nerves. He's perfectly happy now. Indeed he's decided to have all the treatments.'

'What?'

Amiss stared again at the list. 'But he couldn't possibly have understood the descriptions of these.'

'I fancy he's a bit of an adventurer. Wants to try everything.' Amiss wondered if he was right in thinking her smile was rather fond. She couldn't really have succumbed to Ahmed's brutish sexuality, could she? Well, it was none of his business.

She picked up her telephone and pressed a button. 'McIver, the gentlemen are ready.'

She nodded a dismissal and bent to her Filofax. Amiss left the room feeling small.

Even Ahmed could find nothing to object to in his quarters. At a pinch his bedroom could have held a party for a hundred and fifty; the bathroom could have taken an overflow of a couple of dozen and the four-poster could have comfortably slept six. On finding that Ahmed was under the impression that since he was incapable of unpacking, a servant would appear to do it for him, Amiss gritted his teeth and stepped in. Ahmed helped by opening his bags and emptying them on to the floor.

In addition to his normal clothes, he had brought with him a newly-acquired sports wardrobe. This included red, blue and white tracksuits, four pairs of satin shorts with matching T-shirts, three towelling dressing-gowns and two pairs of running shoes.

As he placed on the dressing table six of the seven watches Ahmed had brought with him, Amiss tried to make sense of an approach to life that involved a passionate addiction to time-pieces along with a complete indifference to time.

It took half an hour to put everything away. Ahmed lay on his bed smoking. Amiss reflected that he wouldn't mind being a gentleman's gentleman: it was being a pillock's gentleman that hurt.

Before going to his own much more modest room to deal with his own much more modest belongings, Amiss scanned the brochures and instructions on the desk. 'Right, Ahmed. I'll collect you in twenty minutes. That's when I have my evening meal and you have your hot water.' Ahmed showed no sign of hearing him, and indeed he had not moved by the time Amiss returned. It took a further twenty minutes to get him downstairs to the hall, where this collation was served, and where they were both ticked off for lateness.

Unwilling to expose any of the other patients to Ahmed, Amiss found a quiet corner for them and got a desultory conversation going. He drank his consommé and ate his fruit and Ahmed sipped his hot water. He had lifted out the slice of lemon and was sucking it when the sister marched through looking about her keenly. She caught sight of Ahmed and came over to him, thunderstruck. She leaned forward and slapped his wrist. 'Tut, tut,' she cried. 'I thought you were fasting. That means hot water and nothing else. Have you no self-control?'

She charged onwards, leaving Ahmed behind her muttering darkly of vengeance and blood. It was, thought Amiss, going to be a very, very long week.

26

Rich got up early to look for Plutarch. She had not come home the night before and he felt unable to go to work without seeing her. 'Something urgent's come up, Jenn. Tell Gavs to sort out the groups. I'll be in as soon as I can — noon at the latest.'

He walked round the neighbourhood for an hour and then got his car out and drove to Ned Nurse's house. It was as he and Amiss had left it: there were no signs of Plutarch having paid a return visit. He drove home to check just once more. As he opened his front gate his eye caught a flash of orange under the hedge. It was Plutarch: she had a piece of thick string around her neck and she was not breathing.

'I'm worried about Robert, Ellis.'

'I know, sir. So am I.'

'He's very clever in all sorts of ways —'

'But very naïve in others?'

'Precisely.'

'Of course those threats to Ahmed may be just a hoax.'

'But then again they may not.'

'The sooner I can get some protection for them the better I'll feel. I'm going to try to get Rich Rogers on the phone. I've thought of a plausible excuse to ring him. You get on with boning up on the Nurse mugging.'

Milton called in Pooley a couple of minutes later. 'No good. He probably won't be in till midday. How are you getting on?'

'I've learned that Nurse's neighbour says the supposed mugger was black.'

'That wasn't on file, was it?'

'No, I've only just got it from North-West. I rang them up just to check that we had everything. Apparently he phoned and told them that the day after he made his statement.'

'Well if the fellow really was black, it eliminates all our suspects.'

'Except Ahmed.'

'It'd really be pushing it to call Ahmed black.'

'Or unless one of them had blacked up.'

'Or wore a black balaclava. We must neglect no possibilities, Ellis. Now go away and find out more.'

'Mr Peter Dicks?'

'Speaking.'

'Detective Sergeant Pooley of Scotland Yard. Could I have a word with you about the assault you witnessed on Mr Nurse?'

'The old git's dead now, i'n't he? You'll hardly catch the bloke now.'

'Nevertheless, we must continue the investigation.'

'I s'pose you know what you're doin'. I'm surprised you're botherin' so much. You usually let blacks get away with murder.'

One of those. Pooley took a deep breath and remembered what his job was. 'I wanted to ask you about that, sir. In your original statement you didn't mention that the assailant was black.'

'No. Well, I didn't remember.'

'What made you remember?'

'My wife. She said, "I s'pose he was black, then." Fair enough. They usually are, aren't they? Then I remembered his hat.'

'His hat?'

'Yes, his hat. He was wearing one of them woolly caps like them blacks wear — the ones with the funny ringlets.'

'Sorry, sir. Can we start from the beginning?'

'Any luck, Ellis?'

'No, sir. To summarise Mr Dicks's explanation: the assailant wore a cap reminiscent of those worn by Rastafarians; therefore the assailant was a Rastafarian. All muggers are black; this was a mugger; ergo he was black. Guilty on both counts. The only fly in the ointment is that he didn't actually see what colour his skin was.'

Milton groaned. 'I sometimes wonder if we should believe anything the public tells us. Any further details about size?'

'No. Average was as far as he would go.'

'So it could be the benighted Ahmed, or indeed most of the people at the school?'

'Yes, sir.'

'OK, Ellis. Get down there and start checking alibis. I'd really better chair the resources allocation meeting now that I'm here. I'll put the skids under them and be along to you at noon.'

'See you, sir.' Pooley looked at his watch as he left Milton's office and went to his own desk to pick up the papers he needed. He was on his way out when Pardeep beckoned him over. 'Coffee?'

'Sure,' said Pooley, stifling his slight guilt, 'but I can't spend long.'

'I've something to tell you, Ellis,' she said, as she took her first sip.

'Good news, I hope.'

'I think it is.' She looked down at the table and then straightened and looked him in the eye. 'My parents have arranged a marriage for me.'

Pooley had never before felt the blood drain from his face.

'You look shocked.'

With difficulty he found his voice. 'I am.'

'It's the right thing, Ellis. It was time for me to have children.'

'But why an arranged marriage? What about love? Do you even know this person?'

'I gave it a lot of thought. I wanted someone from my own cultural background and I wanted stability. I haven't got the sort of courage it takes to face all the problems of inter-marrying. I didn't know anyone suitable and I respect my parents' judgement. Love usually follows.'

'I'd have taken the risk.'

'I'm not you, Ellis. You're a romantic. I'm very practical — or maybe I'm a coward.'

'You're absolutely determined?' She could hear the choke in his voice.

'I am. Will you wish me well?'

'Of course I will. I do. I hope you'll be very happy. Now do you mind awfully if I disappear? I'm running very late.'

'Off you go. Bye.' She had tears in her eyes as she watched him leave. His were dry: he hadn't gone to Eton for nothing.

*

Milton and Rich arrived at the school simultaneously and went straight to the office to join Pooley. Rich repeated what they already knew about the threat to Ahmed.

'You really should have told us about this earlier, Mr Rogers.'

'I'm sorry, I didn't really take it seriously.'

'Well, I do. I'll get on to the appropriate people right away.'

While Pooley sat in the lounge checking students' alibis, Milton made a series of telephone calls. He had a long wrangle with his opposite number in the Hertfordshire police, whose view seemed to be that Arabs should be confined to London and kept off his patch. It was out of the question, he said, to provide a police guard. The best he could do was ask the relevant patrols to keep a special eye on Marriners.

Special Branch were not offering protection either, but they agreed to get one of their Arab specialists to visit the hotel.

Interpol had nothing of interest to report. They had failed to get any information whatsoever on Ahmed. Arabs were hell, they pointed out, because of the absence of surnames. However, under pressure from Milton, they promised to redouble their efforts.

Sighing, he walked through to the lounge where Pooley was trying to soothe an outraged Gunther. At the sight of Milton, Gunther rose magisterially to his feet. 'Here now is your superior. I want that you let me to speak with him.'

Milton listened to a couple of minutes of complaints about the impropriety involved in interrogating a man of his eminence in such a manner. When he realised that a large part of Gunther's grievance had to do with Pooley's junior status, Milton interrupted. 'I'm sorry, sir, but I must insist that you answer my colleague's questions. He has my full confidence.' He walked out before Gunther could utter another sound, found Jenn and ordered sandwiches, then returned to the office to put his feet up and think.

Pooley thanked him when he rejoined him in the office a couple of minutes later. 'Not at all, Ellis. Can't have pricks like that telling us how to organise ourselves. Now let's talk things through over lunch and this afternoon we'll split them between us and try to see the lot of them.'

By five thirty the job was done and all alibis checked. They looked in on the Pimms party in the garden in order to double-check a few details, politely refused to stay for a drink and left the building.

'Hellish afternoon, wasn't it?'

'Certainly was, sir.'

'None of mine took very kindly to being suspected of beating poor old Nurse over the head.'

'Nor mine.'

'Well, we certainly did a good elimination job.'

'Certainly did, sir.'

'So if Ahmed turns out to be in the clear as well, we're back to square one.'

'Maybe he won't, sir.'

'We should know tomorrow morning. The locals have promised to go along to Marriners first thing. I hope to hell they act sensitively: I delivered a long lecture on the importance of patience and tact. Went down badly.'

Pooley said nothing.

Milton stopped suddenly. 'What's wrong, Ellis? You've been down ever since I joined you at the school.'

Pooley was so close to tears that for a moment he did not trust himself to speak. Then he said, 'I'm fine, really.'

'Rubbish,' said Milton. 'Is it personal or professional?'

'Personal.'

'Serious?'

'Feels that way.'

Milton looked at his watch. 'We're both off-duty now. Would you like to have a drink and talk it over?'

Pooley had never spoken to anyone about Pardeep and his training in hiding his feelings had been of the best. He hesitated for a moment and looked at the pavement. Then he raised his head and looked squarely at Milton. 'Yes, please, Jim. I'd appreciate that very much.'

163

27

'What is quite extraordinary,' wrote Amiss to Rachel, 'is being in circumstances where the environment is geared to maximum relaxation while events place one under maximum stress. All around me are people who have shed all their everyday worries and are talking at about half normal speed. I have moments of feeling like them — in the sauna or when being massaged especially — but then a knot of tension rises in me at the thought of what devilry that cretin is likely to be up to now.

'At the moment I feel peaceful. He's left me alone for an hour, claiming to be tired and to need sleep. In fact he's probably found someone to screw, but I'm past caring. The last two evenings were awful. On Monday night everyone disappeared immediately after the seven o'clock feast so Ahmed and I were thrown on our own resources. He decided he wanted to play games, so we sat in his room, sipping water and working our way through the stockpile provided by the management.

'First we played Ludo, something I haven't done since I was ten. He lost and became petulant: I shrugged and said Insh'allah and got my head bitten off, I have to say on this occasion quite rightly. Ahmed found out sometime last week that I'm an atheist so he now holds me in contempt (apparently it's infinitely worse than being a Christian or even a Jew), and considers me beyond saving. (Mind you, I find it a bit thick being dismissed as a hopeless case by Ahmed. Compared with him I'm a saint.) That means I'm not entitled to make any reference to any deity, since they're not my property, so to speak.

'Anyway, Ludo was condemned as unfair, so we tried Snakes and Ladders. His problem there was that he could never grasp that the point of the game is that one has to take the rough with the smooth. Ahmed is only interested in a life full of ladders — preferably if someone else carries him up them. We never finished that game: he got so cross when confronted with his second snake that he upset the board. The next game on offer was Trivial Pursuit, at which I drew the line. Even if he understood the questions, he wouldn't know any of the answers, Allah having willed him to be so lazy that he's never acquired any knowledge of any kind other than how to drive a car and where to dip his wick. Then he said he wanted to play cards, which he'd never done. Very astutely, I thought, I introduced him to Snap. He became so hooked on it that we had to play it for hours on Tuesday night as well. It has two major attractions: it requires no skill that might have to be learned and if I say Snap first he can say I didn't.

'Enough about Ahmed for the moment. I want to tell you about this joint. I wish you were with me, because it's the kind of place one wants to discuss obsessively with someone like-minded. You'll have gathered from what I told you about our reception that it's a cross between a concentration camp, a prep school, a home for the feeble-minded glitterati and a five-star hotel whose cooker is out of service.

'It's astonishing how quickly one becomes institutionalised and utterly obedient (except for Ahmed that is) to the timetables and rules that abound. One's world shrinks and the only things of interest are to do with the inmates.

'I don't know if places run on these lines are a purely English phenomenon. There's an all-pervading Nanny atmosphere that makes Marriners especially right for the English: after all it's England, not Britain, that elects Nanny Thatcher. My guess is that they might appeal to Scots but not Welsh and certainly not Irish; to Norwegians and Swedes but not Danes; to Germans but not French; and never never to Italians or Arabs. I could feel sorry for Ahmed if he weren't such a shit that I'm delighted he's having a horrible time.

'What worries me is how quickly I fell into following orders. Late this afternoon four of us were sipping barley water in the Turkish baths (I loathe barley water, but I'd been told to drink it), and discussing the rival merits of dry and steam heat, when a chap called Mick (yes, he's Irish — stereotypes follow me round everywhere these days) said, "Sod this, lads, enough is enough. What do you say we have a little drink before dinner in my room?"

'All three of us mumbled with embarrassment and pleaded health reasons for turning him down. Now think about it: I'm here because of Ahmed; I'm perfectly healthy and I'm thin. So why did I refuse an invitation to a drink I sorely wanted? Answer: because it's against the rules. I suppose I should be glad I didn't find myself reporting him to Sister. The only thing I can say in mitigation is that I came to my senses around six and tried to find out his room number from reception, unfortunately unsuccessfully. They don't know people's first names — or perhaps they suspected what was going on.

'The high spot of the day is, of course, lunch, made particularly attractive yesterday by the absence of Ahmed. He had his glass of hot water in the hall: I had lunch in the dining-room with a book and thought how nice it was to be without Ahmed. Unfortunately today he insisted on seeing Mrs Cowley-Bawdon and persuaded her that he should be put on the light diet. She must be one of those women who fantasises about a brutal sheikh riding off with them into the desert. So my peace was shattered and he came with me to lunch.

'We sat down and were served with soup, which he slurped with every appearance of enjoyment. Then I took him to the table from where one can help oneself from five or six excellent salads. "Where is meat?" Ahmed's broken-hearted cry arrested the attention of every patient in the dining-room. I doubt if they're over it yet: we don't speak of meat at Marriners. Ahmed is in a terrible state: he'd been anticipating great big steaks and he hates salad. So even on the light diet he's not a happy man.

'Now we move to sex. Yesterday afternoon ended the honeymoon period with Mrs Cowley-Bawdon. She called me in at five and announced that Ahmed had propositioned the receptionist, two waitresses and four patients. I didn't add the information that he'd tried me as well, nor that I've a shrewd suspicion he succeeded this morning with a chambermaid. "I am sorry, Mr Amiss," she said, "but I have no option but to ask you to take that person away."

'This was a bit of a facer, but you know my resourcefulness. I assumed an expression of immense gravity and said, "Please, Mrs Cowley-Bawdon, let me explain."

'"There's nothing to explain. He is simply unfit to have in residence at Marriners."

'"I realise that the prince's manners are rather lacking, but he learns fast. It has not been easy for him to adjust to life outside the palace."

'"A prince. Really? Which royal family?"

'"The Sauds."

'"And which branch of the royal family is he from?"

'It was a cinch. I spoke of not being able to give details, Ahmed's father being so close to King Fahd. It was absolutely crucial that there should be no scandal: for that reason Ahmed was incognito.

'"Poor man," she said, shaking her head sadly. "What terrible pressures must be on him. We must be understanding." We agreed that the staff would be asked discreetly simply to ignore his suggestions.

'I thanked her for her great humanity, and withdrew and tried to explain to the libidinous little bastard why one didn't make random sexual overtures: not a lot penetrated, if you'll forgive the pun. The difficulty, of course, is that from his perspective all Western women are what he calls "brostitutes" because they flaunt themselves.

'We proceeded to the Tuesday night party. This is a bizarre occasion when everyone dresses up to the nines, drinks carrot juice and makes small talk about food and treatments. I was far too casually — and of course inexpensively — dressed, but Ahmed made up for me. He's got a new jacket in yellow suede which he wore with mustard cashmere trousers and a gold-coloured silk shirt. It being an early evening party, he confined himself to only five rings.

'He got on very well for the first half hour and I thought my sermon had worked. Then as I was engaged in an animated conversation about aromatherapy with the owner of a Chelsea boutique, I heard the unmistakable sound of a slap: a young woman who I had been told had a small part in a BBC soap was marching away from Ahmed, who was feeling his cheek and looking furious. Most of those present being English, everyone affected not to notice. I grabbed him and dragged him out and demanded to know why he had bropositioned this woman after all I had said to him. Aggrievedly he pointed out that a) she was an actress and b) she was showing a lot of cleavage (or as he put it, "she show me tits").

'With all that as background, guess what he inferred this morning about a woman who for a living stands beside a bath in which a naked man is immersed in water and points a high-pressure hose at all parts of his body, having politely asked him first to protect his organ with his hands? The problem was that he didn't simply broposition this lady; when he had hurtled forth rampantly from the bath he assaulted her. Mrs Cowley-Bawdon was so unamused that I thought I'd have to claim this time that he was the heir to the throne. Instead I soothed her with the offer of a hundred quid to compensate the girl for hurt feelings.'

Amiss looked at his watch and was surprised to see that it was already nine and Ahmed hadn't phoned to summon him to the next phase of their Snap marathon. He surely couldn't still be napping.

He wasn't answering his phone, so Amiss went down to his room: the door was locked and his knock met with no response. He instituted a thorough and fruitless search for him in the public areas. Cursing, he went back to his room and changed out of his dressing-gown into outdoor clothes. Without any real expectation of success, he went out to check the terraces: the night was so balmy that even Ahmed might have been tempted to take a stroll.

He returned by the route that passed by Ahmed's windows and was disturbed to find them open. He went back to his own room and rang reception. No messages. I don't like this one bit, said Amiss to himself. He looked up a number in his address book and dialled Jim Milton.

28

'I don't know how worried we should be,' said Milton. 'We haven't really got much on those death threats. Ahmed eventually admitted to our lot that he'd had three but said nothing useful at all about the caller — just that he wasn't a Saudi. The switchboard operator thought his accent was very peculiar and felt he mightn't have been an Arab at all.'

'If he thinks a killer might be lurking, could even he be fool enough to open his french windows?'

'Search me. You're our Ahmed specialist. You're quite sure they weren't forced?'

'As positive as I can be, but I'm no expert.'

'And he's said nothing to you about being afraid of anything?'

'I tried pumping him this afternoon. I couldn't admit to knowing anything, so I picked up on a revolting conversation about executions that he'd initiated the other day and asked if he had ever met a murderer.'

'Anything interesting?'

'He went all coy on me. Said he knew things he couldn't talk about. I think he's indiscreet only when he's been drinking or snorting.'

'Hmm.'

Amiss took a cigarette from the case his students had given him and lit it with his matching lighter. He felt momentarily ashamed of being so hard on Ahmed: at least the fellow was generous with money. 'Any other news?'

'Sorry, Robert. I forgot that we haven't talked since Sunday. Most important news is that of the eight people who could have laced Nurse's drink, only one could also have mounted that attack on him in the alley.'

'Ahmed?'

'Yep.'

169

'I was afraid so. The others really don't seem the type.'

'It could still be coincidence.'

'Sure. I still can't think of a motive, can you?'

'No, unless he was acting as someone else's agent.'

'You haven't got anything on his background? I mean he isn't a card-carrying member of some international terrorist brotherhood or anything useful like that, is he?'

'Not to the knowledge of Interpol. They haven't found out a damn thing about him.'

'You'd think they'd have something on a prince, even if there are thousands of them.'

'That's why they think he probably isn't one.'

'Well for Jesus' sake don't tell Mrs Cowley-Bawdon that.'

'Mrs Who?'

'The Ubergruppenfuhrerine. Tell you about her some other time.'

'What are you going to do now? Give up the search and go to bed?'

'You don't think I should ring the local Old Bill?'

'I think you'd get very short shrift. They wouldn't get too excited by a grown man being out at ten o'clock.'

'Oh, sod it. He's probably in someone's bed. Or maybe someone with a car took him off to the bright lights. This afternoon he was on at me to take him out tonight, but I refused for his health's sake: he seriously needs to lay off the food and booze.'

'Maybe he's gone off by himself.'

'Couldn't without a car: it's miles and he hates walking. That's another reason he's so furious about not being allowed to drive . . . Hang on a minute.'

'What is it?'

Amiss put his cigarette in the ashtray, went over to his jacket and tried the pockets. He went back and picked up the receiver.

'I'm an idiot.'

'Go on.'

'The turd's pinched the keys to the car.'

'Which is not insured for him?'

'Of course not.'

'Look, there's absolutely nothing you can do, so if I were you I'd go to bed.'

'Will do. You too. How's Ellis?'

'He's all right. Got a bit of personal trouble that he'll no doubt tell you about sometime, but I'm keeping an eye on him. He'll survive.'

'I won't pry. OK. Good-night. We'll talk when there's any news.'

'Good-night, Robert. I hope your encumbrance comes home in one piece.'

'I hope he doesn't. I don't know how I can face another four days with him.'

Amiss finished his letter, went to bed and slept until woken by a young woman bearing muesli and China tea. He immediately telephoned Ahmed. 'Are you all right?'

'Yes . . . no. My head is sick.'

'I'm coming.' He pulled on his dressing-gown and hastened downstairs. Ahmed opened the door looking sheepish. He had a large gash on his forehead. It took Amiss ten minutes to extract from him the information that he'd run the car into a wall (the will of Allah), but had not otherwise been hurt (Praise be to Allah). The car was not bad.

When Amiss had arranged for him to be visited by Sister, he went back to his room, showered, dressed and went out to look at the car. He guessed that at a rough estimate, the bodywork had sustained several hundred pounds worth of damage. Bugger it, he thought. I'll drive it back to London and Rich can sort out the compensation.

He returned to find Ahmed bandaged up, complaining about his sore head and sitting in bed guzzling chocolate.

'Where did you go last night, Ahmed?'

'Restaurant. I have meat and wine.'

'And then?'

'I find a club and a woman. We have sex and I come here.' He took another bar of chocolate out of his pocket and tucked into it noisily. Amiss looked at him with only barely concealed distaste.

'Ahmed, why did you come to Marriners in the first place?'

'I cannot understand.'

'Why did the doctor say you must come here?'

'I am sick.'

'Do you want to be well?'

'Yes.'

'Then why did you drink wine and why are you eating chocolate?'

'Because I want to.'

'But if you have those things, you will not get better.'

'I bay a lot. They must cure me.'

'Oh, fuck,' said Amiss. He turned on his heel and went back to his own bedroom.

To avoid the trouble with the management that ensued from missed appointments, Amiss had been making a practice of delivering Ahmed to his various treatments. On this Thursday morning there was no need, as Ahmed decided to stay in bed and skip his massage and his herbal bath. However, in mid-afternoon he consented to join Amiss for a Turkish bath. Relations were tense between them and conversation perfunctory. Ahmed, knowing himself to be in the wrong, sulked. Amiss, weary from holding back from telling Ahmed what he thought of him, found it a great strain to be civil.

They sat opposite each other naked and alone in the Turkish bath until after five minutes two figures came in and joined them. The steam was so thick that it was impossible to recognise faces, but their first few words identified Amiss's neighbours as the Irish contingent. Amiss was overjoyed to meet them again, and enthusiastically took up Mick's renewed invitation to a small party in his room. 'And you're very welcome too, gentlemen,' said Mick into the steam in which were buried Ahmed and a third newcomer. Two grunts came back, but Mick ignored the incivility and chatted to Amiss and his compatriot of the horrors of the exercise programme for which he had incautiously signed on. He had pulled a calf muscle on his first day and strained his wrist on the second. He stretched out his injured leg for relief and almost tripped up the invisible man opposite who was just leaving. Mick apologised, but this time the man did not even grunt: the only sound was of him opening and shutting the door.

Mick's friend also left after another few minutes, but Amiss, who had a high tolerance for heat, sweated happily and enjoyed Mick's conversation. After spending so many hours with Ahmed it was a pleasure to talk to someone who merely wished to be entertaining. He had no idea how much time had passed when

Mick announced his imminent departure. 'Make sure you come along about six then. Room seventeen.'

'I look forward to it. Thanks very much. Coming, Ahmed?'

There was no answer. 'Ahmed!'

Nothing.

'They didn't both leave, did they?' asked Amiss.

'Don't think so.'

'He must have fallen asleep. Ahmed!'

Amiss stepped carefully over towards the bench opposite and felt around. 'Ah, got him. Ahmed, wake up.' He patted him vigorously on the knee. There was no reaction.

'Mick, I think he must be ill. Will you get the attendant and leave the door open so that the steam clears a bit?'

Mick went off without a word and Amiss waited uneasily. It took three or four minutes before visibility was good enough for the three men to see that Ahmed had a stab wound in his chest, that blood had mixed with the sweat on his body, and that he looked very dead. 'May God have mercy on his soul,' said Mick. 'Now Robert, throw on your dressing-gown and come on upstairs with me. We'd need a quick one to recover from this.'

29

'This is appalling, utterly appalling. It could have a disastrous effect on business. I knew I should have insisted on expelling him from Marriners, but through sheer good nature I allowed myself to be talked out of it by that plausible side-kick of his.'

It was eight that evening and Milton and Pooley were listening to Mrs Cowley-Bawdon. They let her go on talking until she came to a natural halt. 'Now, ma'am,' said Milton, 'we have every sympathy with you and we'll be just as quick as we can, but you must understand that we have to make full inquiries.'

'But I won't have any of the patients upset. They are all busy and successful people who come here to rest. They must have no stress. It undoes all the good.'

Pooley admired the mantle of stolidity Milton donned on these occasions. He seemed able to detach himself from the gibberish and think about practicalities while saying that which had to be said. Mrs Cowley-Bawdon was given her head for several minutes more and then Milton became firm.

'I appreciate all you've said, ma'am, but we have to stay here until we've done our work. We'll need an office and, if possible, accommodation for the two of us.'

'Accommodation? Why do we have to have policemen from London? What's wrong with the other ones?'

'Nothing, ma'am. They're doing an excellent job, but for reasons which I cannot disclose, Scotland Yard is taking over. Now about the office?'

'*They* made do with a corner of the hall.' She clicked her tongue, 'Oh, I suppose you'd better have mine. I hope you're not going to need it for very long.' She stood up, picked up her Filofax, and moved towards the door.

'As long as it takes to conclude our on-the-spot investigation of the murder,' said Milton stiffly.

She winced. 'Please don't use that terrible word.'

Milton's patience tended to wear thin when he was confronted with hypocrisy. 'What word would you prefer? Stabbing? Killing? Or would you like me to say he was put to sleep?'

Relations deteriorated after this, but did not quite break down. She bowed to the inevitable, gave them copies of lists of clients and staff along with the timetables of the day, and telling him he could use McIver to find people, she swept out of the room with her head high.

Milton tried Amiss's number without success. He pressed the PORTER button on his keyboard. 'Mr McIver, do you know where Mr Amiss is, please?'

'Dinna ken, but mebbe he's back with Mr McGuire.'

'Please find him if you can and ask him to come down to Mrs Cowley-Bawdon's office to see the police from London.'

'It's such a relief to see you both.'

Milton jumped up to greet Amiss and gave him a rough embrace.

That his friend's voice was slightly slurred came as no surprise; Milton knew Amiss's propensity for taking to the bottle when confronted by sudden death.

'Come and sit down,' said Pooley, giving him a friendly pat on the shoulder, 'and tell us all about it.'

'Nothing to tell really. Someone stabbed him just two feet away from me and Mick and we didn't see or hear a thing. Mick'll tell you the same thing. Good bloke, Mick. We've been drowning our sorrows together along with his mates.'

'I'm glad you've got support. Now just let's run through the events of the afternoon and then we'll send you back to Mick.'

The local police force had done a great deal of the donkey work, so Milton and Pooley were able to confine themselves to talking to the key witnesses — those who had been in the vicinity of the Turkish bath between three and four. Then they spent a couple of hours going through all the evidence, checking and cross-checking.

'Seems perfectly clear to me, Ellis. Is it to you?'

'Yes, sir.'

'Let's just make sure we got the same answers. Surprise,

surprise, no one admits to being the mystery man and only two male patients have no alibi for that time. Correct?'

'Correct: the American film producer and the Scots barrister.'

'They deny ever being in Saudi Arabia. They haven't even been in London during the time Ahmed was there. Both of them have seen him around Marriners, but have never spoken to him.'

'That's right.'

'With the exception of those on holiday, all the staff were on-duty and have alibis.'

'Right. So it looks almost certain that we're dealing with an interloper.'

'I'm knackered,' said Milton, throwing down his pen. 'It's nearly midnight and I think we should leave it until the morning. I don't suppose there's any chance of getting a drink in this place.'

'Hardly, sir. Unless we try Mr McGuire.'

'His party's unlikely to be going on still.' He dialled Amiss's number and got no answer. 'Where are we supposed to be sleeping, anyway?'

'Mrs Cowley-Bawdon said to ask McIver. I forgot all about it. He's surely off-duty by now.'

Milton pressed PORTER and got a most disgruntled response. 'I've been waiting till ye were ready, so I could show ye to your quarters.'

'I'm very sorry to have kept you, Mr McIver. Perhaps you could show us now. We'll pick you up at your desk.'

He picked up his papers. 'Stupid old bastard,' he said to Pooley. 'All he had to do was to give us the room numbers hours ago. We could perfectly well have found our way ourselves.'

'I expect he enjoys his grievance.'

They found McIver and followed him to the bedroom that had been allocated to them: single rooms were declared to be out of the question. McIver's back was stiff and his accent apparently deliberately impenetrable: they couldn't decide if he was always like that, if he regarded the murder as having been their fault, or if it was because he considered them socially unacceptable.

'Thank you, Mr McIver,' said Milton. 'Now can you tell us where we can find Mr Amiss?'

McIver pointed to a door at the end of the corridor. 'That's his room, but ye'll mabbe may find him in Mr McGuire's, room seventeen down the other end. I warn ye,' his tones were sepulchral, 'I've reason to believe they've drink taken.'

'Well, they have had a very unpleasant shock.'

McIver began to speak of weak vessels and Milton interrupted him. 'Let him who is without sin cast the first stone,' he said firmly. 'Thank you, Mr McIver, that will be all.'

He threw himself down on one of the beds. 'Great God,' he said, 'he's worse than Romford.'

'You shouldn't say something like that until we're off-duty, sir.'

'We're off-duty, otherwise I wouldn't say it. Go and see if Robert's up to a chat, will you, Ellis?'

'Why don't you come too? Mr McGuire might give us a drink.'

'Oh, all right. Mind you, I can't imagine he'll have any left.'

Amiss's room was empty, so they walked quietly to McGuire's door and listened. The low hum of voices emboldened them to knock, and the door was opened by McGuire. 'Come on in, you're more than welcome. How about a drink? Gin? Whiskey? Vodka? Beer?'

There were half a dozen people in the room; the number of glasses strewn round suggested that there had been far more at various times. 'That's very kind of you, Mr McGuire. Actually, we were looking for Mr Amiss. A few things we needed to check on about the deceased, you know.'

'You'll get nothing out of poor Robert tonight.' He waved towards the bed, where Amiss slept deeply. 'He didn't want to be on his own, but he couldn't keep awake, so we put him to bed here. I'll take his later on. Have a drink anyway, gentlemen. And it's Mick.'

'Well, I must admit that's a very attractive idea, Mick. We've had a very long day. Whiskey and water please. And it's Jim.'

'And the same for me, please,' said Pooley. 'And it's Ellis.'

McGuire sat them down on the side of the bed, got them their drinks and introduced them to their fellow-guests, three of whom they had already met. 'You're very impressively equipped with booze for someone on a health farm,' observed Milton. 'Cheers.'

'Oh, I've usually only got the one bottle. But of course we had to have a wake for that poor fellow, so I sent someone off to get supplies.'

177

'Not, I suppose, that he'd approve of our drinking in his honour,' said a fat MP whom Milton and Pooley had interviewed earlier that evening.

'You're wrong there, Gervaise, old boy,' said Mick. 'Robert there told me he wasn't one of your strict Arabs. Great lad for the wine and the women, apparently. Sure, God help him, I'm glad he had a bit of fun out of life while he had the chance.'

'I know it's *de mortuis nil nisi bonum* and all that, Mick,' said a moustachioed old man, 'but I heard a bit about him from one of the girls, and he seems to have been a total sex-maniac.'

'I suppose there's worse kinds of maniacs.' Milton was intrigued by the extent of Mick's charitableness. Was it drink or death, he wondered?

'He was a handsome devil,' observed Gervaise. 'Wouldn't be surprised if women went for him.'

'Handsome is as handsome does,' said the moustachioed man. 'That squint didn't add to his attractions.'

'I never saw him close enough to see a squint. Remember I only arrived this morning. But I saw him in the woods when I went for a walk. And I must say, he'd that kind of lithe grace women go for. You know — animal attraction and all that guff.'

'How did you know it was him?' Milton sounded casual.

'Because he was an Arab, of course. There aren't any others around Marriners, are there?'

'Unless the Ayatollah sent someone to get him,' observed the man with the moustache and they all fell into slightly drunken sniggers.

30

'I'm trying to work out how an outsider could do it,' said Amiss, 'but I see almost unsurmountable obstacles.'

'Yes, I know. Ellis and I chewed them over last night and again this morning for what seemed like hours.'

'Where is he, anyway?'

'He's ferreting around following up a couple of hunches. You know what he's like.'

'Trying out the hypothesis that Ahmed committed suicide but swallowed the knife before he died in order to put the blame on me?'

'Something like that, no doubt.' They reached the woods and began to stroll along the path that meandered through the centre. 'How are you feeling?'

'At least half-human. I think I've slept off most of the booze and I'm pretty well over the shock. Mick's therapy was extremely effective.'

'He seemed to take it all in his stride.'

'It's not surprising: he used to be in the SAS.'

'An Irishman?'

'Why not? They've been a mainstay of the British army for centuries. Mind you, he steered well clear of involvement in Northern Ireland.'

'Well, well. That'll teach me to get as hung up on stereotypes as you. Now, will you take my word for it that it's almost a hundred per cent certain it was an outsider?'

'I have to.'

'And all the staff and students at the school are ruled out. Everyone's accounted for.'

Amiss reflected. 'Even Kenneth?'

'Who?'

'Gavs's chap. They had a joint fling with Ahmed, don't you remember? I'm sure I told you.'

'You probably did, but I found Ahmed's sex-life very confusing. I'll get him checked out, of course, but if we're going to track down all Ahmed's bed-partners, we'll be at it for weeks.'

'So you don't want to be reminded of Di?'

'No. Yes. Who's Di?'

'The call-girl he picked up at the picnic. I told her we were going to Marriners.'

'Oh, God. All right. She might have an Arab pimp.'

They turned off the main pathway and ambled through a large concentration of silver birch. 'It was here that Gervaise Whatshisname saw the Arab.'

'But he's not certain it wasn't Ahmed.'

'No. He said the photograph was inconclusive.'

'You said he used the word "lithe". No one could have called Ahmed lithe; he lumbered.'

'Compared to friend Gervaise, Ahmed was lithe. Still, from what you've said about Ahmed's condition yesterday, I really can't imagine that he took time out of bed for a brisk walk.'

'Has anyone else sighted a strange Arab?'

'I've arranged that everyone be in the hall in thirty minutes so I can ask them that. In fact we'd better be heading back there now. I must have a word with Ellis first.'

Both were deep in thought as they walked back through the wood, but as they emerged into the meadow that separated it from the gardens, Amiss saw Pooley in the distance walking swiftly towards them. 'Look, Jim,' he said. 'That's lithe.'

'It's more Ellis doing his imitation of a red setter who's sniffed a scent.'

'Ahmed's was certainly strong enough.'

'You're clearly not mourning him much, are you?'

'No, though I find it hard to shake off the shock of seeing him dead. It seemed somehow much worse that he was naked. Undignified. And I could wish that I hadn't been so unfriendly toward him during the last few minutes of his life.'

'Considering the way he treated you, I think your behaviour was beyond reproach. Stop looking for reasons to feel guilty.'

180

'Sorry, Jim. My besetting sin. I got a lecture on it this morning from Rachel.'

They met Pooley in the centre of the meadow and he turned and walked with them towards the house. 'It's Interpol, sir. They've identified him at last.'

'Took them long enough.'

'Turns out they didn't bother until yesterday to check on his fingerprints.'

Milton stopped suddenly. 'But we sent them those last week!'

Pooley shrugged.

'Shit! Well, what have they got?'

'He was a Saudi, but he wasn't a prince. His name wasn't Ahmed ibn Mohammed ibn Abdullah; it was Abdullah ibn Mahommed ibn Ahmed and he was wanted at home for murder.'

'Of whom?'

'Some criminal associate, it would seem. Interpol say he had a small international reputation as a tenth-rate assassin.'

'My God,' said Amiss. 'He was even too lazy to kill people properly.'

'Ned Nurse's murder was quite imaginative,' pointed out Pooley.

'Doesn't fit Ahmed's mentality. Coshing him on the head, yes. Lacing a drink to cause an accident, no.'

'There's a limit to coincidence, Robert,' said Milton. 'For the moment we've got to proceed on the assumption that the school's resident assassin did the assassinating, even if it was done in a rather unorthodox way.'

'And who assassinated the assassin?'

'Any new developments, Ellis?'

'Only that I think his french windows were opened from outside. There were no obvious signs, but I managed to do it with a credit card.'

'So someone tried to get him on Wednesday night?'

'Could be. And found the bird flown.'

'I don't get it,' said Amiss. 'Why should anyone kill him the risky way they did, when they could just have waited until the next night and got him in his room?'

'That it, Ellis?'

'I did some more checking on timetables. It would have been very difficult for an outsider to get hold of Ahmed's daily timetable: the only copy was in Mrs Cowley-Bawdon's office, which was always locked when unoccupied.'

'Hell.'

'But every day they pin up, on the notice board in the staff room, the schedule for each treatment centre with the patients' appointments written in.' They were approaching the stairs leading up to the front entrance. 'Now, come with me,' said Pooley, and he led them round to the back of the building and down a discreet flight of stairs. 'Here's the staff common-room.'

'Well, well,' said Milton, stepping into the empty room through the open french windows and walking straight to the large notice-board on the right-hand wall. 'Let's see. Ah, yes, Turkish bath: 3.00, Van Hattem, Inglis, Dodds, Bell, Guy, Le Druillenec.' He came out and joined them. 'Easy.'

'If you know they're there,' said Amiss.

'I didn't,' said Pooley triumphantly. 'I just snooped round.'

'There are lots more unanswered questions,' said Milton, 'but now it's time to talk to the assembled masses. Ellis, come with me and stand respectfully behind me when I speak. Robert, trail along slightly behind us now and then join the audience and revert to being a recent acquaintance of mine.'

It had taken Milton half an hour of oozing charm at Mrs Cowley-Bawdon to gain her agreement to calling the meeting. Once she yielded, she proved highly cooperative and exhibited the terrifying efficiency that made Marriners operate so smoothly. As he came through the front door she was standing there with a list. 'Every member of staff is here, Superintendent, and all the patients except Mr Amiss. Ah, no. I see him now. Come on, Mr Amiss. You're late. Over there, please.'

Amiss scurried obediently to his place. 'Now, everybody. Here is Superintendent Milton to talk to you. Please listen carefully. Superintendent. Over to you.'

Milton stood in front of a crowd which he knew must number seventy-five: forty-five patients and thirty staff. He cleared his throat as quietly as he could. 'Ladies and gentlemen. I shall make this as brief as I can. First, I'd like to thank Mrs Cowley-Bawdon for being so very helpful.' He looked towards her. 'She

182

has made every effort to make our job as easy as possible. We greatly appreciate her efficiency and kindness.' He bowed and she inclined her head slightly in his direction and smiled graciously. Milton was visited by the ignoble thought that such blatant flattery might pay off in the lunch she provided for him and Pooley. The previous night they'd been given nothing but mousetrap cheese and biscuits. 'The purpose of this meeting is to speed up our inquiries, although I can assure you that we will be very sad to leave this haven of luxurious serenity.'

Amiss stared incredulously at Milton.

'You have all been seen individually by Sergeant Pooley and me or by other officers. Now I should like you do something that requires you all to be together. When I've finished, I want each of you to spend a few minutes looking at everyone in this room with the object of finding out if anyone you've seen at Marriners since Monday is missing — other than the unfortunate gentleman who died yesterday.

'Now of course you can't remember everyone you saw, but for one reason or another you might remember noticing someone who you realise is not now present. A gentleman, for instance, might have glimpsed in the distance a Marilyn Monroe look-alike, or a lady might have seen Robert Redford's twin brother, yet as they look around this room they notice that attractive though their companions are, there is no one who quite fits such a description.' He paused for the titters to cease. 'Such a person might have been wearing a white coat, a dressing-gown, a dress, a suit, or if you were in luck, they might have turned up naked in your sauna.' More titters.

'That's it then. Thank you all very much for listening. Any questions? No? Well, in that case, Sergeant Pooley and I will retire to Mrs Cowley-Bawdon's office, for in her kindness she continues to sacrifice it to us. Please come to us if you think you can help.'

'What'd you think, Ellis?' he asked as he unlocked the office door.

'Slightly on the shameless side, sir.'

Milton laughed. 'It was, wasn't it? But in this job you've sometimes got to be a populist.'

Gervaise was the first to arrive. 'Just dropped by to congratulate you. Very neat ploy, that. Means any sightings they come up with will be genuine.'

'And you haven't said anything to anyone?'

'Not a soul. And I'm sure that goes for the others from last night. You put the fear of God into us.'

They heard a knock. 'OK, I'm off. Good luck to you both. I enjoyed our discussion last night. And I lay you ten to one more ladies than men will have noticed the Arab.'

Amiss bolted his lunch and sneaked off to join Milton and Pooley in their office. 'Greedy sods,' he said indignantly, looking at the debris. 'Where did all that come from? A take-away from the Savoy?'

Milton pushed away his plate. 'Don't know what you're talking about. All we've had is a little asparagus, a simple steak, some salad which I expect is no better than what you've had, along with really rather delicious new potatoes and a most acceptable sweet omelette.'

'Not a patch on the Yard canteen,' said Pooley, polishing off the last morsel of the omelette.

'Indeed not,' said Milton, sipping a little burgundy. 'I'd much rather have joined you on the light diet, but I didn't want to hurt Mrs Cowley-Bawdon's feelings.'

'Give me some of that,' demanded Amiss savagely. He grabbed the bottle and Milton's empty water glass and filled it to the brim.

'Be our guest, my dear Robert.'

Amiss took a healthy swig. 'Christ! I thought I was supposed to be the tart around here.'

'You're only a newcomer. I've been at it for years.'

Amiss took a sip this time and put his feet up on the desk. 'OK. What gives?'

Milton became a policeman again. 'Eight women spotted a nice-looking Arab.'

'Who wasn't Ahmed.'

'Yes. They all said he wasn't Ahmed.'

'Men?'

'Four saw an Arab who wasn't Ahmed: two thought he was good-looking.'

'So presumably there may be lots of them who saw an Arab who wasn't Ahmed and think he must have been Ahmed and therefore haven't come to tell you about him.'

'Yes. Now that we've established that there really was a strange Arab, Ellis can do a quick run-around with Ahmed's photo and see if any more who thought they saw him in fact saw the other one, if you follow me.'

'Have you got good descriptions of the unknown Arab?'

Milton helped himself to seconds from the silver coffee pot. 'No, not really. Same colouring as Ahmed, good teeth, slim, dressed unobtrusively. He didn't hang around at all. No one ever saw him for more than half a minute.'

'And was he seen anywhere incriminating?'

'He certainly was.' Milton swallowed another mouthful. 'He was sighted yesterday at about three thirty taking off from the car-park on a motor bike.'

'Sounds pretty conclusive.'

'It does,' said Pooley. 'Now all we've got to find out is why Ahmed killed Nurse, if he did; if he was working for someone and if so who; why and from whom he got death threats; who killed him; were they working for someone else; where the missing Arab is; and a lot of other things I can't think of at the moment.'

'Like did someone kill Wally Armstrong and if so why and who was it?' said Milton.

'I see.' Amiss drained his glass, got up and moved towards the door. 'Well, if that's all there's to it, you obviously don't need any help from me. I'm off for a sauna: don't feel like a Turkish bath today. Then I'll have a massage and a nap. If you sort out everything before I wake up, I suggest you go and look for Lord Lucan.'

31

'I've had an idea, sir.'

'Go on.'

'It's almost impossible to imagine that the killer could have succeeded without having *some* knowledge of Marriners. However clever you were, you couldn't, for instance, guess how the system worked in practice. You'd have to know something of the geography and what the staff actually did. For instance, he'd have needed to know that the Turkish bath attendant was rarely near the steam room but spent his time rubbing people down on the slab next door.'

'Remember he could and did take risks. If he'd been seen around the Turkish bath, he could simply have aborted his mission.'

'Yes, but he wasn't. And that in itself suggests he was well-briefed. Anyway, it's the only lead we've got at the moment.'

'There are any number of people who could have briefed him: staff, patients, ex-patients.'

'We have to narrow it down to the school. Someone there could have put it into Ahmed's head to come here.'

'I thought the doctor did.'

'Not quite. I rang him just now and he said that to the best of his recollection, Ahmed suggested it first. The doctor spoke in generalities about rest, recuperation and self-denial. The patient mentioned Marriners.'

'Interesting. You think someone thought this a better spot for murder than London. I can't imagine why.'

'Nor can I at the moment. Though if we're dealing with a paid assassin, the reason could have been to guarantee an alibi for whoever hired him.'

'So what's your idea?'

'I think we've got to hang on to the school as central to all this.

From what Interpol said, it doesn't sound to me as if Ahmed was being killed by a vengeful relative.'

'I agree. Nothing as romantic as that.'

'And we're agreed that it's possible that the school is a cover for something sinister?'

'Yes, though it seems highly unlikely. A few milligrams of coke doesn't suggest great corruption. Anyway, what's your suggestion?'

'That we get from Marriners a complete list of all the guests they've had during, say, the past year, and get from the school a list of students from the same period. BPs only, of course. Then we compare them.'

'It's a very, very long shot, Ellis.'

'But we haven't any short ones at the moment, sir.'

'I know.' Milton got up and took a turn around the room. 'It'll take ages. They must have a couple of thousand going through here every year, and not a computer in sight.'

'I know, sir.'

Milton looked at his watch. 'We've just got time. OK. You ring Rogers and ask him to fax the stuff down to us. I'll go and beard Mrs Cowley-Bawdon. Don't blame me if we get bread and water for dinner.'

'Christ, I've done some boring jobs in my time,' said Amiss, 'but this takes the fucking biscuit.' He scribbled a name on yet another slip of pink paper and made a tick on a list.

'What a privileged life you've led,' remarked Milton. 'I can think of many far more boring jobs that I've done.'

'Me, too,' chimed in Pooley.

'He's obviously never shadowed anyone and waited for them outside a house for five hours.' Milton ticked the last name on his list and reached for another.

'Or spent the night in a ditch because of a tip-off about a burglary that failed to materialise.' Pooley picked up the two piles of white and one pile of pink slips and sorted them alphabetically.

'Or spent a whole day with his back to a cricket match watching the crowd.'

'Or —'

'Oh, all right, you sods. Stop ganging up on me. My life hasn't all been beer and skittles, you know. I once spent two days writing a forty-minute speech about the future of heat pumps.' He saw Pooley open his mouth and interjected hastily: 'And that was without even understanding what I was writing about.' Pooley opened his mouth again. 'And what's more I had to listen to my minister mangle it.'

'Oh, shut up, Robert. We're nearly finished,' said Milton. 'If everyone gets on with it and no one talks for the next ten minutes it'll be done.'

They complied, and within half an hour Pooley had amalgamated the three piles of slips and sorted them by letter. He gave them roughly a third of the letters each. 'Now sort each letter into alphabetical order.' They did so. 'Right, you still remember what you're looking for, don't you?'

'Just about,' said Amiss, 'though I'm so tired that I might end up thinking I'm supposed to choose which to vote for in the General Election.'

Marriners had yielded well over two thousand names and the school four or five hundred, so the secondary sorting process took the three of them another hour.

'OK,' said Pooley. 'Now we come to the sixty-four thousand dollar question. Is there any name that appears on both a white and a pink slip? If not, we've wasted fifteen man hours on a daft idea.'

'It's time we had a drink, Ellis.' Milton took a bottle of whiskey from his briefcase and poured three stiff measures into the water glasses on the table.

'Brilliant idea,' said Amiss. 'Where'd you get it? Have you and Ellis been raiding Mick McGuire?'

'Raiding? He came and forced this on us this afternoon. Said he'd never be able to finish up all the booze before he leaves tomorrow, so we'd be doing him a favour by helping. He's impossible to refuse.'

'Excellent,' said Amiss. 'Don't worry about that. I'm buying him dinner next week.'

'Now, Ellis,' said Milton, 'your idea was a good one and remains so whether we find some names in common or not. So calm down. Off we go.'

There was only one name that came up twice. At two thirty, Pooley let out a shout. 'Sven Bjorgsson, Knightsbridge School of English December 1988; Marriners January 1988, with Mrs Bjorgsson.'

'Now you're getting over-excited, Ellis. We're agreed that it's a very tenuous link.'

Pooley stopped pacing and sat down again. 'Sorry.'

'Here's what we'll do,' said Milton. 'I'll have a quick word with Interpol now and get them going on the Bjorgssons. Then I suggest we all go to bed.'

'Quite sure?' asked Amiss. 'Nothing else you'd like help with? Ellis might like us to go through the books in the library to see if any of them is hiding a mysterious envelope?'

'Shut up, Robert. It's far too late in the morning for facetiousness.'

Amiss grimaced. 'So it's censorship now, is it? OK, I'll retire once again to the window and have a cigarette.' For perhaps the twentieth time that night, he opened the window, lit a cigarette and expelled the smoke into the moonlit garden.

'Tomorrow morning, I'll head straight back to the Yard to pull together everything we've got and pursue whatever needs pursuing on the Bjorgsson front. Now, Ellis.'

'Yes, sir.'

'You stay here and see what you can find out about the Bjorgssons.'

'And then?'

'Go back to London. Robert?'

'Sorry?' Amiss drew his head back into the room.

'Will you stay on until Ellis is ready and drive him back to London? You might be able to get in a few more massages.'

'Yes to both, assuming the car goes on functioning. It's sounding a bit seedy since it had its night out with Ahmed.'

'And then, if you're both free and so inclined, we can meet for dinner and exchange news.'

'We're really getting into the habit of Saturday being Boys' Night Out, aren't we? Where'll it be this time? Your pad, Jim?'

'No, tomorrow I think you and I should take a trip down memory lane.'

'Not the Star of India? Couldn't we sacrifice sentiment to gastronomy and go somewhere better?'

'I think not. Can't think of anywhere as discreet. I'm no more anxious at the moment to be seen in public with you than I was when we first met.'

Amiss sighed. 'As the Superintendent wills. I'll spend the morning praying they've had a change of management.'

32

Amiss had forgotten to put the 'Do Not Disturb' notice outside his door, so he was woken up as usual at seven thirty with a modest breakfast full of worthy ingredients. He meditated turning over and going back to sleep, but decided that that would be a waste of Marriners' expensive facilities. As he munched his muesli he promised himself that if the Star of India did not actually poison him, he would have a massive plate of bacon and eggs on Sunday morning.

Obedient to his timetable, he attended Sister at nine to be weighed. 'Eleven stone four pounds, Mr Amiss,' she said, appearing to be in deep shock. 'How have you managed to put on weight? Haven't you been sticking to the light diet?'

'I haven't eaten anything not provided on the premises,' he said, feeling it might be tactless to mention all he'd drunk.

'Well, it's very odd,' she said.

He smiled weakly and proffered the remark that metabolism was a funny thing. This inanity failed to impress and he was ushered out coldly.

He went straight to the sauna, which was already full of naked men swapping information on their weight losses. Amiss's news made them all feel better. 'Bet you didn't tell her about the wake,' said a bald man whom Amiss half-recalled from Mick's bedroom.

'I wouldn't have dared. It cost Mick twenty quid to silence McIver.'

'Great fun, though. It really made my week. Usually it's a bit on the dull side here.'

'There's worse things than dull,' said Amiss, as he closed his eyes and began to doze. It was with great reluctance that he responded when the attendant called him. The cold plunge, agony at the best of times, was particularly hard to face this

morning. As he emerged shivering he made a mental note to ask
Pooley if he went in for cold showers. It was a strongly held belief
of Amiss's that they were a first-rate indicator of social class,
being enjoyed only by those who'd been to public school. The
warm shower and salt rub that followed were reprehensibly
hedonistic.

He had an underwater massage from the young lady whom
Ahmed had assaulted and went straight back to his bedroom,
where he crawled into bed and fell asleep immediately. He lay
undisturbed until one thirty, when Pooley knocked at his door
and got him up. 'I'm ready to go, Robert. If you get a move on
we'll have time for an unhealthy snack at the local.' He sat in an
armchair and closed his eyes.

With his mind full with thoughts of shepherd's pie, sausages,
baked beans and pickles, Amiss got himself ready and packed
within fifteen minutes. He had to shake Pooley awake. 'Lunch
ahoy!'

Pooley shook his head to clear it, darted into the bathroom and
could be heard splashing water vigorously. 'Nothing like cold
water to get one going,' he offered as he reappeared. 'What's so
funny?'

'Do you take cold showers?'

'Every morning, after a hot one. Doesn't everyone?'

'You're so predictable, Ellis. Come on, let's get going.'

Pausing only to reassure reception that the Knightsbridge
School of English would pay his bill, Amiss passed thankfully out
of Marriners for the last time.

It took only ten minutes to find a pub. The food was excellent
and the local brew superb. Pooley had a pint and Amiss a half, as
he was driving. 'Role-reversal,' observed Amiss. 'I'm sure
you've never in your life before been a drink ahead of me. You're
so damned moderate, it's sickening.'

Pooley smiled and took another long draught. 'Glad to leave?'

'Yes, in the sense of getting away from the scene of what I
suppose has to be called a tragedy. No, in the sense that I'd love
to have a week or two to do it properly. I never usually look after
my body, and it was getting to like it. I wonder if I could persuade
Rachel to come to a health farm for our honeymoon? Not this
one, of course. Ahmed would cast a bit of a dampener over

proceedings. But one of the others — especially the kind where you're allowed to drink.'

'Are you getting married soon, then?'

'Not till she's been back in London a while and we've lived together for at least a few months. Rachel says that apart from anything else she's not prepared to go through all the hassle of family disapproval at marrying out until she's absolutely certain it'll work.'

Pooley stared at his beer.

'What is it, Ellis?'

'Nothing.'

'No it isn't.'

'You're very persistent, you and Jim. I'm not used to talking about my personal life.'

'Class, old man. Middle class males are getting quite good at talking about all those unimportant things of life like love, disappointment and death. Your lot are still carrying on as if the natives would revolt if they saw a white man's lip tremble. Now come on and tell me about it. We've got all afternoon.'

The Star of India was just the same. The main interior was still caught in perpetual twilight, while from the entrance it seemed as though the tables at the back were plunged in stygian gloom. It took Milton a moment or two of peering towards the far end to identify his guests. He sat down thankfully and let out a long exhalation. 'God, what a day.' He called a waiter. 'Good evening. Your drinks all right? That'll be one gin and tonic, please.'

'I'm touched that they haven't changed anything, Jim. Not the red flock wallpaper, not the tiger pictures —'

'And judging by the stains, not the tablecloths.'

'You know I've never had the full story of your first meeting,' said Pooley. 'How did you become allies?'

'It wasn't quite love at first sight,' said Amiss.

'More like curiosity,' said Milton.

'Of course we found we'd a lot in common,' said Amiss.

'Lots of dead bodies, apart from anything else.'

'Are you going to tell me about it, or are you intending to go on with the cross-talk act?'

'Sorry, Ellis. Let's just peruse the menu and place our orders.

Then we'll tell you the whole story.'

'The food isn't as bad as I remember,' said Amiss. He chewed his last mouthful of Chicken Biryani and put his knife and fork together on his plate.

'Probably because you're still grateful for anything that isn't lettuce,' said Milton, who had stopped eating five minutes before. 'It's pretty bad. All right, Ellis. Have you had enough of our joint autobiography by now? Can we get down to business?'

'Yes, sure. Thanks. I've enjoyed the story. Eventful times you've had together.'

'It gets a bit tiresome always having to meet like illicit lovers. When this is over we must dine flamboyantly wherever the smartest people go,' said Amiss.

'Then we'd be certain of not being recognised.'

'*Touché*. OK. To business. What's happened today?'

'Hang on a moment.' The coffee and brandy were served and the waiter melted away. 'Let's start with you two. Ellis?'

'Mrs Cowley-Bawdon and three of the staff remembered a bit about the Bjorgssons. The consensus is that they were tall, blonde, handsome and kept themselves to themselves. Jogged and played a lot of tennis *à deux*.'

'Identikit Swedes, in other words,' said Amiss.

'You're wrong there,' said Milton. 'At least about her. She wasn't Swedish. Which meant she wasn't Mrs Bjorgsson.'

'Stop being mysterious, Jim.'

'It's quite simple. I took away with me the list of patients at Marriners the week the Bjorgssons were there and set someone to tracking down anyone who remembered them. Got one who had chatted to the female Bjorgsson and who swears she was English.'

'Swedes have wonderful English.'

'This woman said she admitted being English.'

'Oh, all right,' said Amiss. 'Let's assume she's right. Why can't she be Mrs Bjorgsson?'

'I asked the Stockholm police to check up on his two addresses: the one he had given Marriners and the one he had given the school. The first was false: the second was accurate and is known also to be that of a Swedish Mrs Bjorgsson.'

'He hasn't had time to get divorced and remarried since January, I suppose?' asked Amiss. 'Swedes do get around, I understand.'

Milton ignored him. 'I asked them to double-check by finding out where the Bjorgssons were in early January. I must say the Swedish police handled it very well. Asked some questions about a mythical car crash in January and elicited the information that he was away but she was at home.'

'Aha. Back to the impostor. Did the fellow guest have any more gen?'

'No. She said they had only the smallest of small talk. Like your witnesses, Ellis, she remembered them because of their tallness and blondeness. Said the so-called Mrs B reminded her of the young Princess Grace.'

'Anything interesting on Bjorgsson?' asked Pooley.

'Well, I'm afraid he isn't known as an international white-slave trafficker or anything useful like that. But his occupation doesn't rule him out of consideration: he's in import-export, which can cover a multitude. I've got people checking him out in depth.'

'Mmm.'

'I talked to the people at the school about him. They didn't have much to add. Confirmed the general impression of reserve. Rich and Cath said he didn't join in social activities much.'

'Doesn't give us much to go on,' said Pooley despondently.

'No. But the Swedes and Interpol are pressing on. What's the matter with you, Robert? Got a toothache?'

Amiss was supporting his head in his hands and gently rocking backwards and forwards. He shook his head.

Milton dropped his voice to a whisper. 'I've seen this performance before. It denotes serious thought. Ssh for a minute.'

They sipped their coffee and brandy and watched their companion's gyrations. After a couple of minutes he looked up. 'It's got to be Cath.'

They both started forward. In unison they said, 'Cath?'

'Snap,' said Amiss automatically. 'Yes, Cath. The first time I saw her I thought of Hitchcock heroines.'

'You mean the Grace Kelly comparison. Yes, I see that. Anything else?'

'Yes. When I had lunch with Gavs after Ned's funeral, he said something about thinking she'd been involved with someone for several months.'

'Excellent, Robert. Now, how do we discreetly check she was free to be at Marriners?'

'She certainly wasn't working. The school was shut until the tenth. I noticed that on the holiday chart in Rich's office.'

'Right. For the purposes of this conversation we'll assume she's the impostor.'

'It could all be quite innocent,' said Amiss. 'Innocent from our point of view, I mean, not from the real Mrs Bjorgsson's.'

'Of course. But it's intriguing that Cath kept it so quiet. It's hardly as if she thought her colleagues would disapprove. Anyway that's as far as we can go now on her.'

'Have you heard anything on our unknown Arab?' asked Pooley.

''Fraid not. We've pulled out all the stops — nationwide alert, bombardment of the media with his description and of course the ports and airports are on the qui vive. So far no reliable sighting since the car-park. However, there is more on Ahmed, who turns out with every new revelation to be an ever nastier piece of work.'

'I don't see where there was much room for disimprovement,' observed Amiss, 'but then I've lived a sheltered life.'

'He was nasty enough to have the Saudi police cooperating,' said Milton, 'and they're usually pretty reluctant to spill the beans on their citizens. Feel they lose face and all that. But they really disliked Ahmed. Delighted he was dead. Just wished they'd been able to execute him themselves.'

'Yeech,' said Amiss. 'What did he do? And can I bear to hear it?'

'Not a lot of hard evidence, but lots of suspicion of very nasty stuff with young girls. And boys. And drugs. And murders. Versatile chap. Bit of rape, bit of corruption, bit of killing, bit of fraud. He was a small-time villain working freelance for bigger-time villains and doing his own thing on the side.'

'Sounds pretty big-time to me,' said Amiss.

'I take your point, but I mean small-time in the sense of professional success. Apparently the criminal fraternity didn't rate his efficiency highly.'

'But he wasn't caught.'

'You're sounding positively defensive about him,' said Milton.

'Well of course I'd prefer to have been involved with a master criminal. More of an ego boost.'

'I'll give you that he had a good sense of self-preservation. He disappeared at the crucial time. Probably helped by a corrupt policeman, but they're obviously not going to suggest that.'

'And the revenge killing angle?'

'They've no ideas. Think lots of people could well have had reason to kill him but have no information on who might have done it.'

'When did he leave and how has he made a living since?' asked Pooley.

'They lost track of him about eighteen months ago. And someone like him is never short of work. He'd have plugged easily enough into the international criminal grapevine.'

'Who was financing him in London?'

'No one knows as yet, but it was someone sufficiently well-informed to know that he could get a visa through the school.'

'So his involvement with the school might merely have been a matter of getting his visa and keeping his cover while he got on with whatever he'd been given to do,' said Pooley.

'But equally he might have come specifically to kill Ned,' said Amiss.

'Hired by Rich Rogers or A N Other,' said Pooley.

'Possibly,' said Milton.

'Could there be a tie-up with Bjorgsson?' asked Pooley.

'There could be a tie-up with the Queen Mother for all I know.' Milton sounded desperate. 'I'm wilting under the number of "maybes" and "possiblys". Every bloody piece of information that comes in seems to increase the number of variables.'

'Cheer up, Jim,' said Amiss. 'Imagine how much more confused you'd be if the Saudis had declared Ahmed to be a well-known philanthropist and religious leader.'

'Oh, I know, I know. I'm over-reacting. But it has been a long, busy and inconclusive day. I haven't even mentioned Wally. That lad in Central, Doug Layton, has been beavering away and has come up with some evidence that Wally was in an odd mood on the night before he died.'

'What sort of odd?'

'Talking about heavy responsibilities and difficult decisions.'

'From what I've heard about Wally,' said Amiss, 'that meant that he couldn't decide which shirt to wear the next day.'

'Doug thinks there was more to it than that. It came from his son, and Doug thinks he's no fool.'

The three of them sat without speaking for a couple of minutes. Then Pooley asked, 'Where now?'

'Cath, I suppose,' said Milton. 'Though I don't see where it'll get us. If she admits it, what then? Lighted matches between her toes?'

'Maybe I should see if I can get anything relevant out of Rich tomorrow,' offered Amiss. 'I rang him from the car-hire place to clarify a point about the school's liability, and he invited me to Sunday lunch.'

'Relevant about Cath?'

'And Wally. In the light of Wally Jnr's evidence, it might be worth trying to find out what mood Wally was in at school the day before he died?'

'He wasn't at school the day before. He was electrocuted on Monday morning.'

Pooley stared into the middle-distance. 'He wouldn't have been to one of your picnics, I suppose?'

'Christ, no. Only a madman would invite him. Oh, look. I'll see if there's anything to be got from Rich about anything and then I'll ring you, Jim.'

'Fair enough. I'll be at home. Now let's talk about cricket.'

33

Plutarch lay sunbathing on a white silk Chinese rug in front of the long window overlooking Rich's garden. Beside her were two small bowls: one was half-full of milk; the other, Rich told Amiss, contained chopped cooked chicken, her especial favourite. Close by, on the highly-polished parquet, was a spotless white plastic tray of cat-litter.

'Was she very ill?'

'Absolute miracle that she pulled through, poor old love. If I hadn't found her when I did, she'd have been a goner. In fact I thought she was. She was lying there without moving, but I held a mirror over her nose and saw the tiniest bit of mist on it. I rushed her to the nearest vet and a couple of days later I was able to bring her home.'

'What had happened?'

'Someone tried to kill her by lassoing her with a piece of string and pulling it tight. I don't know why he didn't finish the job: maybe he was interrupted or maybe he thought she was dead. The vet says she's a real toughie — especially since it seems as if she'd been out there for ages. I hadn't seen her for twenty-four hours, so God knows when she was attacked. Poor old thing.' He smiled foolishly, squatted on the floor and stroked Plutarch's back very gently. 'Who's a clever girl, then?'

'She certainly seems to be enjoying her convalescence.'

'Well, I'm doing everything I can to make it up to her, of course.' He started guiltily. 'Oh, I'm so sorry, dear boy. I haven't even offered you a drink. Would you care to join me in a little champagne to celebrate Plutarch's survival?'

'Delighted.'

'I've got a half-bottle of a rather nice vintage Moët. We'll have to drink her portion: I haven't managed to persuade her to drink alcohol yet, har . . . har . . . har.'

'I brought you a few flowers. I didn't dare bring wine.'

'Oh, how very kind of you, Bob.' He darted into the kitchen with the yellow roses and emerged with them in a crystal vase a minute later. 'Now let's see. Yes, I think they should go over there on the chiffonier.' It took him a couple of minutes to place the vase, rearrange the flowers, move the vase to the right, take a few paces backwards to consider the effect critically, advance and move the vase a couple more inches, retreat, advance again to tease one rose upwards about half an inch, then nod and return to Amiss. 'Awful old woman, aren't I? Now let's have that champagne.'

He sped back into the kitchen and this time emerged carrying a bottle, an ice-bucket and two champagne flutes. 'Would you like to open it, Bob?'

'No thanks,' said Amiss, shuddering as he looked around him at all the breakables. 'I hate to think what I'd hit with the cork.' Then, remembering his man-of-the-world image, he added, 'I usually open champagne on the balcony or in the garden.'

Rich undid the wire, pushed the cork gently upwards and before it could pop out, pulled it sharply and filled up the glasses without spilling a drop.

'Very neat,' said Amiss, taking his.

'I'm an old hand, dear boy.' He picked up his own glass. 'To Plutarch.'

'Plutarch,' said Amiss gravely. He sat down in an armchair beside her and tickled her ear. 'You two are really getting on well together, aren't you?'

'After a rather shaky start. She was a rather fierce old thing that evening, wasn't she?'

'Is she generally friendly, now?'

'I haven't introduced her to anyone else yet.'

'You mean no one's been round to visit her sickbed?'

'Only you, dear boy. In fact I didn't tell anyone she was ill — too superstitious.' He topped up their glasses. 'Sorry, Bob. Remiss of me. We should also have toasted your safe return from Marriners. What a time you've had; I'm sorry to have been the indirect cause of it. Now tell me all about your week. You sounded a bit het-up when you phoned me from the car-hire place.'

'Come on, Rich. Can you imagine how they reacted when I told them the car had been bashed up by someone uninsured whom they couldn't proceed against because he was now dead?'

'Bit short, were they?'

'Just a bit.'

'Ahmed really was a horrid nuisance all round, wasn't he? It's a naughty thing to say, but I really can't be sorry he's dead.'

'Nor I. I'd have killed him myself if I'd had to put up with much more.'

By the time Amiss had finished his expurgated account, they had finished the champagne and were half-way through the artichoke soup. 'Funny those policemen going all that way to Marriners,' said Rich. 'I really can't see what Ahmed's death has to do with poor Ned's. Or do they think there is a link?'

'They don't take me into their confidence. This soup is absolutely superb, Rich.'

'I'm so glad. I won't offer you any more, because I expect the soufflé to be ready and we must eat it straightaway.' For a few minutes there was silence as he fussed around a little. 'Pour some more Chablis, dear boy, if you're ready.'

Amiss watched admiringly as a perfect soufflé was placed in the centre of the table. 'Please help yourself, Bob.'

They chatted for a while in a desultory fashion, both of them being primarily concerned to do justice to the meal. The soufflé was followed by a medium-rare Chateaubriand accompanied by a half-bottle of Château-Latour. 'I have to say,' said Amiss, as with regret he finished the last morsel, 'that I've eaten some superb meals since I started working with you, but this is the best yet.'

'I'm so pleased, Bob. It's just a small thank you for your great kindness to me when Ned died. Now have some crème caramel and then we'll take our coffee inside to join Plutarch.'

Amiss was suspended in such a state of well-being after lunch that it took him a few minutes to stop thinking dreamily about food and drink and how nice a nap would be and start looking for opportunities to ask some pertinent questions. He moved in obliquely. 'By the way, Rich, who have you got lined up for me next week?'

'The same as before, Bob.'

'You don't mean Galina's still here? I thought she was due to leave last week.'

Rich chuckled. 'Sorry, old man. Though the good news is that she seems to be struck on someone in Gavs's group. You might have an easy time.'

'So it's Fabrice, Galina, Gunther and Simone again, is that it?'

'Possibly someone new in place of Fabrice. She's still pretty shirty with him.'

'I should think she's still pretty shirty with me.'

'You're forgiven because of what happened last week. She's dying to hear the details.'

'No picnic today, then?'

'Not for the want of trying on her side. The wretched woman is insatiable. But I got out of it by insisting it would be offensive to Ahmed's memory.'

Amiss laughed: he picked up his port and took an appreciative sniff. 'The picnics seem like a lot of trouble. Do you have them often?' He tried to sound only half-interested.

Rich shook his head. 'Maybe every eight weeks or so.'

'Aren't you at all worried about being shopped for providing drugs?'

'You mean someone telling the police. Who would? Any student would land not just the school but several other students in trouble. They'd be unlikely to do that to rich and influential people.'

'Staff?'

'The school would be closed down and they'd lose their jobs.'

'I suppose it's pretty watertight. Did Ned mind?'

'Good Lord, Ned didn't know. He wouldn't have been happy with any infringements of the law. Me, I don't see any harm in what we do. I only ever provide hash or coke, and I'd never offer them to people who weren't used to them. It's like the sex. I don't see anything wrong with a bit of depravity as long as no one gets hurt. I'd never have anything to do with corrupting the innocent.'

'Do the students ever want you to go further than you do?'

'Bless you, of course. We get the occasional real degenerate, looking for kids and that sort of thing. Someone who's picked up the wrong idea about our little operation. And I get some wanting to get us involved in drug smuggling. We'd be a very good front, with all that coming and going. There's one chap's been after me for ages. But I've been very firm. I won't tolerate anything I call wrong-doing.'

Amiss took a considering sip and lit a cigarette. 'Don't any of these people ever get, well, heavy?'

'Not really. Well, occasionally. But I've never had any real trouble. Always call their bluff. Finally told that nuisance of a Swede yesterday to get lost or I'd call the police. I would too. Since Ned died I'm not easily frightened.'

'Has Ned's death changed anything professionally, Rich?'

Rich shook his head. 'Not really. I expect I'll go on as before.'

'On your own? Or will you get a new partner?'

'Have you ambitions in that direction?'

Amiss laughed. 'No. I enjoy the job but I don't see myself making a career of it. But I thought maybe one of the others?'

'I wouldn't want to be in partnership with anyone who wasn't simpatico. Frankly, and I probably shouldn't tell you this, Cath wants half the business and I don't want to sell to her. I've always put her off in the past by pleading Ned. I don't know quite what to say now.'

'You don't find her simpatico?'

'Too cold. And greedy. That's why I was wondering about you.'

'You'd better just stall for the moment. She must realise that you shouldn't be making decisions while you're still in a state of shock over Ned.'

'I don't think Cath understands that kind of thing.' The phone began to ring. 'That may be her. She's been at me to have a meeting this afternoon.'

'Don't say no on my account. I'm leaving in a couple of minutes. Got to see a friend at four.'

Rich picked up the mobile phone beside his chair. 'Hello, Rich Rogers . . . Hello, Cath . . . Not really. I've work to do at the school this afternoon . . . Oh, you will?' He raised his eyes to heaven. 'Oh, well, I suppose in that case, yes . . . say about five. But only a few minutes, please. I really am very busy . . . Right, bye.' He jabbed at the off-switch. 'See what I mean.'

'She's certainly persistent.'

'And the more persistent she is, the less likely I am to want her as a partner.'

*

'Ten to one the drug baron's our Sven,' said Amiss to Milton from a call-box at Knightsbridge tube station. 'Two hypotheses. First is that Rich murdered Ned in order to inherit his cat. Second is that Cath murdered Ned so as to leave a vacancy for a partner.'

'But she couldn't have put the alcohol in his drink.'

'Maybe she hired Ahmed to do it. Or Sven did.'

'It's an extraordinarily roundabout route. Why not invest in a different business?'

'Christ, I don't know. You know as much as I do. Maybe he's stubborn. Oh, yes. Wally. Rich was a little vague about picnics, but I gather he usually has them at about two-monthly intervals, so that would fit. I suppose it's just possible Wally stumbled on a picnic. Quite certainly he wouldn't have been invited.'

'I'll brood on that. What are you doing now?'

'Meeting Ellis to play squash. He'll win of course — not being full of rich food and half-drunk.'

'And then?'

'Dropping by the school at Rich's request to interrupt him and Cath. Then I'm going on to Ellis's for an early supper. Or in my case a glass of water. He needs company at the moment.'

'I know. Good luck with the hand-holding. I'll call you there later and we'll talk about how to approach Cath.'

'Good luck with the cogitating.'

'I don't intend to do much of that. I'm off duty. Bye.'

Indeed Milton was fast asleep over the newspapers when the telephone rang with news of more death.

34

'What's the urgency, Cath?'

'I want my future settled. I've been hanging on for ages, hoping to be able to get a stake in the business. I enjoy this job, but I don't want to go on as an employee. I'm ambitious. What's wrong with that?'

'I've promised you that if I decide to sell a piece of the partnership, I'll give the teachers a chance of buying in.'

'But Gavs doesn't want to and there isn't anyone else.'

'There's Bob.'

Cath's control held, but barely. 'You can't seriously mean that. He hasn't been in the school five minutes. I think you're treating me in a very cavalier fashion, Rich, if you'll forgive me saying so.'

'I feel the boot is on the other foot, my dear. You don't seem to understand that I'm still shocked and grieved at Ned's death. I don't want to make any decisions at present. I'll let you know when or if I do.'

'But you always used to say that the only reason for not opening up the partnership was that it would be unfair to Ned.'

'You took me very literally, Cath. Did it never occur to you that I might be using dear old Ned as an excuse?'

'No, it didn't.' She gave a bitter laugh.

There was a long silence. Then Rich summoned up his courage.

'Look, Cath. I promise you I'll think about it seriously as soon as I'm feeling better. Now please excuse me? I've got some more paperwork to do, and then I'm going home to look after my sick cat.'

'I thought it was dead,' said Cath absently.

'No, she's recovered.'

'Oh, good. All right, Rich. If you don't mind, I'll make a phone call or two from the lounge before I go.'

'Of course. See you tomorrow.'

'Yeah. Bye.'

'It's no good. You'll have to think of another angle. Or find another business.'

Dispiritedly, as the angry voice accused her of not having tried hard enough, Cath turned in her chair and fixed her eyes on the Monet reproduction beside the door. She was thus perfectly placed to see squarely the grotesque figure that burst into the lounge and crashed something heavy on to her skull. She had time for only a gasp of terror before the second blow cast her into merciful unconsciousness. It was the sixth blow that killed her.

It was five forty-seven when Amiss found the two bodies. Retching from the sight of Cath's shattered head, he lurched to Rich's side and realised with a sob of gratitude that he was breathing and appeared uninjured.

He ran to the office telephone and managed to speak to Milton before staggering into the washroom to vomit. As he emerged five minutes later, uniformed police were pouring through the front door and Rich was beginning to move. By the time Milton arrived, Rich had been moved to the nearest classroom, where Amiss was ministering to him with tea and sympathy. Milton called him out into the hallway where he was issuing general instructions.

'You get on with the forensic boys, Sammy,' said Milton to Inspector Pike. 'Get someone talking to the neighbours and get one of your lot to keep trying Ellis Pooley at home. Tell him to come immediately. Robert, I'm going to tell Rogers I've sent you home, but I want you to stay in the office. Sammy, make sure no one tells Rogers Robert's still on the premises.'

'Understood, sir,' said Pike, a long-time fan of Milton, encourager of Pooley and friendly acquaintance of Amiss. Amiss, recognising from Milton's tone that there was no point in arguing, retired despondently to his appointed quarters.

'All I know,' said Rich to Milton, 'is that we finished talking about five fifteen. She said she had a few phone calls to make in the lounge. About a quarter of an hour later I packed up ready to go home, looking into the lounge to see if she was still there, and there she was with her head staved in and all that blood splashed round. I was terrified, I can tell you. I don't know if it was horror or fear that made me faint. Next thing I knew, your chaps were all around.'

'Are you suggesting that Miss Taylor let the murderer in?'

'She didn't need to. The front door wasn't locked. Anyone could have turned the handle and walked in.'

'But you heard nothing?'

'Nothing. The office door was closed and it's a longish way from the lounge.'

Milton went over and over the ground with him without getting very far. Rich maintained that they had been having a friendly discussion, albeit with a slight difference of opinion, about whether he would offer her a partnership. 'But if anyone had a grievance it was her, not me, Superintendent. I wasn't prepared to give her what she wanted, at least not now.'

When Pooley arrived, Milton was talking to Amiss in the office, darting in and out when called on by Pike. 'The problem is simple,' he explained. 'Rogers says it must have been done by someone walking in from the street. Evidence in favour of that is that there is no blood on him and we can't find a likely weapon. Evidence against is that the next-door couple were working in their garden, saw Rich and Cath come in and swear no one else did. I discount the faint — easily put on for Robert's benefit.'

'And could no one have got in or out the back way?' asked Pooley.

'Both the back door and the back gate are heavily bolted.'

'You'd think if Rich had done it he'd have faked a back exit for the mythical assailant,' said Amiss hopefully.

'He couldn't. There was a party going on in the back garden of the house on the other side and the door is visible from their terrace because of the slope in the gardens.'

'It's very hard to imagine we've got another mystery murderer coming in out of nowhere,' said Amiss reluctantly.

'Sven?' asked Pooley.

'Because he was cross with her for not becoming a partner? Forget it.'

'Could Rogers conceivably have done it without getting his clothes spattered with blood?' asked Pooley.

'Almost certainly not.'

Pike looked in and called Milton outside for a consultation with the fingerprint teams. Amiss and Pooley sat thinking until he returned.

'A waterproof cape?' asked Amiss.

'Where is it?'

Amiss shrugged.

'He could have done it naked,' said Pooley.

'I thought of that one, Ellis. And it's just possible. If he murdered her within, say, fifteen minutes of her arrival, he'd have had time to strip, kill her, mop himself down, and even dry his hair with the hair dryer.'

'And do what with the blunt instrument?'

'That's our real problem. We've searched the house and garden and anywhere within throwing distance of the windows three times to date, and can't find anything remotely suitable.'

'Hidden safes?'

'Rich says there's only one and we've looked in that: it contains petty cash and a tiny amount of cocaine and marijuana.'

'Gavs might know if there's another.'

'We've already tried him and he doesn't.'

'What do you want me to do, sir?'

'You two stay in this office and think. I've got plenty of people outside dealing with the practicalities. Keep going through Rogers's statement and praying for inspiration.'

Pooley's inspiration came first. As Milton came in to report that a fourth search had yielded nothing, he suddenly said: 'Has anyone tried the Last Number Replay button?'

'What? Oh, you mean on the phone she was using? Christ, I don't know. Let's try, even though she was probably phoning for a taxi.'

'You two go,' said Amiss. 'You're the pros. If you don't mind, I'll stay here and skip the sights.'

Milton strode into the lounge. 'Sammy, has anyone used this phone since we arrived?'

'No, sir. The fingerprint boys have only just finished with it.'

Milton picked up the receiver and pressed the LR button. There was a long succession of clicks and then an unfamiliar tone. 'It's long distance,' he said. It rang twice and then a voice said: 'Hello. Sven Bjorgsson.' It was all that Pooley could do not to let out a cheer.

Opting for discretion, Milton put the phone down without a word. 'It's a tricky one this,' he said, when they had gone back to the office. 'The only sensible hypothesis I can offer is that Rogers attacked her because of something he overheard her saying to Bjorgsson. We need to know from Bjorgsson the substance of their conversation and if it came to an abrupt halt, but I don't want that done on the telephone. I'll have to have someone sent over to see him. Damn. I know it's Rogers. Nothing else makes sense. But where in hell is the weapon?'

Amiss was sitting dejectedly on the floor in the corner of the office, thinking mournfully about his first day at the school. Only three weeks ago and it felt like years. He remembered sitting waiting for Rich as Ned jabbered disarmingly of their travels together. 'Oh, God,' he said to himself under his breath. Milton was on the phone so he spoke softly to Pooley. 'Ellis. Any more details on what she was hit with?'

'Only what I told you earlier — something very knobbly — bit like a blackthorn club only more so.'

Amiss looked in the right-hand drawer of what had been Ned Nurse's desk, nodded, and sat on the corner of the desk and removed his right shoe and sock. Milton and Pooley watched on with fascination as he began to fill his sock with handfuls of coins. He whirled it round experimentally and then handed it over to Milton. 'Try this for size,' he said.

35

'Mr Rogers, I'm charging you with the murder of Miss Catherine Taylor and I must warn you that anything you say may be taken down and used in evidence against you.'

'This is ridiculous. How could I have killed Cath?'

'We've found what could well have served as a weapon, sir.' Milton took Amiss's coin-filled sock from a carrier bag and showed its contents to Rich. 'Could you take your shoes off, sir?'

'I don't understand.'

'I think you do. I think you converted coins into a weapon, probably by putting them in a sock. If not a sock, then something similar. Could I have a look at your socks, please.'

'Certainly, Superintendent. Just one small matter, first. Isn't one supposed to have a motive for murder? Or did I do this for fun?'

Milton closed his eyes for a moment to recall accurately the strategy that Amiss had impressed upon him. 'I think you did it because she was blackmailing you.'

'This is preposterous, Superintendent. I haven't done anything to be blackmailed about. Unless you mean those piddling amounts of drugs. I'd hardly risk life imprisonment to save a small fine.'

'No, sir. Not the drugs.' Milton looked Rich straight in the eyes. 'I believe she was blackmailing you because she knew you'd hired Ahmed to kill your partner. He failed to batter him to death: then you set him up to spike Mr Nurse's drink.'

'Don't even say anything like that. It's a blasphemy. I wouldn't have hurt a hair on Ned's head. I loved him.'

'Yes, sir. So you say. But we deal in facts. You stood to gain a great deal of money from his death and therefore all along you've been the obvious suspect.'

Rich fell into a chair and began to cry. 'I can't bear this,' he sobbed.

'We have evidence of the truth of what I'm saying.'

'You can't have.'

'Miss Taylor's lover, Mr Sven Bjorgsson, is prepared to testify to this.'

'He couldn't.' Rich stopped crying and thought for a few moments. 'I'm wrong, aren't I? He could, of course he could. And everyone will believe him. I'd rather be dead than have people believe I had Ned killed.'

'Well in that case I'd advise you to get your story in fast, Mr Rogers.'

Rich leaned back in the chair and looked from Milton to Pooley. 'All right, Superintendent. You win. One of my socks is damp and though I washed it thoroughly, I'm sure it'll show up something it shouldn't. And of course some of the fibres will be found in Cath's wounds. I had taken the precaution of putting plastic film over the sock, but it split. Give in gracefully has always been one of my mottoes. Or to put it another way, "It's a fair cop, copper,"' he guffawed weakly.

'And your reason for doing it, Mr Rogers?'

'I'd better tell you about it in sequence. While we were talking she gave the game away by saying she thought Plutarch — my cat — was dead, when no one but me, the vet and the would-be strangler had known anything about the attack. I knew then that there was something awful going on. I crept along the hall and listened to her. The lounge door opens without a sound. I realised that the Sven she was talking to was the one you'd been asking about last week. He'd been pestering me to come in with him on a business proposition. Drug smuggling in other words. I said no.

'It all fell into place suddenly. It was around that time that Cath started to try to get a slice of the partnership. Obviously she was intended to be the Trojan horse if I refused to open the gates to Sven. Then she said, "So you wasted your money on Ahmed. It's no help at all Ned Nurse is dead." He said something and then she said, "I never thought he'd crack as easily as you did, though it was worth trying it with the bloody cat. Would you believe it survived? Wasn't Ahmed unbelievable? Glad you had him bumped off."

'I've never felt hatred before. Sharpens your wits, I find. I had everything worked out in a couple of minutes and she was dead within five. Funny, really. I don't know whether she rang Sven from the school because of impatience or tightfistedness, but that's why she died. I'd never have killed her in cold blood.'

'Thank you for your frankness, Mr Rogers. Are you ready to come with us now?'

'There are just one or two things I'd like to get from my office.'

'The sergeant will get them for you, sir. What would you like?'

'If you don't mind, Superintendent, I'd like to do it myself. I probably won't see the office again.'

'Very good, sir,' said Milton. 'Just hold on a moment while I make a couple of notes and I'll take you there. Sergeant Pooley, perhaps you'd go ahead and tell Inspector Pike what's happening.'

Pooley tore downstairs to the office where Amiss was sitting staring at a blank wall. 'He's coming in here in a minute, Robert. If you don't want to be seen you'll have to get out now.'

'Where'll I go?'

'Nowhere downstairs is safe. Just go out the front. And get well clear. We'll be taking him into custody immediately. Come on!' and he bundled him out of the office and down the hallway. A moment after the front door closed, Milton and Rich came in from the lounge and disappeared into the office. When they reappeared, Rich was saying, 'What's really worrying me, Superintendent, is my cat. She's not well.'

'Have you anyone to look after her?'

'The only one I can think of is my young colleague, Bob Amiss. Could you be very kind and ask him to take over? If he could move in with her for a few days, until she's better and I can make arrangements about her future, I'd be awfully grateful.' He took a key-ring out of his pocket and handed it to Milton, who was studiously avoiding Pooley's eye. 'I'll certainly see that that is done, Mr Rogers. I assure you that even if we don't find him tonight, someone will see that your cat is looked after.'

They left the school together. As they reached the car, Rich turned and looked at the building for a few seconds. 'Oh, well,' he said. 'It was good fun while it lasted.' He bent and got into the car. There was unbroken silence until they reached the police station.

36

When they arrived at the station, Milton took Pooley aside. 'You
clear off now, Ellis. Take these keys to Robert and look after
him. He's going to be in a very bad state.'

There was no answer from Amiss's telephone, but Pooley took
a taxi to his flat anyway. The bell went unanswered. Pooley
leaned against the door and tried to guess Amiss's whereabouts.
It was nine thirty, only three hours since he had arrived at the
school. Pub, of course, he said to himself and set off at a brisk
pace in the most promising direction. He found him in the second
one, gazing sightlessly at what Pooley correctly guessed to be his
third or fourth large gin and tonic.

Pooley bought himself a whisky and a dry ginger and sat down.
'Hello, Robert,' he said gently.

'Hello.' It was the barest mutter.

'He's confessed.' He gave Amiss the bones of the story.

Amiss said nothing.

'What's upsetting you most?'

'Being Judas.' To Pooley's relief, Amiss spoke with reasonable clarity.

'By identifying the murder weapon?'

'Not so much. Telling Jim how to get him upset. And all the
snooping and sneaking.'

'He's a murderer, Robert. For all we know he's a double
murderer.'

'Doesn't matter. Ends don't justify means.'

The barman called last orders. 'Get me another, Ellis, will
you? I've run out of money.'

Pooley was grateful to have a couple of minutes in the scrum at
the bar to think.

'Do you know who you remind me of?' he asked as he sat down
with the drinks.

213

'Nope.'

'Lord Peter Wimsey.'

'Ellis, for fuck's sake! This is for real.'

'Listen, will you? When Wimsey caught a murderer, he used to go through hell the night before the execution. Especially if he hadn't got the murderer to forgive him — which I always thought was expecting a bit much. But he still went after the next one because it was the right thing to do. This is your third time, and it won't be your last. You may not believe in God or the Establishment, but you do believe in truth.'

Amiss scratched his head. Pooley wondered if he had been too drunk to follow the line of reasoning. Then Amiss looked at him for the first time and gave a half-smile. 'You're a good fellow, Ellis. Why don't you add a dash of Pollyanna? I should be glad, glad, glad that they've abolished capital punishment. So should you for that matter. Think how much drunker I'd be getting if they were going to hang him.'

Pooley grinned. 'You can't afford to get any drunker, Robert. He's nominated you to look after his cat for a few days. On the premises.'

'You're kidding!'

'I'm not. And you're going to have a busy day tomorrow as well sorting out the school. In fact you'd better ring Gavin Franklyn from Rich's flat. Come on, let's get going. Plutarch will be getting cross.'

Rich's instructions, relayed through his solicitor, were to close the school down with the minimum of disruption. The prefab students were given their fees back and their teachers paid off generously. Jenn, delighted by being in the centre of a drama that got her photograph in a couple of tabloids, worked efficiently at organising the cancellations of all kinds of bookings. To the great relief of Gavs and Amiss, most of the students departed within a couple of days. Only a handful of the most morbid remained to hone their English by incessant discussion about Cath and Rich. Distressed as he was, Amiss got a great deal of black amusement out of seeing Galina's obsession change from sex to violence.

Free of extra activities, he spent one evening with Mick

McGuire and two with Plutarch; on Thursday he was able to send a message to Rich to say that she was back to full health and out on the tiles.

That evening Rachel rang to say she would come over for the weekend and Milton, from Bramshill, rang to invite them to dinner on Saturday along with Pooley to welcome Ann home from America.

That call was followed by one from Rich's lawyer asking Amiss to visit his client at Wormwood Scrubs the next day.

At two thirty on Friday, Amiss and Gavs said farewell to the last three students. 'Goodbye, Bob darling,' said Galina, pressing her lips firmly on his. 'I 'ope you are well soon.'

'I'm fine, thanks,' said Amiss. 'Oh, sorry, yes. You mean that. Of course. It's a very mild case.'

He took a taxi to the prison, arrived promptly at three fifteen and was shown into a tiny room where he was shortly joined by Rich. They shook hands.

'I thought we'd have a warder with us.'

'Well it helps that I'm only on remand and have made a full confession. I think the police put in a word because I'd been so cooperative.'

'How are you, Rich?'

'A bit frightened about the future, but I'm hoping for an open prison. I'll be all right. I expect I'll be the life and soul of the place in no time at all, har . . . har . . . har.'

'You've got great guts.'

'No I haven't, dear boy. That's why I'm in the position I'm in now. If I'd made it crystal clear that I'd never go into partnership with anyone, Ned would be alive today. He was killed because I used him as an excuse to hide behind. And Wally Armstrong also died because I was a coward.'

'Wally Armstrong?'

'Yes. I've got to tell someone about this, and I'm afraid you've drawn the short straw.'

'Please, Rich, don't tell me anything you might regret.'

'How can I regret it? I can't imagine you telling the police. And if you did, it'd be your word against mine and nothing provable. Please, Bob. You'd be doing me a great favour to help take this weight off my mind.'

Amiss looked around the nasty waiting-room and thought of the years Rich was going to spend amid ugliness. He let out a heavy sigh. 'All right,' he said, 'but only if you call me Robert in future. I've never forgiven you for making me Bob.'

He chuckled. 'Mean of me. Used to do that to everyone. It was revenge really. I hated being called Rich but got saddled with it early on.'

'OK, Richard, shoot.'

'I had a picnic that Sunday. I was always a bit nervous in case someone came into the school unexpectedly, but only Ned and Wally had keys and I discouraged weekend work. Also, of course, I always put the snib on the lock. It happened just once that Ned tried to come in on a Sunday and couldn't get in, but it was easy to convince him that he hadn't done the right thing with the keys.

'It was a frightful piece of bad luck that we should be holding a picnic on perhaps the only Sunday that Wally Armstrong decided to come in. It was an even more frightful piece of bad luck that I had left the snib off the lock. Wally had come in to see if he could fix the language laboratory. He wanted to spend the afternoon worrying away at it and then in the morning he'd be able to give a superior smile and say, "You can cancel the electrician. I did it yesterday."

'What happened was that he came in, saw possessions strewn around and heard noises in the garden. Anyone else would have come out to see what was going on. Not Wally. He loved to get information that other people didn't know he had.

'Everyone thinks you can't see into the loggia from the house. But Wally knew something no one else did. He went upstairs to the walk-in cupboard on the third floor, brought in a chair and looked through the small high window which gives a perfect vantage point if you don't mind the discomfort. Wally didn't. He stayed long enough to view me dispensing cocaine and a couple of students having a screw to the great applause of the others: it was a rather raunchy group that week. Then he went home.

'I got back from an exhausting day and had this call from Wally about dreadful happenings that were out of keeping with the distinguished traditions of the Knightsbridge School.

'He was dripping crocodile tears. So sorry he'd witnessed it: the last thing he wanted to do was to put the school in jeopardy. But having said that, he was a man for whom integrity was all and he took a very strong line on drugs and orgies. He'd like to talk things over with me before he spoke to Ned and/or the police.

'I knew just what was going on. For one thing he was mad with envy. He was one of those people who never has fun and never looks for it but always resents not having it. One of the reasons he disliked me so much was that I enjoyed life a lot. He'd have had a sweet revenge by telling Ned he had been wrong about me, and that what was necessary was to get rid of me and take him into partnership. Wally really had a hankering to deal with the BPs and believed he'd have done it just as well if not better than me.

'What I couldn't bear was the thought of how broken-hearted Ned would be. He'd have forgiven me, oh yes, because he was that kind of person, but he'd have been devastated. He took a very simple line against drugs. And the public sex bit he'd have found distressing. Over and above, he'd have been deeply disappointed, though it wouldn't have stopped him loving me. But I couldn't stand the thought of his being so hurt.

'Wally wanted to come over and talk, but I told him my mother was with me. He said if I wanted to see him before he saw Ned it would have to be before nine the following morning. I suggested eight, got in at seven and fixed the wiring. As you know, I'm very practical, and this was easy. I stayed in the lab until he arrived, saying when he did that I thought I nearly had it, but didn't think I'd got it quite right. That made him forget everything else. Within seconds he had moved in purposefully and within minutes he was dead. I skipped out before it happened. I wouldn't have been up to watching. Cowardice again.

'It's interesting, isn't it, that I committed both murders because Ned was such a lovely person. The first time I was determined to preserve his innocence; the second time I felt I had to take revenge on someone worthless who destroyed such goodness.'

Amiss found it impossible to think of anything to say.

'And yet, I was probably wrong about Ned. I should have had more courage and more trust in him. He'd have known from the ancient Greeks about all kinds of depravity: mine was very small

217

beer. I'd forgotten too how unshockable really good people can be. And of course if Wally hadn't worked me into such a panic I'd probably have calmed down and called his bluff.'

'I'm sorry, Richard,' said Amiss. 'I'm really very very sorry.'

'Thank you, dear boy. You're very kind. Funny. When we met first I thought you were a bit of a shit.'

'I felt the same way about you.'

'Now you find I'm not a shit, just a murderer. I must say, Robert, you're a very charitable fellow.' He chuckled.

And to the bewilderment of the warder, who came in to give them a five-minute warning, they both fell into hysterical laughter.

EPILOGUE

Saturday evening at the Miltons was a huge success. Pooley's nervousness evaporated within a very short time of arrival and by the end of the meal he no longer felt like a spare man, but like one of a united group.

When the meal had been demolished, they moved with their coffee and brandy into the living-room.

'Can we wrap this up?' asked Ann Milton as she sat down. 'You know how I like things to be tidy.'

'Things intellectual,' remarked her husband. 'If you look around you, you'll note she doesn't mean things domestic.'

Ann ignored him. 'Right, I think I've got all this straight. Ahmed killed Ned at the behest of Sven and Cath; an as yet unidentified Arab killed Ahmed, almost certainly at Sven's behest; and Rich killed Cath. Seems like rather a lot of murderers.'

'Might be even more,' said Pooley. 'We still don't know what happened to Wally Armstrong.'

'Let's forget Wally Armstrong,' said Milton. 'We have to write him off. There's simply no hard evidence.'

Amiss opened his mouth and closed it again.

'All right,' said Ann. 'Now let's look at justice. Cath and Ahmed have given an eye for an eye; Rich will get life imprisonment for Cath's death; and Sven and his hired hand get off scot free.'

'Up to a point,' said Milton. 'I doubt if we'll ever catch Ahmed's assassin. He had plenty of time to leave the country. And Rich's evidence isn't good enough to have Sven Bjorgsson extradited. But he doesn't get off scot free, Ann. Although he admitted next to nothing, he couldn't deny the affair with Cath. His wife says she's leaving him and the Swedish police will keep a very close eye on him from now on. His legitimate and illegitimate business will suffer greatly.'

'Poor old Rich,' said Rachel. 'Will he really get life?'

'Yes,' said Milton. 'But he might get out in seven years or so. The premeditation was slight and the provocation severe. How's he getting on anyway, Robert? You haven't told us about yesterday. What did you talk about?'

'The past and the future,' said Amiss slowly.

They all looked at him curiously. 'Something happened, didn't it?' asked Rachel. 'Something that's hard to talk about.'

Amiss said nothing. After a moment Pooley leant forward and touched his hand. 'Robert, we started this together. Don't you think I deserve to be in on the finish?'

Amiss looked round all four of them. 'I'll tell you only on the condition that you tell nobody. This is off the record. In other words, anyone who quotes me is betraying our friendship.'

'You're certainly making yourself clear,' said Milton. 'I agree. Anyone not?'

No one did and in silence they listened to the story of the murder of Wally.

When it was over, Milton reached for the brandy and refilled their glasses. 'I'm glad I haven't heard about Wally Armstrong being murdered,' he said. 'I might find it difficult to pursue his murderer with much enthusiasm.'

'Me too,' said Pooley.

'Except for Ned Nurse,' said Ann, 'the victims seem worse than the murderers.'

'Nonsense, Ann,' said Milton. 'Half the victims were murderers — and vice versa, of course.'

'I haven't finished about yesterday,' said Amiss.

'Uh, oh,' said Rachel. 'I know that tone of voice and it presages trouble. What else is there? Tell me quickly.'

'He wants me to adopt Plutarch.'

'Oh, Jesus!'

'And I agreed.'

'Oh, Christ!'

'Because I didn't know how to say no.'

'The story of your life, Robert,' said Rachel.

'He says she's quite old — about fourteen. So it won't be for long. He wanted to pay me to do it — even offered me a diamond tie-pin, but of course I refused.'

220

'Of course,' said Rachel. 'The very idea of a man of your wealth accepting such an offer.'

'It's the Judas business.'

'So Judas, he gets thirty pieces of silver. Robert, he gets a cat.' Amiss looked at her miserably. She leaned over and kissed him. 'I'm sure I'll learn to love her. She sounds divine.'

'What'll you do now, Robert?' asked Ann.

'Register for the dole, I expect.'

'Will you get it this time?' asked Pooley.

'Ah, interesting theological question here: Have I still to work through my twenty-six week suspension for leaving the Civil Service without good reason? Or can I get the dole immediately because the school closed down through no fault of mine?'

'Sorry, Robert,' said Pooley. 'It *was* your fault. If you hadn't thought of the foreign coins, we mightn't have nailed Rich and the school would still be open.'

'My God, you're absolutely right. Don't tell the benefit office, will you?'

'Be serious for a moment,' said Milton. 'What are you really going to do?'

'I'll tell you what he's going to do,' said Rachel, 'and he's going to do it before that beastly cat moves in and before either of you gets another bright idea. He's going to enrol on Monday for a training course in assertiveness.'

They all looked at Amiss. 'Well,' he said. 'If you say so.'